Joe Joyce is the author of seven novels including the *Echoland* series of spy thrillers set in neutral Ireland during the Second World War which were chosen as Dublin's One City One Book in 2017. He is also the author of a history of *The Guinnesses* and co-author with Peter Murtagh of *The Boss*, the classic account of Charles J Haughey in government in Ireland. He lives in Dublin.

# Also by Joe Joyce

**The *Echoland* series of WW2 spy novels**

*Echoland*
*Echobeat*
*Echowave*

**Other Fiction**

*1691: A Novel*
*The Trigger Man*
*Off the Record*

**Non-Fiction**

*The Guinnesses: The Untold Story of Ireland's Most Successful Family*
*Blind Justice* (with Peter Murtagh)
*The Boss: Charles J Haughey in Government* (with Peter Murtagh)

**Plays**

*The Tower*

**www.joejoyce.ie**

# NO SECOND TAKE

Joe Joyce

Published in 2021 by
Cove Books
7 Ballygihen Avenue
Sandycove
Co Dublin
Ireland



ISBN: 978-1-9162951-7-9



*All characters in this book are fictitious, and any resemblance to actual persons, living or dead, is purely coincidental.*

# One

The arrest was carried out so smoothly that it barely registered, no more than the blink of an eye on the sunlit afternoon.

I had left work early and was walking home along the Promenade des Anglais. On my right, the full tide was bashing the stones with a last-minute fury as if it just realised they were stopping its onward roll. The sun was still high in the cloudless sky, burning a blinding path across the beautiful blue of the Mediterranean and keeping away the freezing air that came off the snow-topped mountains to the north.

There were lots of strollers out, taking advantage of the daytime heat. The locals were muffled in coats and scarves, the newcomers obvious in their heavy northern suits. There was little traffic on the road, mainly bicycles, a lone bus, and a couple of cars with gazozene tanks on their roofs.

I became aware instantly of the one car without a tank, a low-slung black Citroën that was hugging the edge of the promenade like a sleek black panther on the prowl. It was moving slowly, little faster than walking pace. The driver was alone: at another time on another road, out near the studios in the evening perhaps, I might have assumed he was cruising for a prostitute. But not here in the warmth of the bright afternoon. And not in a petrol-driven car.

A well-honed instinct for survival, sharpened again after all the years by the times we were living in, knew what was happening.

I maintained my pace, checking as much of my surroundings as I could without looking around. Nobody seemed out of place among those coming towards me: elderly people out for a walk, mothers with small children, two governesses chatting as they pushed high prams. The hairs on my neck stiffened at the thought of what might be behind me but I resisted the urge to look around. Besides, I reassured myself, I wasn't guilty of anything these days. Certainly not here.

The car kept moving ahead, stretching out the distance, and I relaxed. I wasn't the target.

It was a hundred yards away when a movement among the strollers caught my attention. Two men linking a young woman suddenly turned towards the road. She looked from one to the other, surprised, as if she couldn't decide which to choose as a dance partner or suitor. The one on her right smiled back at her. She didn't struggle or protest as they led her to the kerb and showed her politely into the back of the Citroën.

The car moved off as if it had all the time in the world. No squealing of tyres, no hint of a hurry, no celebration of a successful detention.

The arrest barely cast a shadow on the afternoon but it chilled the air nonetheless. Nobody paused or glanced after the car. Everyone was aware of it but pretended they were not. As if there had been a momentary eclipse of the sun, a blink in the beauty all around, the blue of the bay, the green of the palm trees, the smooth elegance of the buildings across the road, the dozy heat of the afternoon. A passing thought dismissed with haste.

I wondered idly who the woman was and why she had been seized. She had been too far away and it had happened too quickly to get a good look at her. Just an impression of shoulder-length black hair and a dark, belted coat. No hat and no protest. Someone who had been arrested before or perhaps expected to be. Someone who knew the game. Probably a local. A critic of the new government. Or possibly an Italian anti-fascist that our new masters in Rome wanted back. Anyway, she was none of my business.

There was no way I could have known she was going to change my life.

# Two

Nice was a strange place then. The tourists were gone. The English, all but the ancient and harmless, had been evacuated in cramped coal boats to Gibraltar after the collapse of the French armies eighteen months before. The Americans had now disappeared too after the US joined the war at the end of the previous year. The pre-war holidaymakers were replaced by the hopeful and the desperate, new refugees from the Nazis in occupied France and elsewhere in the spreading Reich. As well as the longer-term refugees from Mussolini's Blackshirts.

And the Niçois were in a strange place too; stuck in a demilitarized zone; ruled by the new national government in Vichy; ordered about by the Italians under the terms of the armistice. The Italians wanted to return the area to Italy but hadn't yet occupied it like they'd annexed Menton along the coast. Nobody, not even the Pétainists who accepted France's defeat by Germany, acknowledged that France had been defeated by the Italians. There was a lot of talk of backstabbing and the enemies within, the large number of Niçois who were of Italian origin. On top of all the bitterness of who was to blame for the German disaster.

I heard it all at work and let it wash over me. It was not my war. I'd had my fill of war and political passions about republics a long time ago in Ireland.

I touched my inside pocket to make sure my wallet was safe. Not for the francs it held but for the piece of paper with its official stamp that confirmed that I was the citizen of a neutral country, Ireland. It had taken a month in a civilian internment camp to get it and I had no desire to go back there. My old American passport was safely stowed behind someone else's electricity meter in the basement of our apartment building. It was of less use now, although the US still didn't treat the Vichy lot as an enemy, as the British did.

The Promenade was thinning out, the pleasure of the afternoon sun spoiled by the slouching Citroën. The foreigners drifted away slowly across the lanes of sparse traffic, as nonchalantly as if they were pre-war tourists deciding it was time for an aperitif, but they were actually seeking the illusion of greater safety in the shadowed streets.

I found myself following their example, dodging across the road to Rue Meyerbeer where wooden scaffolding enclosed another new apartment block rising on the ruins of an old villa. A man in a suit was arguing with a foreman at the corner, holding up a plan against the rough cross beams of the scaffolding and stabbing an angry finger at some design feature. The foreman was frozen in a shrug, his lips pursed and his hands held wide.

The temperature dropped as the shade closed in and I moved faster and turned into the Rue de France and crossed the road to the Café du Raisin. Mrs Mac was leaning on the zinc, *Le Petit Niçois* spread out before her. She raised an eye as I entered. 'Marty,' she said as a greeting. 'You're early.'

'Not much work to do. We're still waiting for the rumours to come true.'

Her name was Kathleen MacCloskey and we, all the English speakers, called her Mrs Mac, although her French customers knew her as Mme Bonnard. She had come to Nice before the last war as a nanny with an Anglo-Irish family, caught the eye of a dashing local, Lucien Bonnard, and was left widowed with an infant son when her husband killed himself racing a rival on the *moyen corniche* to Monaco in an old Ferrari that he had rebuilt with wires and a prayer to an unheeding god. There had been hints at the time that it wasn't an accident but nobody mentioned them anymore. It was a long time ago, fifteen years or so. Before I arrived in the city.

'That's a pity,' she said, picking a glass and holding it under the beer dispenser. 'We need the picture factory now more than ever.'

'That we do.' She always called the Victorine film studios the picture factory and was ever eager to hear gossip about the stars, the scandals of their relationships, the ones whose acting ability was limited to throwing tantrums. 'There was another rumour today,' I offered her.

She straightened the glass as the beer foamed near its rim. 'Anyone interesting?'

I leaned across the bar and dropped my voice. 'Claude Dauphin.'

She pursed her lips and waved her head from side to side in a so-so expression. 'Although he wasn't half bad in that Cinderella one.'

I smiled at her typically Irish roundabout praise, thinking not for the first time that you could take the woman out of Cavan but you couldn't take Cavan out of the woman. But for the fact that the counter was zinc, the tobacco smoke still had a nostalgic hint of Gauloise, and the newspaper wasn't *The Anglo-Celt*, she could have been in a pub in her native village. She gave me a hard eye that questioned what I thought was so funny. People were very touchy those days, their nerves raw behind the bland façade of daily life: the defeat was still an open sore, made worse by apprehension about what might yet be to come.

'Is it a comedy too or what?' she asked as she pushed the glass across the counter with a force that almost spilled some beer.

'I don't know. I didn't ask. It's just today's rumour.'

She gave a dismissive 'humph' and turned back to her paper, clearly narked at my amusement.

I raised my glass to the blue-eyed old *Maréchal* whose framed photo now stood on the shelf where she used to keep the Paddy and the other spirits before whiskey became impossible to get. I had begun to develop a taste for pastis as a suitable substitute until the *Maréchal* banned it too. All part of his campaign to stamp out the decadent republic that he blamed for France's current predicament. All part of his new *état Français* and its national revolution replacing *liberté, egalité, fraternité,* with *famille, travail, patrie.*

'I saw Solange at mass this morning,' Mrs Mac said without looking up from the paper.

I didn't say anything, knowing what was coming next. I drank some beer and felt the urge to light a cigarette but couldn't be bothered with what passed for them now. I looked around the bar to see if there was anyone I knew well enough to interrupt. The printer from the building next door was crouched over a long proof and didn't look like he'd welcome an intrusion.

'Really, Marty,' she said, closing the paper and folding it with an air of finality, 'you can't go on like this, especially these days. You have to do the decent thing.'

The 'especially these days' caught my attention. A dark thought crossed my mind. Could Mrs Mac be the source of the anonymous letters Solange had been receiving? I dismissed it as unworthy.

'What did she say?'

'Nothing. She never says anything about why you won't marry her.'

'It takes two people to get married, Mrs Mac.'

'What does that mean? Are you telling me she won't marry you?'

I sighed, trying to keep my patience. 'We've been over all this before.'

'And I've never got a proper answer. Why won't you marry her?'

I drank more beer and glanced at *Le Petit Niçois*. The upside down headline said something about more new laws.

'Are you just using her?'

'No.' I put down the glass harder than I intended. 'She doesn't think so, does she?'

'How can she not think that?'

'Is that what she says?'

'She's says nothing but it doesn't take a genius to see she's not happy.'

'You're wrong.' I lit a fake cigarette after all, to calm myself with the gesture, wondering why she was pursuing the issue now. Usually she contented herself with a few vague comments about our living arrangements, giving me a fool's pardon because I'd spent a few years in heathen Hollywood.

She was shaking her head. 'Time's running out,' she said, loading the phrase with heavy emphasis.

Oh Jesus, I thought. 'She's told you she wants a baby.'

'No,' she lied.

'There's plenty of time.'

'No, there isn't. What age are you now?'

I couldn't help laughing. 'I don't know if anyone ever told you, Mrs Mac, but my age …'

'What age are you?' she demanded in a schoolmistress voice.

I shook my head and admitted that I'd be forty-one this year. 'There's plenty of time,' I added. 'Solange is a lot younger than me.'

Mrs Mac gave me a look which suddenly reminded me of my mother's face when I did or said something stupid as a child, a closed-down look that mixed disappointment and despair.

I climbed the flights of stairs to the third floor in the gloom of the weak bulbs that were on every second landing to save electricity, and opened the door to Solange's flat. The smell hit me immediately, re-awakening a hungry memory from another age. Whatever was cooking smelt like food used to.

Solange was in the small kitchen and turned from the cooker with a spatula in her hand and a look of triumph. She leaned forward to be kissed. I glanced over her shoulder at the pan. Some kind of fish was frying in the midst of sizzling butter.

'What's that?' I asked after I'd given her a perfunctory kiss.

'*Un loup*,' she replied as if the sea bass was a normal sight on our table. 'You're happier to see a fish than to see me?'

'*Evidement*,' I said with an attempt at a Gallic shrug.

She tapped my forehead with the spatula and I put my arms around her and kissed her properly.

'That's better,' she said, turning back to the fish and flipping it over. 'It's nearly ready.'

'Where'd you get it? Signora Mancini?'

Solange was a cook and worked part-time for the widow of an Italian industrialist who had retired to a mansion on Cap Ferrat more than a decade earlier. He had sold up and left Italy after Blackshirts had burned one of his furniture factories in Milan when he criticised Mussolini. Luckily for him, he had died before the war or he would have been one of those in danger of being picked up those days by the *Organizzazione per la Vigilanza e la Repressione dell'Antifascismo* and repatriated against their wills. His widow, in her late seventies, could easily afford black market prices, a fact that benefited us regularly.

Solange pointed at the ceiling with the spatula. 'From Madame Lecroix.'

Mme Lecroix's husband was one of those who spent their nights fishing from the beach or the edge of the *Jetée-Promenade* which carried the casino out into the bay. So many people fished along the coast now that it was difficult to claim a spot, even more difficult to hook an increasingly rare fish.

Solange turned back to me. 'She wants your help. Her cooker keeps blowing a fuse.'

'Ah,' I said, trying to remember if I had interfered with the Lecroix fuse board when hiding my American passport. I was fairly sure it was behind somebody else's.

'And the butter?' Butter had become even scarcer than fish and was certainly more expensive on the black market.

'Signora Mancini,' Solange admitted. 'She had a little *bof* left over.' The search for butter, eggs and cheese was so all-consuming that their acronym from the French words had gone into everyday parlance.

'You've got cheese too?'

'No. Don't be greedy.'

'I was just hoping to be surprised again.'

'No more surprises tonight,' Solange said with a smile.

That was a relief. I had wondered on the way home if Mrs Mac's onslaught had been the opening shot of a plan to soften me up for a difficult conversation with Solange. Or even a warning of what was to come. But there was no sign that she was preparing for that. Nor did she appear unhappy, as Mrs Mac claimed.

Solange had made a melange of some indefinable vegetables, probably rutabaga, the all-purpose bulker-up of most meals those days. But she always managed to spice it up in different ways to hide its boring origin and make it taste new. She had now turned it into a tasty accompaniment to the butter-fried fish. I was a lucky man to live with such an imaginative cook, as Jean-Luc constantly reminded me.

I poured us each a glass of white wine and we ate slowly, savouring the meal.

'I met Mrs Mac this morning,' she said.

'So I heard.' I braced myself, noting that she called her Mrs Mac. Up to recently she had always referred to her as Mme Bonnard. Did that indicate that they'd been having a candid chat?

'You saw her?'

'Left work early and dropped into the café.'

'Did she ask you about Gerard?'

I shook my head. Gerard Bonnard was Mrs Mac's surly son and a trial to her. He seemed to blame her for his father's death, although he could barely remember Lucien. The mother and son relationship turned especially sour when he interpreted her desire to move back to Ireland before the war as a betrayal. Ever since, he refused to speak English to her, although he had grown up bilingual, albeit with the hint of a flat Cavan accent in English. Lucky enough to be too young to be conscripted into the army at the start of the war, he was now about eighteen.

'She wondered if you might be able to get him some work at the studio again,' Solange added.

'She never mentioned it.' She knew better, I thought. Thanks to Jean-Luc, I had got Gerard a job helping the carpenters build sets when he was sixteen but he had irritated everyone with his laziness and unhelpfulness, especially the communists who ran the carpenters' union and appreciated his political views even less than his work shyness. Conflicted as they had been about Stalin's deal with Hitler just before the war, they hadn't appreciated his insistence that they were now all on the same side. His outspoken fascist sympathies always seemed to me to be more a way of irritating his workmates than a political stance. In any event, he hadn't lasted long.

'There's no work available,' I added. 'Unless a new film comes in.'

'He's joined the Legionnaires.'

I looked at her in surprise. 'But he wasn't in the army.'

The *Légion Français des Combattants* had been set up after the Armistice for veterans by a Niçois hero of this war and of the previous one, Joseph Darnand. It was devoted to Vichy's Revolution Nationale, and quickly became more xenophobic and fascist than Marshal Pétain's supporters. It was violently anti-communist and anti-semitic.

'They have a youth section now for those who were too young for the war,' Solange said. 'Mrs Mac found out only when she saw his khaki shirt, black tie and beret.'

'I can see why she's worried.'

The Légion was a growing presence on the streets with torch-lit rallies and their chants of 'France! France!' They were becoming more aggressive, randomly stopping people who looked foreign and demanding to know if they were Jews. I didn't look foreign but I kept out of their way. I was very aware these days that my accent in French marked me out as an English speaker and, to the excitable and paranoid, a potential spy. Which would be the kind of black joke – me being beaten up as a British spy – that life likes to throw at you for the fun of it.

After dinner I got my toolbox and went upstairs to the Lecroix flat and patched a cable whose rubber insulation had melted and caused a short circuit. I thanked Madame for the fish and promised to make a more permanent repair as soon as I could get the necessary material. I could snip off another short length of cable from something in the studio and maybe earn another sea bass in gratitude.

Later, I lay in bed beside Solange, listening to her barely audible breathing and the creaks of the old building, wondering about the future. Solange had said nothing about wanting marriage or a baby. But it was obvious that she had discussed it with Mrs Mac, who in turn had told her about her problems with Gerard. They were both informing me of the other's wishes. I didn't have any answers for either.

Life was still good in spite of the traumas this country and its people had endured and were still enduring. People were more closed than they used to be. Fear and apprehension hovered beneath the surface, ready to break through at any moment. Food and other shortages were getting worse and darkening the public mood. But Solange and I could get by all right. Imaginative cooks and efficient electricians were in as much demand as ever, possibly more so; we could make a living even without formal jobs if we found ourselves among the growing numbers of unemployed. And the war had to end sometime, settle down into some new normality.

But none of that was what was really gnawing at me. It would soon be twenty years since I had left Ireland. More than ten years since I'd left America. It was too risky to go back to America and I couldn't decide if I wanted to go back to Ireland. Or even if I could. But I didn't know if I wanted to stay in France either. It had always been a temporary refuge without any real thought of where my permanent home should be. But some biological clock of my own was beginning to tick, urging me to move on. Or at least to make a decision.

I'd been running for so long that I was now drifting and I knew it. But it wasn't the worst of fates. There were a lot worse to be seen all around us every day.

# Three

A few mornings later I was sitting in the canteen at La Victorine reading a Peter Cheyney novel in French and sipping the concoction of acorns and roasted barley that now passed for coffee when Jean-Luc Lebret sat down opposite me with a 'Bonjour, Martin.'

I placed the novel on the table upside down to keep my place and he turned it around to read the blurb on the back cover. 'Any good?' he asked.

'You wouldn't like it.'

He gave a disinterested shrug and lit a brown cigarette. We'd had this conversation before. Why was I always reading those pulp novels? Because it passed the time on the set when I wasn't needed. In my early days in Hollywood with Rex Ingram I used to pay attention to what was happening, to how he directed the actors, placed the cameras, assembled the shots, built the story. I had some notion back then that I'd like to do what he did, be a director. But that notion had faded years ago. Now I just did my job and had no greater ambitions.

Jean-Luc was about my age, a dark-skinned southerner whose good looks often led visitors to assume that he was one of the stars at La Victorine rather than one of its carpenters. He had even been asked to sign an autograph or two in the pre-war days. He was the closest I had to a friend in Nice, thanks partly to a shared experience of internment in France, and partly to one late night's drinking session when I had unwisely dropped my guard and told him something of my war in Ireland. I had never made that mistake a second time and he had never asked me about it again or mentioned what I had told him.

Shortly afterwards, when this war was declared, he was interned as the head of the communist union representing the carpenters in the studio. He had renounced the party in disgust at Stalin's pact with Hitler and was eventually released. Most of the union's leaders hadn't followed his example and were still locked up. Then, after the Armistice, when Vichy turned anti-British, I was interned briefly as an enemy alien until I managed to establish that I was a neutral. Jean-Luc helped me get my job back at the studio.

'The rumour is true,' he said.

'Which one?'

'Marcel Carné. A story set in the Middle Ages.'

'Ah,' I laughed. 'Lots of sets. Lots of work for you.'

'And maybe for you,' he smiled. 'Recreating candlelight.'

'Flickering light's no problem. But the cameras don't like it.'

But that was definitely good news. We needed a feature film with an established director to get the studio working properly again. Instead of ticking over with cheap propaganda films about rural pursuits and the interminable newsreels of Marshal Pétain visiting villages and artisan workshops.

'Not another false start, is it?' I asked, becoming cautious. There had been a lot of those in recent months.

Jean-Luc shook his head. 'The Germans and Italians are funding it, Continental and La Scalera. Work has already begun in Paris. They're moving here soon.'

So it was real this time. The German involvement meant we would get the supplies of film and other essentials that were increasingly scarce. 'Who's in it?'

'Arletty. It's a medieval tale involving the devil.'

'Gabin, too?' Carné had already made a film before the war with Jean Gabin and Arletty that had made her name, *Le Jour Se Lève*. She was now one of the country's best-known stars, even though the film had been banned by the Vichy government as demoralising.

'There's been no mention of him, so he mustn't be included.'

We left our cups on the counter and headed back towards the workshops. Jean-Luc mentioned that the rough cut of the latest newsreel was about to be shown. He turned towards the screening room but I couldn't be bothered. Besides, I had just remembered that I hadn't yet snipped a length of flex from somewhere to fix Mme Lecroix's cooker properly.

'By the way,' I said, stopping him as something else occurred to me. 'You remember Gerard Bonnard? Mme Bonnard's son?'

'That young pup. What's he doing now?'

'Looking for a job.'

Jean-Luc gave a dismissive laugh.

'He might have settled down a little by now,' I offered. 'He was very immature the last time he was here.'

'You could take him on as an apprentice electrician,' Jean-Luc smiled, then clapped me on the shoulder to demonstrate no hard feelings and added, '*À bientôt*,' as he walked off.

***

The Café du Raisin was busy with the after-work crowd. Solange wasn't there yet so I went up to the bar where Mrs Mac was pouring red wine into four glasses on a tray for her waitress, Ange-Marie. She began pouring my glass of beer as soon as she'd finished.

'We're back in business,' I said as I waited and told her about the Marcel Carné film.

'It's a pity Gabin isn't in it,' she sniffed.

'Maybe he will be. I don't know all the details, but you'll like it. It's about the devil.'

She gave me her don't be cheeky glance and said, 'So they'll keep you on for another while then.'

'It appears so.'

She passed the beer to me and I lit a cigarette. I inhaled out of habit and coughed up the smoke again as its harsh tang caught the back of my throat. They were useless. The only part of the smoking habit they satisfied was the ritual of lighting and holding cigarettes. It was something but it wasn't much without the satisfying hit of nicotine.

'You'd be as well giving those things up altogether,' Mrs Mac said.

'I know.' I stubbed the cigarette out in the old Pernod ashtray on the zinc. 'I made some inquiries about a carpentry job for Gerard on the new film but …' I shrugged.

She sighed, a sound of resignation, and thanked me, which made me feel guilty at the feebleness of my approach to Jean-Luc. But I had no intention of trying to take on Gerard as an apprentice electrician either: he was nothing but trouble.

'Solange told me he's a Legionnaire now. Can you get someone to talk to him?' I knew there was no point in his mother trying to dissuade him. Or me for that matter, or, indeed, any of her friends.

'Who?' she asked with a look of desperation.

'Some of his father's old friends,' I suggested.

'Out of the frying pan and into the fire,' she snorted and turned her attention to Ange-Marie again as the waitress called out another order and plonked some empty glasses on the counter. It was the closest I'd ever heard Mrs Mac come to confirming the rumours about Lucien Bonnard's involvement with the gang that controlled the port area, emulating the mafias from across the border in Italy.

I checked my watch. Solange was late, which was very unlike her. The café was full, mainly with familiar faces, even if I didn't know all their names. One of them, a professional gambler, caught my eye and raised his wine glass to me. I raised my beer in return. The hubbub of conversation and the soft glow of the lights reflecting off the dark windows created a cosy atmosphere that challenged the realities of the outside world. But for the absence of real tobacco smoke and glasses of spirits, we could have been back in the pre-disaster days of the Third Republic.

'Solange hasn't been in earlier, has she?' I asked Mrs Mac when she was free.

'No. I haven't seen her today.'

'I was due to meet her here but she's late.'

I thought for a moment that Mrs Mac was about to launch into her marriage lecture again but she changed the subject. 'There's an Irish diplomat here at the moment,' she said. 'From Vichy. Staying at the Hotel Suisse. I'm hoping he'll update my passport and include Gerard on it.'

'Will he go to Ireland with you now?'

She avoided the direct question. 'I want to make the arrangements. Have them in place.'

I knew that persuading Gerard to go would be another day's work, a hard day's work. But I didn't want to discourage her. 'There shouldn't be any problem with the passport,' I said to sound encouraging.

'He's still underage. I can get him included on mine without his involvement. Or so I thought. But this fellow says it could be complicated because Gerard was born here and is French.'

'But surely he's Irish too?'

'He says it's not as simple as that. Not these days with so many people trying to claim they're something else. There are a lot more procedures to go through. So he says.'

It sounded like he was giving her the run-around for some reason. 'I don't know,' I said. 'It mightn't be the best time to try to go home now.' Like everyone else, I was aware of the thousands of refugees in Nice, some happy to stay in the belief that it was a safe haven, most hoping to move on, if they had the money and contacts. Ideally, to get out of Europe altogether, to America. 'It's not easy get back to Ireland even if you have the passports and Gerard agrees to go.'

'You've thought about it yourself?'

'No.' Which wasn't entirely true. I'd given it some casual thought but not any serious consideration. Still, I knew enough to know it would require travel permits for Spain and Portugal and then some luck to get on a coaster from Lisbon to Dublin. There was a flight from Lisbon to Foynes but the word was that you had to be very rich or very well connected to have any chance of getting on board. 'It's probably better to wait out the war here.'

'I don't know about that,' she said, her eyes sweeping over the café as if she could see beneath the surface of the apparently contented social scene before her.

'You don't think so?' I felt a sense of unease. Mrs Mac knew much more about Nice than I did, from her nearly thirty years here, and from her vantage-point behind this bar.

'I think ...' she paused and changed her mind about what she had been going to say. 'Maybe it's just Gerard.' She sighed.

'Things would look brighter if you could get him fixed up properly.'

'That's true,' she agreed.

A man came to the counter to pay and she exchanged some light banter with him as she rang through the coins. Maybe I should do what Jean-Luc suggested and see if I could take on Gerard as an apprentice, I thought, feeling guilty at not doing more to help her. I watched four old men concentrating on a board game as if the fate of the world depended on its outcome.

'Anyway,' Mrs Mac said, changing the subject again as she returned, took my empty glass and poured me another drink. 'This diplomat fellow, Seamus O'Casey, was asking about you.'

'About me?'

She nodded. 'Wanted to know if you were still in Nice and where you live.'

I didn't like the sound of this. I had had nothing to do with Irish officialdom for nearly twenty years. The last time I'd come up against it, someone put a Webley revolver to my head and offered me a choice of leaving the country or getting a bullet in the head in the Dublin mountains. It wasn't a figure of speech. I had known some lads who hadn't taken the choice seriously and whose bodies were found in the mountains or never found at all. I had chosen New York.

'What exactly did he say?' I asked, feigning only a casual interest.

'Just that. Is Marty Harris still in Nice? And where's he living now? I didn't give him Solange's address.'

'Did you give him my other address?'

She gave me a wry smile. 'I didn't know you still had that other address -- that little place on the rue de la Republique? Why haven't you got rid of it?'

I could see the shadow of suspicion cross her face and knew she was thinking it had something to do with my intentions towards Solange but it hadn't. I simply hadn't gotten around to it and then the poison pen letters had started arriving. I changed the subject. 'What did you say his name was again?'

'O'Casey. Seamus O'Casey. He also pronounced it the Irish way. Ó Cathasaigh.'

The name meant nothing to me, neither in English nor Irish.

'He sounded like he was a friend of yours,' she said, becoming aware that I was not delighted by this man's interest. She knew nothing of my departure from Ireland, probably assuming that I was just another emigrant who had washed up in America in search of a job and a better future. 'But I didn't tell him anything. I said you came in occasionally but I didn't know where you lived.'

I gave her a reassuring smile and resisted the temptation to ask for a description of O'Casey or any more details about him. I looked at my watch. Solange was now very late, more than forty minutes. 'I'd better go and see what's happened to Solange,' I said.

It was cold and dark outside. I pulled up the collar of my jacket and jammed my hands in my pockets as I made my way down by the Albert Park to the Promenade des Anglais. The sound of shouting came down on the wind from the old casino on Place

Massena and I caught sight of the flickering of torches. The Légion was at it again, another rally.

A pale moon cast a ruffled white path across the swell in the bay. The tide was out and the white foam of the breaking waves was lined with fishermen, some with little lanterns hanging by their seats. A group of them were gathered around a small fire, its flames bent horizontal. Behind me the lights of the Palais de la Jetée hovered above the water on its invisible iron latticework.

I kept my head down against the cold mountain wind, dominant now that it no longer had to compete with the daytime sun. I was thinking of Seamus O'Casey, running every variant of his names in English and Irish through my memory. James, Jim. Jimmy. Jem. Shamey. Shay. Nothing struck a chord. Which was even more worrying. It was possible that some former comrade was now working for the government in Dublin since our side in the civil war had finally got into power. But the odds were that their diplomats were still dominated by those who had sold out the republic.

Why would one of them at Vichy want to meet me? How did they even know I was here? I'd had nothing to do with them for nearly two decades and should have disappeared off the face of the earth as far as they were concerned. But Mrs Mac had confirmed for O'Casey what he presumably knew already, that I was indeed in Nice. And he had called me Marty, so she said. Nobody had called me that for a long time, except herself. Which was probably why she had used it. Or so I hoped.

I glanced at the Hotel Suisse, nestled into the side of the huge rocky outcrop at the end of the Promenade, as if O'Casey might have been standing there watching for me. There was no sign of life other than a dim light glowing through the glass in its hall door. Whatever O'Casey wanted with me, I certainly wanted nothing to do with him.

I hurried on around the hill and turned my worry to Solange instead. It was very unlike her to be so late or not to turn up at all. She had said she would be finished work early; Signora Mancini was going out to dinner at one of her neighbours' and didn't need her for the afternoon. Which was why we had agreed to meet in Mrs Mac's and probably go to a film.

I ran up the stairs and let myself into her apartment. It was in darkness. My worry turned to fear. I stepped into the kitchen, wondering what this might mean, and became aware of a figure sitting by the table at the window.

I must have uttered a curse or something because Solange said, 'Sorry I frightened you.'

'Why are you sitting in the dark?' I asked, my relief sounding unintentionally aggressive.

She said nothing. I reached back to the wall and flicked on the light switch.

Her eyes were red and the tears began to flow again when she looked at me. She had a handkerchief balled in her hand and she pushed it into one eye and then the other. I put my arms around her and kissed the top of her head. 'What?' I said. 'What is it?' But I could see what it was as soon as I asked the question.

On the table before her there was a strip of brown cardboard. Scrawled across the top was the word 'Abortionist!' And under it in crude capital letters the words, 'You Were Warned. You are a disgrace to the New State. The State Tribunal will deal with you now!'

I picked it up and turned it over. It was part of one of the ubiquitous posters of Marshal Pétain against the colours of the French flag. They were everywhere around the town, lines of them on hoardings, now beginning to fade and lose their colours after a summer's sunshine and another winter. It was the same photo as the one framed in Mrs Mac's café.

'It was nailed to the door,' Solange said.

'For fuck's sake,' I muttered, trying to scrunch the cardboard into a ball. A chunk of plaster was still stuck to one side of it where it had been pasted on a wall. It was too stiff to ball and I tore it into strips and dropped them into the bin under the sink.

'It's just more of the same shit,' I said, pulling over the other kitchen chair and sitting down beside her. She had already received three letters in the last year telling her she was a disgrace to the Maréchal and the wholesome world of Family, Work and State that France needed after the debauchery of the Third Republic. 'Don't let it upset you.'

'You don't understand,' she said.

'It's the same sick person, saying the same old stuff.'

'It's not the same.' Her tears began to flow again. I put my arm around her and she sobbed into my shoulder. She said something that I didn't catch. She straightened up and looked at me. 'You don't read the papers, do you?'

I shook my head.

'There's a new law. You can be executed for abortion.'

'You're not an abortionist,' I pointed out.

'You can be executed for having an abortion,' she corrected herself.

I stared at her. 'That's madness. They can't execute everyone who's had an abortion.'

'They won't have to. Just make an example of a few women.'

'But you haven't had an abortion.'

She sighed as if I was being obtuse. 'I will be denounced for having had one and I'll be brought before the State Tribunal.'

'But you haven't had an abortion,' I repeated. 'They can't convict you for something you didn't do.' But even as I said it, I knew how feeble it sounded. The State Tribunal had been set up to try communists and probably wasn't all that diligent about evidence. It sounded a lot like the military tribunals of my youth that had had only one sentence, death, for anyone found with a weapon. A fate from which I had had a lucky escape.

I pulled Solange closer and held her tight. We sat like that for a while in silence, angled awkwardly together on the kitchen chairs. Over her shoulder I could see an open fishing boat with a lantern in its bow heading out of the port. The weak lights of a couple of bars across the harbour broke the dark bulk of Mont Boron rising behind it.

Solange eventually broke the silence. 'You should leave. For a little while.'

I released her and stared at her in surprise.

'Just for a little while,' she repeated with a pleading tone. 'Until this blows over.'

I shook my head. 'We can't give in to this kind of blackmail. It's just some bitter old person in the building.' We had talked about it at length the year before when the first scribbled note on a copybook page had been pushed under the door. We had gone through everybody in the building and identified a few likely suspects, especially those who ignored me on the stairs. But it seemed that this wasn't going to blow over: whoever was nasty enough to send these messages appeared determined to go on doing it indefinitely.

'Look,' I said, trying to calm her, 'we've talked this through every time and agreed that it doesn't mean anything except that somebody is bitter and jealous of us. And there's no evidence that they've ever denounced you to anyone, is there?'

'This is different.'

'How is it different?'

'Because this is a police matter now, not just politics. It's the death penalty.'

'But you haven't had an abortion!'

'I don't want the police investigating me.'

'Nobody wants the police investigating them. But the worst that can happen is that they do and find you're innocent.' I had no idea whether it was easy or even possible to prove that a woman had or had not had an abortion.

'It would be just for a little while.' She put her hands on the side of my face and kissed me tenderly. 'It won't change anything between us. I still love you.'

'We can't let this come between us.'

'It won't. Really.' She managed a smile. 'Nothing will change, just that you don't stay overnight. So nobody sees you leave in the mornings.'

I wondered whether there was more to this than met the eye. Did she know more about this threat than she was telling me? Was it something to do with Mrs Mac's warning that she wanted marriage and children?

'We shouldn't give in to this kind of intimidation,' I said.

'I know,' she said with the air of resignation of a mother explaining the unfairness of the world to a child. 'But … .'

I hugged her close again and she pulled back her head to kiss me deeply. This was much more difficult for her than for me, I knew. She was the one in the line of fire. She had lived in this building and known the neighbours for a decade or more. I was the interloper, unattached to any of them, a foreigner who had no respect for the customs of this new era, no understanding of or concern for the pressures and tensions that had been exposed by France's defeat.

'Okay,' I whispered eventually. 'Whatever you think is best.'

She increased the pressure in her arms and whispered back, 'Thank you.'

'But there's no reason why you can't stay overnight in my place.'

She released me with a look of mock horror. 'I'm not staying in that place. In that little bed.'

'It would make us feel young again. Like we were avoiding our parents.'

'Don't be silly.' She stood up and pulled me to my feet.

She led me into the bedroom and we undressed each other, something we hadn't done for a long time, and made love like it was a new experience, rediscovering each other all over again, thanks to some malicious busybody. I dozed off afterwards luxuriating in the feeling of wellbeing and the irony that the busybody had improved our lovemaking, recreating something that had been lost in routine.

When I opened my eyes, Solange was bending over me, her hair tickling my nose. 'Ah no,' I said as I came to consciousness and deciphered her unspoken message. 'Not now.'

'Yes,' she said. 'We have to start now.'

I grumbled and groaned but eventually put my feet onto the cold floor and began to get dressed. She watched me in silence, lying on her side, her head propped on her hand. It occurred to me that perhaps this was her way of saying goodbye, of ending our relationship. But I dismissed it out of hand. Solange was straightforward and did not beat around the bush, which was one of the reasons that I didn't take Mrs Mac's urgings of marriage and children too seriously. If that was what Solange really wanted, I was sure I would have known it from her.

I put on my jacket and felt the coil of electric wire in the pocket. I took it out and said. 'I got the flex to fix Madame Lecroix's cooker. I might as well do it now.'

'Good idea,' she said. 'I'll make something to eat while you do it.'

The Lecroix were in their late sixties or early seventies and lived in the apartment above Solange's. Madame was more or less housebound but to be seen occasionally inching up the four flights of stairs as if every step was a major hurdle. She was surprised to see me and I knew immediately she had heard about the threat pinned to Solange's door. She was friendly, thanking me profusely for coming back to make the permanent repair, but she was embarrassed too, avoiding my eye. It took me only a few minutes to replace the flex.

'How is Solange?' she asked as I was leaving.

'She's fine.'

'Good. I'm glad to hear it. Tell her to call up if she needs anything.'

I thanked her, taking her words as a message of support.

'See,' I said to Solange after I told her, 'you're overreacting. This is just one nasty bastard who has it in for us for some reason. Or for no reason.'

She had made some pasta with a pesto sauce and something else and we ate it mostly in silence. I made small talk, as if everything was as usual, telling her what was happening in the studios; Jean-Luc and the other carpenters were busy creating some medieval rooms and I was to check all the electrics so there were no breakdowns and delays when Marcel Carné and his actors arrived in a couple of days.

'Once shooting begins, I'll be leaving very early in the mornings,' I pointed out hopefully. 'Nobody will see me going.'

She shook her head with a half-smile. 'Please don't make it harder than it is,' she said.

I gathered up some clothes and my shaving equipment and we embraced at the door.

'Thanks,' she said. 'I just want a little time on my own.'

That sounded ominous, a change of reasoning from earlier, but I let it go; there was no point getting into an argument. Or, perhaps, I didn't want to hear what I didn't want to hear. It was best to let matters play out as they would.

The streets were dark and empty and the temperature felt colder as I headed towards the single room I hadn't visited in weeks. I walked quickly along rue Cassini, facing into the cutting wind that swept down from the mountains, trying to stay warm and come to terms with the uneasy feeling that things were beginning to fall apart, although I didn't know how or why.

# Four

It took me a couple of days to find Henri Tillon, a policeman who frequented Mrs Mac's and for whom I had done a favour a few years earlier. I'd arranged to have his star-struck daughter included as an extra in the last feature film at La Victorine.

I found him in the café the following Wednesday. I got my usual beer and chatted with Mrs Mac for a few minutes while observing him. He was standing at the other end of the bar with a couple of men in civilian clothes who also had the look of policemen: tough-looking men in their thirties with an aggressive swagger to their wide-legged stances. Tillon was older, in his late forties or early fifties. He had a more relaxed air and was beginning to run to fat. I didn't know exactly what he did but assumed he was a deskman at the municipal police headquarters on the edge of the Old Town.

'You want me to tell him you'd like a word?' Mrs Mac asked. She hadn't inquired why I was looking for him.

I thought about that, then nodded.

Tillon looked over when Mrs Mac spoke to him and sauntered across a minute later. 'I hear you're busy out there again,' he said after we shook hands. 'Big names back in town.'

'Yes, at last. How's Laurence?'

'Still has a headful of Hollywood nonsense.'

I gave a polite laugh and got down to business. 'I would like to ask your advice on something, if I may.'

He invited me to go ahead with a spread of his hands.

'My friend Solange has been receiving anonymous letters.'

He raised his eyes upwards in a gesture of impatience. 'Denunciations! We're overwhelmed with them.'

I had heard as much but it was reassuring to learn it from him. The police were hardly likely to pay much attention to them if they were that common. 'She is very upset by them.'

'Most of the complaints are about the wives of prisoners of war having relations with other men,' he added. 'It's a real difficulty.'

I wasn't sure whether he meant that the difficulty lay in the denunciations or the relationships but I could see the problem. There were nearly two million French soldiers still held in German prisoner of war camps, hostages for the country's acceptance of its fate and its good behaviour. Which left a lot of women without husbands or boyfriends.

'She's worried about this new law on abortion.'

'That's why she's being denounced? She's not carrying out abortions, is she?'

'No, of course not.'

'Then she has nothing to worry about.'

'She says the law includes women who've had abortions. Not that she has had one.'

'The government is just issuing a warning,' he said dismissively. 'There's been a big increase in abortions for obvious reasons. The authorities want people to behave themselves.' He raised his eyes in an indication that he didn't think that was likely to happen. He didn't appear to be a committed supporter of le Maréchal's obsession with the country's morals.

I signalled to Mrs Mac and she took our empty glasses and began to refill them.

'I'll keep an eye out,' he said. 'If I see anything about her, I'll throw it in the bin.'

'Thanks,' I said. 'That'll ease her mind.'

'Tell me about this new film.'

'*Les Visiteurs du Soir*. A medieval romance involving the devil.'

'Doesn't every romance involve the devil,' Mrs Mac said, putting Tillon's full glass in front of him.

'Oh, Madame Bonnard, you are too cynical,' Tillon said with a laugh.

'Too long in the tooth,' she muttered in English.

Tillon looked confused and I explained. 'She's too worldly to be easily fooled.'

'Nobody would try to fool Madame Bonnard,' he said.

'They wouldn't be wise to try,' I added as she put down my beer in front of me. She shot me a narrow-eyed look and went to deal with another customer. I told Tillon there was almost certainly going to be crowd scenes in the new film if his daughter was still interested.

'Oh, no,' he said. 'I thought the last time would open her eyes after you told me how boring it would be. Waiting around, being herded here and there, doing the same thing over and over. But she didn't find it boring at all. It only encouraged her nonsense.'

'I'm sorry.'

'Wasn't your fault. But don't give her any help if she comes to you again.'

'No, I won't,' I promised. So much for thinking that he owed me a favour.

He took a long slow drink of his beer and smacked his lips as if he was tasting it for the first time. He put his glass on the zinc with care. 'Do you know a man called Jean-Luc Lebret at La Victorine?'

My heart sank. I couldn't deny I knew him. I didn't know what Tillon knew about our friendship. It was conducted mainly in the studios; we rarely met outside of there, partly because he lived over in the Var. 'He's one of the carpenters,' I said, non-committedly.

'Is he still a communist?'

'I wouldn't know,' I said, cursing inwardly for having landed myself in this situation. 'I've never had a political conversation with him.'

'You know he was a communist?'

'I knew he was involved in the carpenters' union.'

'And that he was interned as a communist?'

'He was away for a while.'

'And he renounced the party,' Tillon added, filling in the gap I had left.

'So I heard. But I don't talk politics with him or anyone else. Not my place as a foreigner in your country.'

Tillon nodded a couple of times. 'That's very sensible. We'd all be much better off if we followed your example. It's politics that's got us into this mess. Too much politics.'

It was a common theme after the fierce political divisions between left and right during the thirties. I said nothing, demonstrating my refusal to become involved in such debates. And it wasn't just because I was a foreigner. I'd had enough of politics in my own time and place and had no desire to become immersed in all that again. All it did, as I had learned to my cost, was to inflame passions, and ignite hatreds and violence.

'Don't worry about your girlfriend,' he added, picking up his glass. 'She has nothing to be concerned about.'

'Thanks. She'll be relieved to hear that.'

'Politics,' he shrugged. 'Just politics.'

He went back to his colleagues, leaving me unsettled. I didn't like the turn the conversation had taken. I should have known better than to ask a policeman for a favour. They always turned it back on you, looking to use you in return. He hadn't pressed me about Jean-Luc but that was no reassurance that he wouldn't come back to me later with more questions. Or was I just being paranoid, I wondered. Tillon didn't sound all that enamoured of politics or the Vichy regime.

'All right?' Mrs Mac asked me with a look of concern.

I nodded and held out my glass. 'I'll have another one please.'

Calm down, I told myself. He didn't know Jean-Luc was a friend. Or did he? Were his questions a test of my veracity? Or, more worrying, a test of my willingness to provide information? With any luck I'd said enough to dissuade him from thinking I'd be his informer, but part of me knew that that was wishful thinking.

'Henri is a good man,' Mrs Mac said as she put down my drink. 'Reminds me of a RIC sergeant we used to have at home. A countryman at heart who had a lot of common sense. Never came down too hard on anyone. Always tried to help people out of their difficulties.' She paused. 'Still, he was shot during the troubled times.'

'Killed?' I asked, feeling some response was expected of me.

'Yes,' she said. 'It was said that some outsiders did it, not local lads.'

I wondered if there was more to that story than she'd said. Whether he had been some relation of hers, perhaps. Whether his killing had something to do with her departure from Ireland. She had left during the war of independence, about the time it would have happened. I knew as little about Mrs Mac's background as I hoped she knew about mine. And I wasn't about to open any avenues into sharing our family histories.

'He's a help to me,' she said about Tillon. 'Keeping an eye on Gerard.'

'That's good,' I reassured her, although I didn't necessarily think it was. But that might have been my sudden suspiciousness distorting my judgement. 'Can he persuade him to give up the politics?'

'He's tried. To no avail.'

'That's a pity.'

She gave a resigned sigh and changed the subject. 'Seamus O'Casey has been asking about you again.'

'Why?' I asked in surprise. 'What does he want with me?'

'He didn't say and I didn't ask. He went out to the studio looking for you yesterday.'

'He what!'

'They wouldn't let him in. They wouldn't even pass a message on to you, he said.'

Security at La Victorine had become stricter now that the stars were beginning to arrive. A few people were turning up outside every day to catch a glimpse of them or even to weasel their way inside. O'Casey had obviously fallen foul of some officious security man who wouldn't accept the 'I'm a friend of one of the crew' line. Thankfully.

'Would you talk to him? For my sake?'

'You want me to talk to him? About what?'

'About whatever he wants to talk to you about.'

'And what might that be?'

She gave a helpless shrug. The look of pleading on her face was a close relation of the anguished look that appeared whenever she discussed her worries about Gerard.

'He's putting pressure on you,' I said.

'There are difficulties with visas and travel permits, he says. Especially for someone who's only half-Irish.'

Bastard, I thought. Who was this guy? 'Are you sure he's a diplomat?'

Mrs Mac looked confused. 'That's what he says. You think he's not?'

'He doesn't sound very diplomatic.'

'Who would he be then?'

'I have no idea,' I admitted. There was only one way to find out. If he was that persistent, he would catch up with me sooner or later. And if Mrs Mac thought she needed my help, I couldn't refuse it. 'Okay, I'll talk to him.'

She squeezed the back of my hand and the lines on her face dissolved. 'Thanks, Marty,' she said.

Solange didn't seem greatly reassured when I told her what Henri Tillon had said. 'How would he know?' she asked.

'He's a policeman. He knows what's going on. What he sees around him at work.'

'A deskman.' She dismissed him with an expressive flick of her hand. 'He's only putting in his time there. He knows nothing.'

I wondered again why she was so determined to make such an issue about this latest anonymous missive. But I didn't want to have a row about it. She was clearly upset about something; I just wasn't convinced that it was the threat of denunciation.

Work was busy now. I was at the studio from early in the morning, arriving before the winter dawn and leaving after dark. All the supplies and replacements that could not be had up to now suddenly became available. Rolls of new electric cabling, selections of bulbs for the arc lamps, replacement lenses for cameras. Anything that was requested was available, thanks, we assumed, to the German producers. Marcel Carné, the director, was known to be a perfectionist and had a reputation for being particularly impatient with those of us who were supposed to make everything work. Everything had to be in perfect working order, the managers told us, you'll know all about his sharp tongue. More likely they feared it themselves. Either way, we were kept busy repairing or replacing anything that might cause a problem and hold up filming.

The cast had arrived in a reserved carriage from Paris, trying to live up to their glamorous images as they disembarked after an exhausting 20-hour journey from a train that was a far cry from Le Train Bleu, the pre-war luxury sleeper service. Still, there was a crowd outside Nice Ville station to see mayor Jean Medecin greet them in a ceremony that hankered back to the old days of not so long ago. Then they boarded a fleet of cars for the Negresco Hotel.

They began to appear at the studio over the following days as preparations reached a climax of hammering and a crew of painters were sent up the hills to Tourrettes-sur-Loup to change the walls of its medieval castle from grey to brilliant white. The director wanted a sharp contrast for his outdoor scenes.

I saw Jean-Luc on the sound stage from time to time as the carpenters mocked-up parts of rooms. It was a couple of days before I got the opportunity to talk to him in private. I found him leaning against the outside wall of the studio where shooting was taking place, smoking and soaking up the noonday sun.

'There's the devil.' He gestured with his chin to where Jules Berry was walking up and down forty yards away with a script in his left hand, mouthing something we couldn't hear. 'He's in trouble already. Can't remember his lines.' Berry was a hooded-eyed actor in his fifties who had been a star of the silent screen, which may have been why he had problems learning lines. He was wearing a black doublet with horizontal stripes over white hose and had his tricorn hat tilted back on his head.

'I hear he's a big gambler,' I said, taking up position at the wall beside Jean-Luc. 'At the baccarat tables in the Palais de la Méditerranée every night since he arrived.'

'He and Arletty had a shouting match on set yesterday. She walked out of the scene because he kept fluffing his lines. He said he was interpreting the script rather than sticking to the literal words, which were not important. She wasn't having any of it. Neither was Carné.'

'I can imagine.' Arletty didn't look like someone prepared to put up with any nonsense. She was in her early forties now, a small bundle of energy with the ability to dominate every scene; the camera found in her an even greater presence than was visible to the naked eye. And she was already quite a presence in real life.

We watched Berry throw up his hands in an unlikely gesture of devilish frustration. He gave up his pacing and sat down on an upturned drum, dropped the script on the ground, and lit a cigarette. The sweet smell of real tobacco drifted over to us a few moments later.

'Do you know a policeman called Henri Tillon,' I asked Jean-Luc casually. 'He's a regular in Madame Bonnard's.'

'Don't think so.'

'He was asking about you the other day.'

'Asking you?' Jean-Luc turned to me. 'Asking you what?'

'If you were still a communist.'

Jean-Luc searched my face as if he was trying to see whether or not I was joking. His look said it wasn't funny if I was. 'Why did he ask you that?'

'I don't know. I told him we never talked about politics.'

'I mean why did he ask you?'

I sighed. 'Because I had asked him something.' I told him about Solange.

'That was a mistake,' he said when I had finished.

'I know that now,' I admitted, 'but I thought you should know.'

He nodded what I took to be approval, even thanks. 'What else did he ask you?'

'That was it. Were you still a communist? I said we never discussed politics. That French politics was none of my business.'

He dropped his cigarette butt on the ground and rubbed at it with his foot until it broke up. 'He'll ask you again,' he said after a moment, as if he was choosing his words carefully.

'And I'll tell him the same thing.'

'That won't satisfy him.'

'Too bad. I'm not going to spy on you for him. You don't need to worry about that.'

He gave no sign that he believed me or had even heard me. In the distance Berry stretched a hand down to pick his script off the ground and went back to his lines.

'You're wrong about politics,' Jean-Luc said. 'It is your business. It's not even French politics anymore. It's everyone's business now.'

It was my turn to give no indication that I had heard him. I had no desire to go down that road.

'I know you've had your own war,' he went on after a moment, his first allusion to what I had told him that drunken night a long time ago. 'But this is different. A different scale. Nobody can sit on the side-lines now.'

I closed my eyes and felt the warm sun on my face. I had no desire to become immersed again in a cause that took over your life and justified things that should never be done. Which side did them didn't much matter. What mattered was the beliefs that permitted them. I no longer had any such beliefs.

The door away to our right opened and the slim young Italian assistant director, Michelangelo Antonioni, stepped out, beckoned me and called to Jules Berry. The actor stood up, straightened his hat, squared his shoulders and marched towards us with a scowl worthy of the man in charge of hell. I followed him inside.

I thought of Berry that evening as I squared my shoulders and approached the Hotel Suisse. I had made one attempt to talk to the Irish diplomat after my promise to Mrs Mac. He hadn't been in when I called and I had put off trying again for a couple of days. But it was better to get it over and done with.

Seamus O'Casey was seated in the small residents' lounge overlooking the Quai des Etats Unis to which the receptionist directed me. My first impression was of a small, compact man, soft-faced, with dark hair swept backwards and beginning to grey around the edges. He was writing on a pad with a fountain pen and a warm smile spread across his face when I introduced myself, as if I was an old friend whom he was genuinely pleased to see again. I had never seen him before.

He stood up, shook my hand and asked me if I'd like a drink. I nodded and he told me to take a seat. He went out without asking what I wanted to drink. I took the small armchair across a low table from his seat. He had left down his pad and pen on the table and I could make out the Gaelic lettering of what he had been writing but I couldn't read it upside down. The room was cosy, warmed by a small fireplace burning wood. It had heavy wallpaper with a floral design against a dark crimson background and there was a small roll-top desk beside the window. Through it I could see the dome of the Palais de la Jetée, its dim lights shimmering like a mirage in the night sky.

O'Casey came back several minutes later with two glasses and a jug of water. He sat down and opened the flap of a briefcase beside his chair and took out a small flat bottle of Jameson. 'One of the perquisites of the job,' he said with a smile as he poured a careful measure into the glasses, neither too mean nor too generous. He turned the water jug to me and I splashed a little water into the whiskey and gave him back the jug.

'*Sláinte*.' He raised his glass to me.

I raised my glass too and took a drink of the whiskey. It went down very well, whetting a long unsatisfied thirst.

'So,' he settled back in the chair, 'how are you getting on?'

I ignored the question. 'Madame Bonnard said you wanted to talk to me.'

'Yes, indeed.'

'And that you're making it difficult for her and her son to return to Ireland.'

'Oh, no,' he said with a startled look. 'She doesn't think that, does she? There are certainly difficulties, as you can imagine, these days. But I'm not creating them. I'm doing my best to circumvent them.'

I took another sip of the whiskey and waited for him to get to the point.

'Have you ever thought of going back to Ireland?' he asked.

'It has crossed my mind from time to time,' I lied. It had rarely crossed my mind since I'd been forced out of the country. There was nothing there for me. My parents were dead, my mother sent to an early grave by my guerrilla activities, according to my father. He had followed her some years later. I had no brothers or sisters. There were uncles, aunts, and cousins but I had had no contact with them since my sudden departure for America. It was questionable whether I would recognise them if I went back, but it did not seem like the time to close off any options.

'And?'

'There was never a particular reason to do so.'

'And now?'

'What about now?'

'The situation here. The war and so on.'

'It doesn't affect me.'

'Thanks to Ireland's neutrality.'

I nodded, conceding what he seemed to think was a point in his favour.

'You know, things have changed a lot back home in the last decade. Since our side got into government and have undone much of the damage caused by those who accepted the so-called treaty?'

So we are supposed to be on the same side, I thought, those who fought against the treaty with Britain and held out for a genuine republic. Whatever that meant.

'People speak highly of you,' he continued. He paused to give me an opportunity to ask the obvious question. I didn't take up the invitation and he went on after a moment. 'It was a pity that you were forced to leave the country. You were the kind of person badly needed to help build it up.'

*Plamás*, I thought, resisting the temptation to ask him again what he wanted. He'd get to it eventually, but I wasn't going to help him along the way. Meanwhile, the whiskey was going down smoothly and I wondered if I would get another.

He nodded to himself as if I had confirmed something. 'I was told you were always a good man in a tight spot. A cool head.'

More flattery, I thought.

'You've been here a long time now,' he went on. 'How long has it been?'

'Long enough.' I held my glass up to the light, swirled the last mouthful of the golden liquid, and drank it.

He took the hint and fished out the bottle from his briefcase. 'Long enough to know how things work here,' he said, pouring a more generous shot this time. He replaced the bottle without helping himself and straightened up, signalling unconsciously that he was ready to get down to business. 'We hope you will be able to help us with something.'

'I doubt that,' I said, topping up my glass with water. 'I'm very busy at the moment. As you probably know. Long days at La Victorine.'

'It's just a matter of keeping an eye on someone. An Irishwoman who's got herself into a spot of bother here.'

I shook my head. 'I'm not in a position to keep an eye on anyone. Whatever that means.'

'It would just mean looking out for her. Keeping her out of trouble until the paperwork is completed for her travel back to Ireland.'

'Why can't you do it yourself?'

'Because I'm not here. I have to be in Vichy.'

'I'm sure there are lots of other people here who could do it.'

'Not any longer. There are still a few Irish people but none that we could rely on, if you know what I mean.'

I did know what he meant but I wasn't going to agree with him. There were a couple of gamblers and con men who claimed to be Irish but whether they really were or not was another matter. 'I'm sure Madame Bonnard would help you,' I said. 'She's a great person for looking after everyone.'

'I think she has her hands full with her own problems.'

I couldn't argue with that. 'Why does this woman need someone to keep an eye on her?'

'She got herself arrested by consorting with the wrong people,' he said. 'We can get her released but we need someone to have a talk with her. Explain the realities of life here. That she has to be careful whom she talks to. And she mustn't get involved in matters that don't concern her.'

'Surely you can have that talk with her yourself.'

'I can and I will. But I can't be coming here every week. That's why I want someone on the spot to keep an eye on her, make sure she stays on the straight and narrow.'

'What's she doing here?'

He sighed heavily as if the answer to that was the most ridiculous part of the whole business. 'Passing through. On her way back to Ireland from Austria and she fell in with some hotheads here.'

'Hotheads?'

'You know. Young people getting excited about things they know nothing about. Political matters that are better left to their elders.'

I suppressed a laugh. Was he talking about his own younger self? He was certainly talking about my younger self whether he knew it or not. Although I didn't agree that such matters were best left to the elders. As I remembered it, it was the elders who got us fired up and chasing their fantasies about mystical republics and suchlike. All ending up in nothing much but causing numerous deaths and disasters along the way. 'What political matters?' I asked.

'You know young people. Against the government. Think they know it all.'

'Right or left?'

'I'm not sure. Not sure they know either.'

'The Free French?'

He shrugged. 'They don't appreciate the difficulties Marshal Pétain is labouring under trying to hold together a defeated and demoralised nation. To create an independent future for it against heavy odds. Defeat is a difficult thing to come to terms with, especially for a proud ancient nation like France.' He drained his glass. 'As we know from our own history.'

Centuries of defeats and despair, of arguments between realists and idealists, of uprisings and rebellions, of oppression and depression, I thought. I certainly didn't wish it on the French but I had been there in my own little way and wanted no more of it. 'I keep well away from politics here,' I said. This was suddenly becoming my regular refrain. one I'd rarely had to voice aloud previously in the years I'd been in Nice.

'That's the proper position for a citizen of a neutral country in the present circumstances.' He nodded approval. 'And one you could usefully explain to this young woman. It would carry much greater weight coming from you with your experience of living here than from a blow-in like me.'

He was a shrewd negotiator and I'd walked into a trap. 'How long would this be for?' I asked, opening my own pitch to him.

'A couple of weeks.' He showed no sign of satisfaction at the turn in my tone. 'Until I can sort out the visas and permits for her to travel on to Lisbon.'

'And on to Ireland?'

He nodded.

'And you could get all the necessary papers and permits for Madame Bonnard and her son at the same time?'

He pursed his lips in a pretence of thinking about that. 'Yes,' he said at last. 'That might be doable.'

'Only "might".' I shook my head with disappointment.

'No. Yes, it should be doable.'

'Should be,' I repeated.

'Yes, it is doable.'

'Definitely?'

'Definitely.' He reached across the table and I shook his hand. 'Deal,' he said.

He gave me the woman's name and an address in the Musiciens area, the part of Nice where all the streets were called after composers. Then he mentioned a few names of old comrades whom he said were now thriving in Ireland in politics and business. I expressed no more than a polite interest in them, as you would in people with whom you had once chanced to share a classroom. Which, in a sense, I had, though it sounded like they had learned different lessons there than I had.

When I got up to leave, he took the Jameson bottle from his bag and handed it to me. It was half full. I thanked him, happy to let him conclude that I might have a problematic taste for alcohol with which he could manipulate me if necessary.

A half-moon hung in the dark sky, marking a feeble path across the bay, as I turned up the hill towards the port and Solange's place. Faint lights of a couple of small fishing boats bobbed on the swell. Behind me the curve of the shore was drawn by the white foam of the breaking waves, dotted here and there by the glow of the beach anglers' fires.

I had no idea what I was getting myself into. O'Casey's story had as many holes as a trawler's net. But I imagined Mrs Mac's delight when I told her she and Gerard would get what she wanted in a matter of weeks. I'd be sorry to see her go. In some ways, she had done for me when I first came here what O'Casey was asking me to do for this Irish woman. She had taken me under her wing, explained how life worked here, identified the people to avoid, and provided a social base away from Rex Ingram's Hollywood crew with whom I'd arrived. And she was a link with where I had come from, a small village like herself, the only one I had. When she left, I would miss her chat and her country accent and the reminders of my childhood.

Part of my reason for doing O'Casey's bidding was to keep my own options open too, in case I wanted to go back to Ireland. He was the man who could arrange that if I decided to do it. And if Solange would agree to come with me.

# Five

I was crossing a street in New York and walking along the opposite footpath, my eyes fixed on the car cruising to a halt in front of our building. I had my left hand in my trouser pocket and my right hand hanging by my side, pressing the Webley hard against my thigh. I was moving casually, unhurried. But the sense of inner dread was overwhelming. A voice in my head was saying, no, no, stop, stop. But that wasn't possible. I couldn't stop. I thumbed back the hammer and cocked the gun in mid-stride.

I opened my eyes and the sense of dread, the knowledge of impending disaster, hung over the bedroom as I came to consciousness and realized where I was. Solange was shaking my shoulder. 'What?' I muttered.

'You're shaking,' she said.

'You're shaking me.'

'Before that. You were shaking.'

'Why are you shaking me?'

'You were having a bad dream.'

I opened my eyes wide and looked around to rid myself of the dread. The bedroom was dark, the thin gaps in the shutters barely brighter than the blackout.

'What was it about?' she asked.

'I don't know,' I lied. 'I've forgotten it already.'

She leaned over and kissed me on the forehead. 'You have to get up. It's nearly two thirty.'

'Ah, no.' I closed my eyes and groaned. 'This is madness.'

I rolled over to embrace her but she had shifted back out of reach. 'You have to go,' she said.

'In a little while. Just let me doze for a moment. I'll be gone by four anyway.'

That wasn't quite true. I didn't have to be in the studio early today. The film crew had moved into the hills to Tourrettes-sur-Loup to film the exterior scenes outside the repainted castle. One of the other electricians was travelling with them. I had argued that various jobs needed to be done in La Victorine: Marcel Carné had lived up to his reputation, having expressive fits of anger if anything broke down and upset his artistic schedule.

I drifted off into a dreamless sleep. Solange was shaking me again and I came to, muttering that I was getting up. Then I saw the fear in her eyes and heard the knocking at the door. 'You stay here,' she whispered as I sat up and swung my feet onto the floor. 'And keep quiet.'

I sank back onto the pillow and watched her wrap her dressing gown around her. The early morning sun was now oozing through the slats of the shutters and painting yellow lines on the wall above me. I looked at my watch: it was just after seven o'clock. From the hall door I could hear a male voice and Solange replying but not what they were saying.

She returned a moment later, closing the bedroom door behind her. She put her finger to her lips to stop my obvious query and bent down to whisper, 'It's the police. They want me to go with them.'

I mouthed a 'why?' and she shrugged. 'Something routine,' she whispered. She got dressed quickly, taking her blue floral dress from the wardrobe, fastening it, and tightening its narrow belt around her waist. She put a white cardigan over it and brushed her hair. I grabbed her hand as she turned to leave and pulled her down and kissed her. She managed a wan smile and then was gone.

That bastard Henri Tillon, I thought as I got up and dressed in a state of agitation. This was all my fault. I'd left her open to the accusation against which I'd been trying to protect her. How could I have been so stupid? Why wasn't I thinking straight? It's not as if I didn't know not to involve the police in anything.

It was no wonder that dream was back.

The market in the Cours Saleya was doing a desultory business, its stalls scattered with the debris of former lives. There were chipped dinner sets, incomplete collections of cutlery, once fashionable oriental ornaments, rusted tools and garden implements, religious statues and pictures. The potential customers were browsers rather than buyers, more interested these days in food than artefacts. At the back of the area, near the Prefecture, the horses and carts of the country people who had brought their wares to the market were gathered in a random group. Some owners were huddled with townspeople among the carts, doing black market deals for food.

I passed by, inhaling the smells of animals, hay and horseshit which reminded me of long-ago fair days, and made my way to the municipal police headquarters where I asked for Henri Tillon. I was left waiting for twenty minutes on a hard bench before he appeared and gestured me into a room that was pretending not to be an interrogation room. It had a scattering of chairs around a dark brown table and its window looked out on the street.

'Solange Delmas has been arrested,' I said once we were seated.

He looked genuinely surprised. 'Why?'

'I don't know. I hope it wasn't because of the talk we had the other day.'

'No, certainly not. Who arrested her?

'I don't know.'

'Where and when?' I gave him her address and told him when.

'Let me see what I can find out,' he said and left me alone for another twenty minutes. I walked around the table, looked out the window and thought dark thoughts.

I remained standing when he came back. 'Well, she's not here,' he said. 'Not in this building. She's in Victor Hugo.'

My heart sank. As far as I knew, the police station in Boulevard Victor Hugo was where the Sûreté detectives and those involved with political matters worked. 'Why would she be there?'

He put up a hand to stop my imagination running away with me. 'Don't worry. I'm told it's only routine. She may even have been released by now.'

'What's routine?'

'It is as you feared. A denunciation. I'm sorry. It didn't come here or if it did I didn't see it or I would have thrown it in the bin like I told you.'

'But you told me nobody paid any attention to these denunciations.'

'Generally, no. But they have to check out an occasional one. To show they're doing their jobs.'

'Why her?'

'I don't know. Just unlucky probably. But I don't think she has anything to worry about. As I say, she may well have been released by now.'

But she wasn't. I hurried back to her flat; it was as empty as I had left it. I couldn't just sit there and wait and I left again and headed for Mrs Mac's. The café was empty and Ange-Marie was behind the counter. I asked for Mme Bonnard and she went through the door behind the bar and called upstairs.

'What are you doing here this time of the day?' Mrs Mac asked when she came down. She looked radiant, as if she had lost several years.

'The crew are up in the hills.' I dropped my voice and leaned across the zinc to her. 'Do you have any real coffee?'

She gave me a curious look and then lifted the counter flap to let me through. 'Come upstairs,' she said and called to Ange-Marie who was now wiping down tables, to tell her she was going back up.

I had been upstairs in her home perhaps half-a-dozen times or so in all the years that I'd known her. She brought me into the kitchen and turned with a look of delight. 'I've just got good news,' she said. 'That diplomat fellow I told you about was in first thing this morning. He says he can get us all the travel documents we need to go to Ireland. Gerard and me.'

'That's great,' I said, happy for her.

'We'll have them in a couple of weeks.' She took a coffee pot from the dresser and a fistful of coffee beans from a closed tin. She dropped them into a grinder and turned its handle.

'What'll you do with this place?'

'Ange-Marie will look after it while I'm away.' She poured water on top of the coffee and lit the gas under the pot. She turned to me as she finished. 'Maybe you'll keep an eye on things for me too.'

'Me? I know nothing about running a café.'

'You and Solange,' she said. 'She'd love to run her own place.'

I was about to protest that I didn't think what Solange had in mind was effectively a bar but Mrs Mac was still talking. 'I don't know if we'll want to stay in Ireland,' she was saying, voicing her second thoughts now that Ireland was becoming a real possibility. 'Until the war ends probably. But after that I'm not sure. It's been a long time since I was there.'

'When did you last visit?'

'Gerard was two. It was before Lucien died. That's a long time ago now. It mightn't be like I imagine. What do you think?'

'It's even longer since I've been there. I've no idea what it's like now.'

The coffee pot began to bubble and she turned down the heat. The smell of the coffee was overpowering my deprived senses. She got a jug of milk and put some in a small pan with a spout. When it was ready, she half-filled a bowl with coffee and poured the warm milk on it. She put the bowl on the table in front of me.

'Do you have any real cigarettes?'

'God, you're very demanding today.' She took a step backwards and looked at me for the first time. 'What is it?'

'Solange has been arrested.'

'Oh, Marty.' She stared at me for a moment and left the room. She came back with an opened pack of Gitanes and a box of matches and put them alongside the coffee.

I lit a cigarette and she sat down opposite me. I inhaled deeply and the strong smoke made me light-headed as I told her what had happened.

'Oh, Marty,' she said again when I had finished. I was grateful that she didn't point out it was all my fault, for not marrying Solange, for telling Henri Tillon about the denunciation. 'I'll call Henri,' she added.

'I talked to him a little while ago. He said he knew nothing.'

'You don't think he knew about it in advance?' she asked in a worried tone.

'I don't think so,' I said, although I was not entirely convinced. 'Unless he's a very good actor.'

'Henri's not an actor, but I'll see if he knows any more now.'

She disappeared downstairs to the phone box in the café. I smoked the cigarette and drank the coffee and looked out the window at the church of the Sacred Heart, which was boxed in between the backs of the houses on the rue de France and the rue Buffa. Solange went to mass there sometimes, met Mrs Mac at her daily attendance, and came back to the café for a coffee afterwards. Probably a real coffee here in the kitchen, though she never told me so and I had never thought to ask.

I never asked her either why she continued to go to church and even to confession, moving around the town's many churches as if God wouldn't notice the repetition of our sinfulness. It wasn't a subject I wanted to bring up. She had asked me once why I wouldn't come to church with her and I had given her some vague explanation about losing my religion in what Mrs Mac called heathen Hollywood. Explaining why the church had banished me would have meant going into things I didn't want to go into. As far as she and everyone else knew, I had been just another Irish emigrant to America in search of a job, not running there for my life.

Except for O'Casey, of course. But he didn't know what had happened in New York. Or I didn't think he could know.

Which reminded me that I was due to meet him shortly at the address he had given me in the Musiciens area. I checked my watch; there was almost an hour to go.

Mrs Mac came back and poured me another half-bowl of coffee. She drained the last of the pot into a cup for herself and sat down. 'Henri doesn't know anything more,' she said. 'He swears he had nothing to do with Solange's arrest. And I believe him.'

'What about her release?'

'He can't find out anything definite. He thinks she might have been released already.'

She took one of the Gitanes and I lit it for her. 'They can't guillotine every woman who's had an abortion,' she said, blowing out the smoke without inhaling it. 'It's madness.'

I lit another cigarette for myself, feeling my heart race again from the unaccustomed dose of nicotine.

'Has Solange heard anything about her brothers?' she asked.

'No.' Two of her brothers were prisoners of war in Germany. The third and youngest had managed to avoid capture before the armistice and make his way home to the family farm in Provence.

'I don't see why the Germans won't release them all now. It's causing nothing but trouble for everyone. All those women without their husbands, children without their fathers.'

I turned the conversation back to her own good news. 'Has Gerard agreed to go to Ireland?'

'That's the next hurdle.' She sighed. 'Please God I'll cross that one when all the arrangements are made.'

'This is Gertie Maher.'

O'Casey introduced us when I finally arrived a little late at the address he had given me in rue Berlioz. It was a classic mellowcoloured belle epoque building with a decorative façade, romeo balconies with intricate ironwork, and a double entrance door worthy of a palace. Gertie Maher's apartment, however, was tiny and fashioned out of what once had been a servant's quarters far from the beautiful front of the building.

She was about twenty, tall and with black hair curling upwards just short of her shoulders. Her dark eyes stared back at me without expression. She gave no indication that she was happy to meet me, which was not surprising in the circumstances. I wasn't exactly delighted to be her minder either.

'I know the waiting will be boring,' O'Casey turned back to her. 'but there's no way around it, I'm afraid. Everything is more complicated these days. Martin here will advise you on things to see, places to go, and so on. To make the time pass more quickly and make sure that there is no repetition of your unfortunate experience.'

I hadn't envisaged being a tourist guide but I thought I'd better make clear that I was not going to be at her disposal daily. 'I'm very busy at work these days,' I said. 'So my time is limited.'

'Yes,' O'Casey agreed. 'But he'll be able to help you out with advice and so on. As frequently as he can. I'd like you to stay in touch with him and let him know all is well on a regular basis.' He turned to me. 'What would be the best arrangement for regular contact?'

'I'm at La Victorine all day every day.'

'That's the film studios here,' he explained to her. 'Not very convenient.' He turned back to me. 'Perhaps you could look in on Miss Maher on your way to and from work.'

'I doubt if she'd appreciate that,' I said back to him. O'Casey clearly hadn't given much thought to what he wanted from me. Which led me to wonder once again what this was all about. 'I normally go to work about five in the morning. And I'm not back sometimes until seven in the evening or even later.'

I thought I saw a hint of a smile on her face but it disappeared as soon as she caught my glance. Perhaps I'd imagined it.

'Well, you could arrange to meet somewhere regularly,' he went on. 'Is there somewhere she could leave messages for you?'

I thought for a moment and then turned to her. 'Do you know the Café du Raisin on rue de France?'

'No.' It was the first word she had spoken since I had arrived.

'Yes,' O'Casey nodded as if that was a great idea. 'You'll find it easily. And it's run by an Irishwoman, Madame Bonnard. A good friend of Martin's.' He turned to me again. 'You could introduce Miss Maher to Madame Bonnard and she could assist.'

I gave him a sceptical look and said to Gertie Maher, 'I'll drop into the Café du Raisin about five this afternoon and we can have a chat then.'

'Excellent,' O'Casey clapped his hands. He looked like a man who had had a weight lifted off his shoulders.

As soon as we left, I practically pushed O'Casey against the wall and demanded to know what was going on. He looked at his watch and said, 'I have a train to catch.'

'What the fuck is going on?' I repeated, spreading out the words.

'It's a matter of state.' He started walking up the street towards the station and I fell in beside him.

'What does that mean?'

'Just that. I can't talk about it.'

'That doesn't tell me anything.'

He paused as if deciding whether to impart a secret. 'It's important to important people that she gets back safely to Ireland as soon as possible.'

'Who's she related to?'

'All you need to know is that it is important that she gets back to Ireland. And that important people will be grateful for your help if you ever want to go home. You'll find doors opening for you. And for your friend Madame Bonnard too.'

'What important people? How did you know I was here?'

'You remember Timmy Monaghan?'

I nodded. Timmy Monaghan had been my commanding officer for a period during what was now called our civil war. How had he known I was in Nice? But as soon as I asked myself that question, I knew it was not surprising that he did. Monaghan always made a point of knowing everything about everyone.

'He's a member of the Dáil now, you know,' O'Casey said.

I didn't know that but it didn't surprise me that Monaghan was now a politician. He was one to capitalise on his role in the independence struggle, make sure that it advanced himself. 'Is he one of the important people you're talking about?'

He smiled as if I'd made a joke. 'No. They really are important. You should think about going home, you know. It's not the country it used to be. Our war is over and we'll be all right as long as we're left to look after ourselves and not be dragged into this business.'

I presumed 'this business' meant the present war. 'I hear you're still interning republicans.'

'Some people never learn,' he sighed. 'But that needn't worry you. Keep Gertie Maher out of trouble till she leaves here and you'll be welcomed back with open arms.'

'I'm not sure I want to go back.'

'Well, it's always good to have friends in high places.'

We crossed Avenue Thiers towards the station. 'What exactly do you want from me?' I demanded as we reached its entrance.

'What I told you.' He looked at me in surprise as if I was slow-witted. He put his briefcase on the ground, took out his wallet, and extracted a business card with his name on it. It had a phone number and the legend Legation d'Irlande and the name of a hotel in Vichy. 'Just keep an eye on her. Phone me if there are any problems. Make sure she is not picked up off the street again. And you will always have friends in high places in Ireland.'

The penny dropped. I remembered the afternoon I was walking home on the Promenade, the Citroën slouching by, the young woman in the distance being steered towards it by two men. She had been too far away to recognise but she was probably Gertie Maher. 'Off the Promenade des Anglais,' I said.

He looked at me in surprise. Then he clapped me on the shoulder and smiled. 'I knew you were the right man for the job.'

I watched him disappear into the gloom of the station and turned westward to go to work.

# Six

I raced through the various jobs I needed to do. The studio was relatively quiet, reduced to routine work with the absence of Marcel Carné's crew on location. But the air of excitement and purpose generated by the feature film still lingered. Jean-Luc passed by my workshop, stopped, entered, and watched me for a few moments.

'Alors,' he exclaimed, 'the director has even terrorised the lazy Irish into working.'

'At least I've been spared his wrath,' I retorted. 'Unlike you and your falling door.' The door on one of his sets had collapsed as an actor made an excessively angry exit at the end of a scene, causing hilarity among everyone except Carné.

Jean-Luc gave a dismissive shrug. 'He got over it. Did you hear about the banqueting scene in Paris?' he asked, clearly in a mood to chat.

I shook my head and continued what I was doing, dismantling a camera whose power unit kept giving trouble. I had skimmed through the script when I was on standby on the set and knew that a big medieval banquet was one of the central scenes.

'The set was all prepared with this long table full of food. Bowls of fruit, roast chickens, piglets on spits, sides of beef, lots of bread. They let in the extras, all in their costumes, to take their places. And they immediately started scoffing everything in sight. Shoving anything they couldn't eat on the spot into their pockets. All the food was gone in an instant. Nothing left but bones and crumbs.'

I laughed at the image, not doubting that it was exaggerated, but I could well believe that the food had disappeared. It was obviously too good an opportunity for hungry extras to miss. And the producers and directors never thought of what would happen: they and the stars lived in their own world, well looked after. They even had their own dining area in La Victorine, and in their hotels, where rationing did not apply to them. 'I thought that scene was done,' I said. The script I had read had it ticked off as completed.

'They had to do it all over again. Getting the food was no great problem for Continental. But they took precautions. Used some phoney food and painted the real thing with carbolic acid. Everyone was warned their mouths would burn and they might even die if they as much as bit into an apple.'

'Very appropriate in a film about the devil,' I suggested. I had identified the loose connection causing the problem in the power unit and had fixed it quickly. Jean-Luc watched me in silence and finally asked, 'What's your hurry today?'

'Meeting Solange early.' I didn't want to tell him about her arrest, because that would have delayed me even more. And increased his fears about Tillon's intentions.

'Like a date?'

'Something like that.'

'Wonderful to see romance still alive these days.'

'Never needed more than now,' I said. It struck me that there was something JeanLuc wanted to tell me. That he wasn't standing there because he had nothing better to do. Whatever it was, I hoped he didn't get to it now.

'I'm off,' I said when I had finished, making it clear that I did not want to be delayed.

He nodded and left without saying anything.

It was another glorious day, although the sun was beginning its descent into the west from its winter height. The bay still sparkled with spots of sunlight dancing on the azure water. The incoming tide toyed with the beach stones, teasing them as it rolled them to and fro, advancing and withdrawing, and then surprising them with a sudden surge inland. I hooked my jacket over my shoulder and walked quickly, looking back occasionally in case a rare bus appeared. None did.

Back near the centre of the town the Promenade was still busy with strollers. Refugees in their heavy northern clothes occupied the blue chairs lining the edge, their backs to the bay, watching the passers-by, alert for any threats. A number of people had stopped opposite the Hotel Negresco as a line of black limousines drew up outside. There was a small crowd across the road from the hotel door, mainly women, applauding the film stars as they emerged from the limousines. Wolf whistles broke out as Marie Déa and Simone Signoret and the other young actresses appeared from the last two cars, accompanied by the older Arletty.

A shout of '*collabo*' broke through the scattering of applause. A young man on the edge of the crowd with his hands cupped around his mouth repeated the shout, but it wasn't clear whether he was accusing one actor of being a collaborator or all of them. Several women in the crowd began to remonstrate with him but he repeated his 'collabo' over their heads. One of the policemen left his position at the hotel door and made his way towards the man. The man shouted '*Vive la republique*' as the policeman came closer. Then he turned and ran at speed up the road and around the other corner of the hotel. The policeman thought better of chasing him.

The crowd and the onlookers on the Promenade dispersed and I hurried along to the port to Solange's place. As soon as I opened the door, I knew she wasn't there. It had the unmistakeable air of an empty home.

The sun had gone down in a bloody sky in the west, taking its heat with it, and leaving the night to the cold north wind as I made my way back to the Café du Raisin. My sense of helplessness had sharpened my mood close to anger. I didn't know what to do to get Solange released. I knew nobody with any real influence here -- the price of deliberately remaining uninvolved in French life. Henri Tillon clearly didn't count. I had no desire to talk to Gertie Maher as I had promised. I was sorry I had got myself involved with her, that I hadn't just told O'Casey what to do with himself.

Gertie was waiting for me, sitting at a table by the window with an untouched cup of coffee. I said hello to her and told her I was getting a drink. Mrs Mac noted the exchange as she noted everything that happened in her café but said nothing about it. She was already pouring me a glass of beer before I reached the bar. 'Any news?' she asked with a concerned look.

'No. She's not home.'

She finished pouring the drink. 'What are you going to do?'

'I don't know. Maybe call around to the place on Victor Hugo and see if they've got her there. But first I have to talk to this woman. Gertie Maher,' I said, taking the glass from her and answering her next question before she asked it. I explained that

O'Casey wanted me to help her while she was waiting for her travel documents.

'She's Irish?'

I nodded. 'One her way back to Ireland. From Vienna.'

I took my drink and went back to Gertie before Mrs Mac could ask me anything more. As soon as I sat down opposite her, she said, 'I don't know what Mr O'Casey told you but I don't need minding.'

'Good,' I said, happy to mirror her hostility with my own. 'I'm not a great minder. Except of my own business.'

'And what's that?'

'What it says. My own business.' I took a long drink of the weak beer. 'What did O'Casey tell you about me?'

A spark of interest broke through the bland exterior she had presented since I'd first met her. 'You don't work for him?'

'He told you that?'

'No. He said you've been here a long time and knew everything that happened in Nice.'

I snorted into my beer. 'I know nothing that happens in Nice and care less about it. Unless it affects me directly. Which very little does.'

We lapsed into silence as we got over asserting our mutual antagonism. I pointed at the untouched coffee and asked if she wanted to change her mind. She asked for a glass of red wine and I caught Ange-Marie's eye and passed on the order.

'Look,' I said. 'O'Casey thinks for some reason that I can keep you out of trouble. What kind of trouble he hasn't bothered to tell me. And even if he had, I'm not the person to do it. I mind my own business here.'

'I'm not in any trouble. It was just a misunderstanding.'

'Your arrest on the Promenade?'

'Yes. I was released as soon as it was cleared up.'

I couldn't remember exactly when I had seen her being arrested but it was at least a week earlier, if not more. And her release had required the intervention of a diplomat from Vichy. Some misunderstanding, I thought. 'You're not going to get yourself into another misunderstanding, are you?'

'Of course not,' she said in a tone rising with indignation. I had been trying to place her accent and it fell into place now. Cork.

'Good.'

Ange-Marie brought her glass of red wine and she sipped at it. The silence lengthened and she looked around the café as if she had just arrived. It was beginning to fill up as the working day ended and the regulars dropped in on their way home. 'Why are you …' She didn't know how to finish the question since I had made it clear I was neither her minder nor her helper. '…here?'

'Because I owe O'Casey a favour,' I said. 'Not out of friendship or anything like that. More like blackmail than a favour.'

'You want to go back to Ireland too?'

'No.'

'What then?'

'That's my business. Just as why someone wants you back in Ireland is none of my business.'

'Okay,' she said, drawing out the word.

I took my empty glass and pushed back my chair. 'Keep out of trouble,' I said as I stood up. I nodded towards Mrs Mac. 'Leave a message here with Madame Bonnard if you want me.'

As I turned towards the bar, Mrs Mac's son Gerard was coming from behind the counter, dressed in his Legionnaire's uniform. Most of the clientèle pretended not to notice as he went by.

'Bonsoir Gerard,' I said as he passed me. He ignored me and glanced at Gertie Maher as he went out to the street.

Mrs Mac raised her eyes to heaven in a gesture of despair as I reached the counter. 'He's off to another rally,' she said. 'Won't be back till all hours, stinking of drink.' She refilled my glass. 'There was blood on his shirt the other morning. When I asked him about it, he laughed and said it wasn't his.'

'You'll get him out of here soon,' I said, a reassurance for myself as much as for her. If O'Casey came up trumps with the Bonnard travel documents, at least my deal with him would be worthwhile. 'Have you told him about going to Ireland?'

She shook her head and it struck me suddenly from the look on her face that she was afraid of Gerard. 'You'll have to tell him soon,' I pointed out.

'What if he won't come?'

'You'll have done all you can for him.'

'I can't abandon him here. He'll get himself into terrible trouble if he goes on hanging about with those types.'

'There's only so much you can do.'

She shook her head again as if I wouldn't understand. To me, Gerard was just trouble waiting to happen, the kind of young lad whose anger at the world would keep driving him until he hit some kind of brick wall. And, with any luck, he would calm down as he grew older. He wasn't my son but I didn't think I'd feel any different if he was. But then I didn't know what having a son was like.

'He's too like his father,' Mrs Mac said, as if she could read my thoughts. 'Impatient. A bit fiery. But great company too.' I wasn't clear whether she was talking about Gerard or her husband Lucien or both. Gerard never struck me as great company but I hadn't really known him as a child. 'He's a good lad at heart, just a bit lost.'

She moved away to attend to other customers and I stared at the portrait of le Maréchal while I finished my drink. I came to a decision and told her when I was paying that I was going to check the police station on Victor Hugo. 'That woman you were with paid Ange-Marie for your first beer and her own drinks,' she said.

'She did,' I said in surprise. I hadn't bothered checking if she had left.

'Let me know what you find out from the police,' Mrs Mac said.

There were few people about as I went up rue Meyerbeer towards Boulevard Victor Hugo. The cafés and bars on the way were busy, casting warm glows into the cold night. As I approached Victor Hugo, I noticed a few Legionnaires gathered around a girl at the corner. I assumed they were trying to chat her up until I recognised Gerard and then saw that the girl was Gertie.

I crossed over to them and said, 'Bonsoir Gerard. Qu'est ce qui ce passe?'

He hadn't seen me approach and he swung around as if I had hit him. 'What do you want?' he demanded. Two of the others were his age and the fourth was older. The older one was holding a green passport in his hand and examining it closely.

'I'm looking for my friend Gertie.'

One of the others laughed and said, 'You're too old for her.'

'Come with me,' I said, addressing Gertie in English.

'Wait a minute,' Gerard interjected, stepping between her and me. 'This is official business. We're talking to her.'

'She's a friend of mine,' I said. 'You saw her with me in your mother's café a few minutes ago.'

'Did she walk out on you?' the other talkative one said. He at least appeared to be in good humour, probably alcohol-induced.

Gerard gave me a dirty look, unhappy at the mention of his mother in front of his colleagues.

'Where's she from?' the older one demanded.

'She's from Ireland,' I said with a man-to-man air, as if I was relieved to be talking to the person in charge. 'Her name is Gertie Maher. She's on her way back to neutral Ireland.' I doubted that they knew or cared anything about Ireland's neutrality in this conflict but they might understand that she was not a refugee.

'I've never seen her before,' Gerard said.

'That's because she's just arrived in Nice.'

'She's a refugee,' Gerard exclaimed as if I had proved his point.

'She is passing through,' I said patiently. 'On her way to Ireland, like I told you.'

'She looks like a Jew to me,' the drunken one said. He closed his eyes and raised his head to sniff the air ostentatiously.

'She's Irish,' I repeated. 'I've told you.' I turned to the older man. 'Her passport proves it.'

'And you?' the drunk said to me. 'You sound like an English backstabber.'

'Gerard can tell you all about me. I'm a friend of his mother.' The drunk began to laugh and poked Gerard in the ribs. I took Gertie's hand and she stepped around Gerard. She held out her other hand to the older man and he gave her back her passport after a moment's hesitation. I wished him good night as if we had been having a civil conversation and we walked away.

'What about the other one you're fucking?' Gerard shouted after me as we crossed the empty boulevard. 'Does she know about your Irish whore?'

The drunk said something about Gerard's mother that I didn't catch. Gerard responded with an angry curse and then fists were flying. I glanced back to see the older man trying to separate

Gerard and the drunk without getting hit by either. The fourth one, who had said nothing, was watching us and ignoring the scuffling beside him. Gertie let out a deep breath as if she had been holding it in all the time.

Maybe Gerard wasn't all bad, I thought. Mrs Mac would be delighted to know he had defended her honour with such alacrity. Although she wouldn't be happy about his methods. But it was not something I was going to tell her.

I held on to Gertie's hand and she made no attempt to withdraw it as we went into the Musiciens area and up rue Gounod. The way the fourth Legionnaire had observed everything and said nothing worried me. He could well be the most dangerous of that lot, the one who would follow us, and find out where Gertie was staying.

We rounded a corner towards rue Berlioz and I looked back and dropped her hand. There was no sign of them.

'Are you a friend of that fascist?' Gertie demanded.

'Gerard is Mme Bonnard's son.'

'Is she one of them too?'

'She's the mother of a difficult son.'

'A fascist son.'

'His fascism has little to do with politics. Everything to do with his own problems.'

'A fascist is a fascist.'

We walked on in silence. I checked behind us regularly but there was no sign of anyone following. 'What were they saying?' she asked.

'Do you speak any French?'

'Very little.'

I told her what they had said about her.

'I thought I heard the word *juif,*' she nodded to herself when I had finished.

We reached her apartment building and she took out her key and stepped up to the door. 'Keep away from these people,' I said.

'You want me to lock myself up in this little place?'

'No, but be sensible. Don't walk the streets when there's nobody else about except thugs looking for strangers to harass. You saw them. That situation could have easily developed to the point where you ended up bloodied on the ground. Or worse.'

She opened the door and stood facing me in the opening.

'You know about the Légion?' I asked.

'Yes, I know about them.'

'You've encountered them before?'

'Not like tonight. But I know they're extreme fascists.'

'Avoid them like the plague.'

'Thank you for your advice,' she said as if I had just told her the best way to get to Place Massena from here. She went inside and closed the door.

She's either very innocent or has strong nerves, I thought as I made my way back towards the boulevard. Apart from that one release of breath, she had given no indication of being frightened by Gerard and his friends. Strong nerves, I decided.

My visit to the police station on Victor Hugo was a waste of time. The policeman in the public office had that mixture of boredom and impatience that such people adopt to deal with civilians. He went through the pretence of consulting a book and said Solange was not there. He'd probably have said the same if there were five Solange Delmas listed. 'What did she do?' he asked.

'Nothing.'

'Then why would she be here?'

I made my way back towards Mrs Mac's dispirited by my helplessness. I couldn't think of anything to do to get Solange released. I would just have to wait until they decided to let her go. Gerard and his friends had disappeared. A line of faded posters with the Marshal's portrait had been defaced with a black X painted across each. Which symbolised neatly his fading reputation as the public's support for him in the uncertain days after France's defeat turned into growing opposition as food became scarcer and the demands of the victors increased.

The moment I walked into the Café du Raisin I saw her. She was at the bar, wearing the dress in which she had left that morning. She had her elbows on the zinc, talking to Mrs Mac, who saw me enter and said something to her. Solange turned to me and I embraced her and breathed, 'Thank God,' into her hair.

'It was nothing,' she said. 'They let me go after an hour.'

I stepped back. 'Where've you been all day?' I asked, my tone taking on an involuntary touch of anger.

'At work,' she replied with a patient smile, as if the answer was obvious.

'Jesus, you might have let me know.'

'I did. I phoned the studios from Signora Mancini's. Left a message for you.'

'I didn't get it.' I took a deep breath to calm myself. Relief was making me angry; I had spent the whole day worrying needlessly.

'I'm sorry,' Solange said, squeezing my hand. 'I called about ten o'clock.'

Mrs Mac passed me a glass of beer and asked in a low voice if I'd like something stronger. I shook my head.

'They brought me to their station on Victor Hugo,' Solange was saying. 'Left me sitting in an office for an hour. Then a detective came in and said they had received a letter saying that I'd had an abortion. I told him that wasn't true. He said that there was unfortunately a lot of lies being spread these days. He apologised for the drama of getting me out of bed and said I was free to go.'

'That was it?'

'That was it. I went home but you had gone. So I went to work too.'

'All's well that ends well,' Mrs Mac murmured.

I wasn't so sure. It was unlikely that the Sûreté was dragging every woman accused of having an abortion out of their beds and into custody all over the Marshal's latest edict. Solange gave me a quizzical look. 'What is it?' she asked.

'Did he show you the letter?' I asked.

'No. He read out part of it.'

'Who wrote it?'

'I don't know. I presume it was anonymous. He didn't say.'

'What are you getting at, Marty?' Mrs Mac interjected.

I admitted that I didn't know.

'Then let us put it behind us,' she said.

We moved to a table but didn't take Mrs Mac's advice entirely. Solange told me in greater detail what had happened but it cast no more light on the incident. She was in good spirits, clearly thinking that the matter was closed. That whoever had sent the anonymous letters and pinned the note to her door had done their worst and could be ignored from now on. 'You can move back in,' she said.

'Good. I might give up that other place altogether. I had forgotten what a dump it is.'

'Then you'll have to pay some of the rent.'

'Fair enough.'

She had another glass of wine and I had another beer. I told her about Gertie Maher and the altercation with the Legionnaires, dropping my voice so nobody heard me mention Gerard.

'I don't understand. What are you supposed to do for her?'

'I don't really know. But I'm afraid she's going to get herself into trouble.'

Out of the corner of my eye I noticed Henri Tillon coming into the café and could see him approaching us. We greeted each other and he asked if he could have a word with me.

The café was less than half full and we stepped away from the table to an empty area. Tillon was out of uniform and looked tired and pale, as if he had had a long day. He stood close to me and handed me a piece of paper folded in two. 'I'm sorry,' he said in a quiet voice.

I unfolded the slip of paper. There were five names typed on it. The first one was Jean-Luc Lebret. The other four were of men who worked at La Victorine too. Painters and carpenters.

I tried to hand it back to him but he kept his hands out of the way. 'I'm sorry,' he repeated. 'This is not my idea.'

I tried to push the note into the top pocket of his jacket but he covered it with his hand. I dropped it on the ground and went to turn away. 'It's no use,' he said. 'They'll just come back to you again.'

I knew he was right and waited while he picked up the slip of paper and handed it back to me. 'Bastard,' I muttered and put the paper in my pocket.

'It's not my doing. I have no choice either.'

He went over to the bar and I sat down with Solange, feeling sick.

'What was that about?' she asked. She hadn't seen him give me the list; I had unintentionally blocked her view.

'I called on him on this morning to see if he knew where they had taken you,' I said. 'He just wanted to tell me there was nothing to worry about.'

'That's a secret?' she laughed.

'*Les flics,*' I said. 'They like to turn everything into a big mystery.'

But there was no mystery at all about the message he had delivered; do their bidding or Solange would be arrested again.

# Seven

I was glad Marcel Carné was so demanding over the following days. He was pushing ahead with filming *Les Visiteurs du Soir,* working from early morning until late evening as if there was a deadline hanging over him. Some of the actresses grumbled, complaining that he was too demanding and ignoring their dissatisfactions. It was clear to all that he had more time for the actors than the actresses. And, of course, even less time for us hired hands.

Being busy suited me fine but it failed to take my mind entirely off my dilemma. What to do about the police demands was keeping me awake at night and occupying any daytime moments when I was not preoccupied with work. Solange's good mood made it worse. Her brief arrest and release had persuaded her that she had nothing further to fear from anonymous denunciations. The poison pen had done its worst and was now ineffectual. I hadn't realised how upsetting the letters had been until her relief at their removal became obvious.

One night as we lay in bed, I asked her if she would be willing to come to Ireland with me.

'You want to go back there?' She turned on her side to face me in the darkness. I had never suggested it before; indeed, it had not often been on my mind, but it now seemed like one way of getting out of my problem. I had no illusion that Henri Tillon's colleagues would leave us alone if I didn't spy for them.

'Thinking of it. If you'd come with me?'

'What would I do there? I don't speak English.'

'Same as you do here. A French cook would be in huge demand. You'd have no difficulty getting work. Make much more money there than here.'

'And you'd live off my money.' Her voice was playful and she wasn't taking me seriously. I suspected she was smiling but I couldn't be sure.

'That's right. You'd be a master chef and I'd be a gentleman of leisure.'

She punched me gently in the chest as if it was all a joke. 'Sweet dreams,' she said and turned away to go to sleep.

Sweet dreams indeed, I thought. It could work. But O'Casey would have to help. And move quickly. That was questionable. Would he agree to get travel permits for Solange if she wasn't Irish? Doubtful, if he was making an issue of getting a passport for Gerard, who, at least, was half-Irish. And did Solange have a passport? I didn't know. It had never arisen before. If we got married, that might solve some of the problems.

I sighed. As I stared at the strips of dull grey showing through the shutters' slats, I knew this plan was a pipe dream. Even if it could work, it would take too long to get all the pieces in place. It would require O'Casey's full co-operation, which was unlikely.

And the *flics* would be looking for answers long before we could arrange it all.

I lay awake for a long time trying to find a way out.

I was in the canteen next morning, having a cup of the ersatz coffee and inhaling the real cigarette smoke which was drifting over from the next table. Jacques Prévert, the scriptwriter and chain smoker, was sitting there, redrafting the dialogue in a scene. He must have heard me inhaling the smoke because he glanced over and smiled. He shook out a cigarette from his blue packet of Gauloise Caporal and I took it, thanked him, and lit it.

Jean-Luc came over, carrying a glass of water. 'I can't drink that piss anymore,' he said, indicating my 'coffee'.

'I'm only drinking it out of habit.'

Prévert got up and left with a fresh cigarette hanging from his mouth. Jean-Luc picked up my book and read the blurb. It was Simenon's *Les Inconnus dans la Maison*. 'Any good?' he inquired.

'I can't get into it at the moment.' I checked there was nobody within earshot and took a deep breath. 'There's something I need to tell you.'

He froze and the look on his face told me he knew what was coming. I gave him the slip of paper Henri Tillon had given me. He read the names and passed it back. 'What is this?' he asked in a neutral voice.

I explained what it was and how it had had come about. 'I haven't told them anything,' I went on. 'I have no intention of telling them anything. In fact, I don't know anything to tell them. And I don't want to know anything. But,' I paused, 'they're threatening Solange.'

Jean-Luc put his head in his hands and rubbed it vigorously, as if he had developed a sudden itch. 'You're becoming a *collabo*?'

'No, I'm not.'

'Then why are you telling me this?'

I looked at him in confusion. It was obvious to me. 'To warn you.'

'And the others?'

'To warn them too. If you want to.'

'Warn them of what?'

'That the police are inquiring about them.'

'Why do you want to warn us?'

I felt a strong need for another real cigarette. 'Because you are my friend,' I said as patiently as I could.

'Did they ask you to tell us?' he persisted.

'No.' I shook my head in irritation. 'For fuck's sake.'

I had seen this before, the sliver of suspicion that could grow and grow until it became a bullet in the back of the head and a crude sign saying 'informer' around your neck. There had been a young lad, bare;y eighteen, in a neighbouring Irregular column back in Ireland who had fallen under suspicion of giving information to the Free Staters. He had protested his innocence but an ad hoc court found him guilty and offered him his life if he confessed and left the country. He confessed and was executed anyway. Nobody wanted to talk about it afterwards. About whether it was a genuine confession or he thought he was buying a ticket to America with a lie.

'You shouldn't have involved that policeman friend of yours,' Jean-Luc said.

'He's not a friend of mine.' There was no point in arguing that Henri Tillon wasn't the cause of the trouble. I had thought about it and concluded that he was not masterminding the attempt to force me to collaborate with them. He was just the messenger.

'Your controller then,' Jean-Luc shot back.

'You don't believe me?' I demanded, feeling myself redden with anger. 'I'm giving you information because I thought we were friends. I'm not giving them any information.' And I'm putting Solange at risk, I thought, but I held back that thought.

Jean-Luc pursed his lips and sighed. 'I believe you,' he said at last. But somehow he managed to make it sound conditional. For the moment, his tone implied.

I was still angered by Jean-Luc's response to my information as I left La Victorine that evening. There was a black Citroën parked across the road from the gates. The driver stared at me and my heart leapt, half-expecting him to pull over to my side of the road. At that moment, the first limousine of the convoy of actors' cars emerged and paused before entering the road. The Citroën revved up and moved in front of it to escort the convoy to their hotels, the Negresco on the Promenade and the Grand up the hills in Vence.

Paranoia, I told myself. Don't let yourself become paranoid. But that was easier said than done.

I took avenue de la Californie back into town, keeping to the northern side to shelter from the cold wind. It was dark and people had their heads down, hurrying home. The street eventually led into the rue de France and Mrs Mac's. I pushed open the door, sweaty from walking fast but my nose was frozen. I unwound the scarf from my neck as I glanced around, relieved that Henri Tillon was not there.

'Marty,' Mrs Mac said, as usual. 'Cold out there, is it?'

'Bitter.'

'Your new friend was in, looking for you.'

'Gertie Maher?'

'Yes. That's her name. I couldn't remember it.'

'What'd she want?'

'She wants you to call around to her as soon as you can.'

'Why?'

'She didn't tell me. Just said it was very urgent.' She passed me the usual glass of beer. 'A bit bossy, isn't she?'

'That's one word for her.' I didn't like the sound of that 'very urgent'. It could only mean trouble.

'What other words would you use?'

I laughed. 'You wouldn't expect me to use any words about a young lady.'

She snorted at the 'lady' bit. 'You're looking very tired.'

'We're being worked hard.'

'So what's the gossip from the picture factory?' she asked, getting back to our normal conversation. 'Any romances?'

'You know we're not allowed to talk about the film. It'd only spoil it for you when it comes out.'

'God, you're being very awkward today,' she said with a grin that belied her words. 'Off-screen romances.'

I thought for a moment. 'All the young actresses have their eye on the Italian assistant director. A good-looking young lad called Antonioni.'

'And who has he his eye on?'

'That's the question.'

'Is it true about Arletty? That she's a *collabo à l'horizontale*?' She used the French phrase for women who slept with German soldiers.

'So they say. She doesn't make any secret of it.'

'What's he like?'

'Her German? I haven't seen him.' At least, I wasn't aware of having seen him. There were always people coming and going at the studio -- producers, accountants, friends of important people. 'They say he's a major or something in the Luftwaffe.'

'A flier? He's here with her at the moment?'

'Is he?' It didn't interest me very much. *Collabos à l'horizontale* were not of much concern in Nice for the simple reason that there were few Germans here. Not in uniform, at any rate. There were probably some Sicherheitsdienst types undercover and some holiday-makers in civvies among the few genuine tourists. But it wasn't like Paris or the German-occupied zone.

'God, you're useless today.' She shook her head in mock disgust and went to move away.

'By the way,' I stopped her, 'any word from Seamus O'Casey.'

'Not a peep. But I wouldn't expect anything yet. He said it would take a couple of weeks at least.'

I finished my beer and left the centimes on the zinc.

Maybe I should stay away from Mrs Mac's for a while, I thought as I made my way to rue Berlioz. Then Gertie Maher couldn't contact me and Henri Tillon couldn't conveniently run into me. But I knew that wouldn't work, not with my main problem: the police. Tillon and his masters obviously knew where Solange lived and where I worked.

It took so long for Gertie Maher to answer her doorbell that I was about to go away when she opened the door a tentative slit. She pulled it back to let me in, looking relieved, and I followed her up the flights of marble stairs to her room.

'Thanks for coming,' she said when we got there. A pot was bubbling on one of the two gas rings that constituted the kitchen corner and a plate with a spoon stood on the tiny table beside it. A narrow bed took up most of the rest of the room. It almost made my own place look spacious. 'Would you like something to eat?'

'No, thanks.' I knew she'd asked out of politeness. Presumably she didn't have enough food for two because she couldn't have expected me to call right now.

'Do you mind if I do?'

'Not at all.' This was a different Gertie Maher, polite and surprisingly vulnerable, instead of the hostile and aggressive person I had met previously. 'You go ahead.'

She turned off the gas and tipped the contents of the saucepan onto the plate. It was difficult to tell what it was, a reddish concoction of rutabaga, what we used to call swede; we used to feed it to cattle in Ireland when I was young. This still looked like rutabaga: Gertie either didn't have Solange's culinary creativity or had nothing with which to disguise it. She tipped a little salt from a small bottle onto her palm and scattered it over the food.

'Please sit down,' she said, pointing to the bed. She took the only chair, by the table.

'Do you have a ration book?' I asked.

'I can get by all right,' she said, avoiding the question, which suggested that she didn't have a ration book. There were charities that distributed limited amounts of food, mainly rutabaga, to refugees who had no official papers or residency qualifications.

She tasted the food and then stirred it with the spoon to cool it.

'You said it was very urgent,' I prompted.

She concentrated on her stirring for a moment. 'I have a problem.'

'Another misunderstanding?' I asked, reminding her of her explanation for her arrest.

The new Gertie ignored that and I regretted my tone, but only a little. I wasn't happy to be summoned here on 'very urgent' business. She kept her eyes on her plate. 'I need help,' she said.

This, whatever it was, was not easy for her. I waited, and she continued after a moment.

'I need someone to keep something safe for me.'

Whatever the something could be was almost certainly something I didn't want to know about or have anything to do with.

'There's no one else I can ask,' she said, looking up at me at last. There was an air of desperation about her that went beyond manipulation.

I muttered a curse to myself and gave in. 'What is it?'

She reached across to the bed without leaving the chair and took a small black cloth bag from underneath the pillow. She handed it to me.

It was closed by a drawstring and felt weighty for its size. The contents were loose and shifted in my hand. I pulled open the top and looked in. 'Jesus Christ!' I said.

'It's not what you think,' she said quickly.

I handed her back the bag. 'No,' I said.

'Let me explain,' she pleaded, not taking the bag. 'It isn't what you think. They're not stolen. I'm only minding them for their owners. To give them back to them.'

I dropped the bag on the pillow and it began to slither downwards as the collection of gold and silver rings, diamonds, brooches, earrings, and necklaces tipped over under their own weight. It ended on its side on the top blanket beside me but the drawstring kept everything intact.

'Please,' she said, 'let me explain.'

Get up and walk out of here now, my sensible voice told me. Whatever the explanation, this is not something you want to get involved in. Especially not now.

'I swear to you they're not stolen,' Gertie was saying, talking quickly. 'They were stolen. But we're giving them back to their rightful owners. There's nothing criminal about them. But we need them kept in a safe place until we can return them. That's all. They're not safe here.'

'We. Who's "we"?'

She went to say something, then thought better of it. 'Some people I knew in Vienna,' she said in a quiet voice as if she was making a confession.

'They're in Nice now?'

She nodded.

'Refugees?'

She nodded again.

'Why can't *they* mind it?' I gestured towards the bag.

She hesitated again. 'Because it's not safe.'

'They don't want to be caught with it.' I said with a mirthless laugh.

'They're in hiding,' she added.

I shook my head, putting together the story she wasn't telling me. 'Your dinner's going cold,' I said, wondering who her friends had stolen the jewellery from, a jeweller or a black marketeer. Probably a jeweller, I thought. That would be easier and safer. And had she been involved in that? 'Does O'Casey know about this?' I asked.

'God, no,' she said. 'Please don't tell him.'

'Why is he helping you?'

'Because my father knows a lot of influential people back home.' She sighed as if she was admitting to a personal failing. 'It wasn't my idea.'

'How were you planning to get back to Ireland without his help?'

'I wasn't in a hurry back.'

'And are you in a hurry back now?'

'I thought I could be of use here,' she said ambiguously.

'Helping your friends from Vienna?'

She nodded.

'To steal back jewellery from people who'd bought it from refugees at knockdown prices?'

'Yes. They were the ones who really stole it in the first place,' she retorted. 'Stealing from desperate people.'

I didn't dispute that but it wasn't how the law would see it. There was no shortage of desperate refugees forced to sell anything they had of value to keep body and soul together, to stay on in a hotel, to buy food, to pay bribes, to find dodgy documents, and whatever else they needed to survive.

'How can you find the original owners?' I asked.

'It's not as difficult as I expected.' She hesitated, staring at me, weighing up whether to come clean about everything or not. 'I go around the hotels with some rings or necklaces, asking if they had belonged to anyone there. When I find an owner, I give it back to them. They generally know someone else who went to the same buyer. Word gets around.'

'Are the buyers jewellers?'

'Mostly.'

'Then your friends know who to rob and who to give the stuff back to.'

She said nothing but continued staring at me.

'And what part of this was the so-called misunderstanding that got you arrested?'

'Somebody saw me with one of the men who's now in hiding, but I said that I knew nothing about what he was up to; that he was just someone who started chatting me up in a café.'

'And they believed you?' I found it difficult to believe anyone would have bought her story, especially not a professionally suspicious *flic*.

'They were suspicious but they let me go when Mr O'Casey arrived.'

'Have the police approached you since then?'

'No. But, I can't risk them finding this stuff.' She gestured around the tiny room. 'There's nowhere to hide it here.'

'So you want me to take the risk instead?'

'You're not under suspicion. You're not a refugee.'

'Neither are you.' I felt a desperate need for a real cigarette. 'You should eat your dinner,' I said, to stop her staring at me while I tried to decide what to do. I was being sucked into things I didn't want any part of. It wasn't a question of rights and wrongs. I didn't want to be part of this damned war, of its poisonous politics, its determination to force everyone onto a side. I'd had enough of that, had been running away from that for nearly twenty years.

But that wasn't the whole truth either, and I knew it. What I'd really been running away from was a wrong. An accidental wrong, but still a wrong.

I watched her eating the now cold rutabaga. She took half-spoonfuls, ate the mush methodically, neither liking it nor disliking it. Something that had to be done. For some reason, Jean-Luc's story about the extras scoffing all the real food on the banquet set in Paris came into my mind. And the special dining rooms with their blackmarket food at the studio and the hotels for all the film's stars. The bag of jewellery lying on the blanket would buy any amount of food on the black market. Fuck it, I thought. I don't want to do this.

'What were you doing in Vienna?' I asked.

'Working for a family. Teaching the children English.' She tilted the plate to scrape up the last of the food.

'They're your friends here?'

'No. That family are still in Vienna. My friends here were neighbours of the family I worked for.'

'They're Jewish your friends?'

She nodded, stood up and held her plate under the tap in the sink. She put it down on the draining board and turned to me. 'Does that make a difference?'

'No. Are they on their way somewhere else?'

'To America.' She shrugged as if that was an impossible goal.

'Was this part of their plan?' I indicated the jewellery. 'To make enough money to get to America?'

'No. They're upset at the way refugees are being treated. They decided to do something about it.'

'And you agreed with them?'

'They were doing it before I got here. They asked for my help to find the owners.'

So, we're both in the same situation, I thought. Both asked to help with something that's already happening. Or so she would like me to believe. I stood up and picked up the bag. 'How long do you want me to mind it?'

'Thank you,' she said formally. 'I hope it won't take long to find the owners.'

'I hope not.'

'Can I have it for a minute?' I handed her the bag and she opened it and tipped out some of its contents on the table. She tried on a couple of rings until she found a gold one engraved with a snake like pattern that fitted the third finger on her right hand. Then she selected a silver brooch with a distinctive pattern and a pair of earrings that looked like pearls but could be fakes. 'I'll try and find the owners of these,' she said, holding them out to me on her palm. 'And that'll lead us to the owners of the other pieces.'

I put the bag in the pocket of my jacket and felt it weigh heavily as I left.

# Eight

I went down to the basement of Solange's building, to the cellars where the electricity supply came in and the meters for the ground floor and common areas were located. I unscrewed the panel covering the main fuse board and then the board itself. I pushed the bag of jewellery into the crude hole which accommodated the large cable feeding the main fuse. It should be safe: there was no reason anyone would look there if they needed to change the fuse. I screwed the board back into place and the panel that covered it.

'What was the problem?' Solange asked automatically when I got back upstairs.

'Just a fuse about to burn out.' I had told her one of the ground-floor occupants had asked me to check his lights, which were flickering on and off.

'So we can knock him off our list too.' She was still trying to figure out who had denounced her but it had become more like a parlour game now that she was no longer frightened by them.

'I wouldn't assume that.' The man I had mentioned was a retired low-level bureaucrat who had worked in the *mairie*. He was always very formal and stiff and notably unfriendly towards me. It wouldn't surprise me if he was the poison pen.

'He'd hardly be seeking your help if he was denouncing me for having you here, would he?'

'That doesn't follow.'

She tilted her head and gave me a shrewd look. 'You're becoming very suspicious these days, Martin. I don't think I like it.'

I resisted the urge to tell her it was the French habit of denouncing neighbours that was the problem. I laughed instead, to hide my growing suspiciousness. 'Yes,' I said, taking her in my arms. 'I think you wrote those letters yourself. To try to get rid of me.'

'So why have I let you back?' she said, smiling.

'That's what I'm trying to work out. You're just toying with me. Playing cat and mouse.'

Later, I lay awake trying to sort out my real suspicions. Did I believe Gertie Maher's story? It sounded plausible but how much of it was true? It was unlikely that she was a straightforward thief. But why not? Or her friends were. A jewellery thief was practically a recognised profession on the Riviera. Besides, there were lots of people justifying their dubious actions with high-minded motives these days. Or what they could claim were high-minded motives. Even young Gerard wrapped his anger at his missing father in a flag.

And what was I to do about Henri Tillon's Sûreté friends, and Jean-Luc? That was a much bigger problem. I hoped Seamus O'Casey would get Gertie out of here soon, but the Sûreté wouldn't go away. I knew that. I could only hope that they would leave Solange out of it now that they'd got my attention. But there was no guarantee they would. And the only way I could make sure they left her alone was to do what they wanted. Inform on Jean-Luc and the others. I had no intention of doing that. But that wouldn't necessarily protect me from either side.

I closed my eyes and was back in New York crossing the street towards the Italians' cruising to a halt outside our building, intent on robbery and worse. I was moving towards them, thumbing back the hammer on the Webley as I walked. Two of them were getting out of the car on the pavement side. I raised the gun and squeezed the trigger. The revolver bucked in my hand and I woke up with a jerk, covered in sweat.

Solange was lying on her back, snoring quietly. The smudge through the shutters was a brighter shade of grey and I looked at my watch. It was almost six o'clock.

I slid out of the warm bed, washed, and got dressed. I broke off a chuck of hardening bread and spread the paste that Solange had made on it. It tasted of olives. I drank a glass of water. I looked in on her before I left. She was still asleep, lying on her side, with what might have been a half-smile on her face but was probably the result of relaxed muscles.

Downstairs, I opened the door and the rain was hammering down, dripping in an almost continuous sheet from the overhang. The sky was a uniform grey and throwing down heavy drops that bounced on the road and pocked the water in the harbour beyond. I cursed aloud. I had a hat but no coat and would be soaked to the skin before I got far. But I had no choice.

A black Citroën swished up to the door and the driver stretched across to roll down the passenger window. 'Get in,' he said.

'Are you from the studio?' I asked, acting the innocent while my stomach sank.

He gave a hearty laugh as if that was genuinely funny, gestured with his hand to come on, and rolled up the window.

There was nobody else in the car. I dashed out and got into the passenger seat. Not an arrest, I thought. There would be at least two of them for that. But I was looking for straws to clutch.

He held out his hand and I had no choice but to shake it. 'Pierre Benetti,' he said. He was in his mid-forties, a bit older than me. He had a round face that was beginning to turn a little jowly and a body tending to extra weight. Which was unusual these days. His name, a French Christian name and an Italian-sounding surname, suggested he was from these parts. Which could mean he was either a French patriot or an Italian fifth columnist happy about Mussolini's victory. Or, more likely, a career policeman; one who had served the left-wing Third Republic before Vichy. Which meant he was probably not a political zealot. That was a good thing, I told myself. I was still clutching at straws.

'Does the studio usually send cars for electricians?' he asked as if he really wanted to know.

'I live in hope,' I said.

He thought that was funny too, let in the clutch, did a smooth u-turn, and drove up rue Cassini to Place Garibaldi. The restaurants around the square were preparing to open, receiving supplies from carts. The few people out were staying under the shelter of the arcades. We circled around the slum of the old town down to Place Massena and cut across to rue de France and headed westwards. The streets were empty, full of rainwater failing to find escape in the overwhelmed gutters. The windscreen wipers swished slowly as if they too were defeated by the downpour.

'So, Martin Harris,' he said, pronouncing my name as the French did. 'You've been in Nice fourteen years.' He glanced at me, indicating that that had been a question.

'About that.'

'Thirteen years, ten months and three weeks to be precise,' he said. 'You came with people from Hollywood.'

'Yes.' We were still heading west, not turning north towards his station on Boulevard Victor Hugo as I had expected. But he could turn right at any of the cross streets.

'You stayed on when they tired of our little Hollywood on the Mediterranean. Because you met the lovely Mademoiselle Delmas, was it?'

'That was later,' I said, playing along with this game. He had obviously read my file.

'And why did you stay on?'

'Because I like it here.'

'You came with the Americans but you are not an American.'

'Most of them weren't Americans either. Not originally.'

'You were an Irishman.'

'Still am,' I said. 'You can't change where you were born.'

He nodded as if that was a profound insight. 'Why did you go to America?'

'To find work. There was very little in Ireland at the time.'

'But that was after Ireland won her independence,' he said as if the country should have been transformed overnight. 'Were you involved in that?'

'In what?'

'The fight for independence.'

'No. I was too young.' Which was strictly true but not the whole truth.

'And if you had been old enough?'

'Probably.' We were still going west and it appeared that he was driving me to work, to La Victorine. The rain was still sloshing down, the wipers making their exhausted efforts to sweep it away.

There was no other traffic: he didn't bother slowing down as he drove across Boulevard Gambetta.

'Why didn't you stay then? After independence?'

'There were no jobs.'

'It wasn't a happy country? Happy with its independence?'

'No.'

'The fighting went on. Between the Irish this time.' He nodded to himself as if that was a pity. I couldn't tell whether he was showing off his knowledge or if he knew something about my past. Perhaps both. 'And were you too young for that too?'

'I needed to get a job,' I said carefully. 'And there weren't any.'

'Why were the Irish fighting among themselves?'

'Because they disagreed over what the English had offered. Whether it was real independence or not.'

'Ah, the English,' he said with a dismissive poof. 'Never wise to trust them. As we found out too.'

So he was more Pierre than Benetti, I thought, more a Frenchman than a secret Italian ally. Or pretending to be.

'Henri Tillon tells me you've been avoiding him,' he said, switching subjects while maintaining the same conversational tone. 'Which is a disappointment.'

'I haven't been avoiding him,' I said. 'I haven't seen him recently.'

'He hasn't seen you in the Café du Raisin.'

'I'm not there all the time. The studio is very busy at the moment.'

He nodded as if that was a reasonable excuse. 'So you can tell me what you've found out about the people on the list Henri gave you.'

'There's nothing to tell.'

'You've found out nothing?' He glanced at me, raising a sceptical eyebrow.

'I'm sure you know more about them than I do. I don't talk politics with anyone here. It's none of my business.'

'An admirable position in normal times. And you have kept out of trouble for nearly fourteen years here. Except for your accidental detention as an enemy alien a couple of years ago.'

'I'm not an enemy of France.'

'I'm glad to hear that. But there is only one legitimate government of France. The government of Marshal Pétain.'

I said nothing.

'You know your friend Lebret is a communist?' he went on. 'He owes his allegiance to Moscow.'

'I know he was a communist before the war.'

'And still is.'

'I thought he gave it up.'

'Is that what he tells you.'

'I never discuss politics with him. Never have and don't now.'

'Then how did you know he was a communist before the war?'

'It was common knowledge.'

'And what's the common knowledge now?'

'That he left the party over the agreement between Hitler and Stalin.'

He gave a humourless laugh. 'But there's no agreement between Hitler and Stalin now, is there?'.

'Obviously not.'

'So where does he stand now?'

'I don't know. I assume he had enough of politics before the war started.'

We drove past the entrance to La Victorine. He gave no sign that he had noticed it. 'You can drop me off anywhere here,' I said casually.

'Would you like me to drive you in the gate? So your friends see us together?'

I said nothing.

'Maybe you're a communist yourself,' he said. 'I hear there were lots of them in Hollywood too.'

'I'm not,' I said. 'I have no interest in politics.'

'Why is that?'

'Because I saw too much of it in Ireland. And the hatreds it leads to.'

He turned into a side road and let the car coast to a halt. He looked at me with what appeared to be genuine interest. 'Tell me more.'

What could I tell him about our civil war? That it was about the meaning of words. About real and imagined betrayals. Disappointments and disillusionments. Or I could try and put it into rough French terms; the new *ancient régime* against the ever-present *sans-culottes*. Or I could go one better and make a stab at my own truth –that it was about my difficult relationship with my father and my desire to hurt him by taking up the cause he hated.

'There's nothing more to tell. Like you said, it ended up with Irishmen killing one another.'

'And you were involved?'

'Only on the edges. I saw enough to know that I didn't want to see any more.'

'Interesting,' he said. 'I hope Frenchmen will not start killing Frenchmen at the behest of foreigners. You can understand that.'

The windows began to fog up, fading out the outside world like a slow dissolve in a film. The wipers were barely moving, exhausted by their efforts. The rain beat on the roof like an over-enthusiastic drummer bringing a song to a climactic conclusion. But there was no sudden silence, no conclusion to this tune.

'You'd better walk back from here,' Benetti said after a while. 'You're going to get wet, but it's safer that way.'

As I opened the door, he added: 'I hope Mademoiselle Delmas' mind was put at rest about that abortion nonsense.'

I stepped out and pulled up the collar of my jacket and set off quickly towards the studio. I had scarcely gone a hundred yards before the rain was seeping through my shirt and coming through my shoes. It chilled me but not as much as the dread I felt. Benetti's friendly-sounding conversation, pretending that we understood each other, didn't fool me for a moment. I knew his parting shot about Solange was a warning wrapped in an apparent reassurance.

The only straw to clutch at now was to get out of France, to return to Ireland, as quickly as I could. But that was a long shot. It would be difficult to persuade Solange to come with me. And I had probably left it too late to set the process in motion for a quick departure.

I was leaning against the wall in the gloom at the back of the studio later. On the sound stage Jules Berry in his devil's outfit was instructing his young emissary, Alain Cuny, to seduce the beautiful bride Marie Déa. Berry, as usual, was making up his lines, causing Cuny to fumble his as he tried to adjust his own responses to what Berry was saying, rather than what he was supposed to say. Marcel Carné was being unusually patient as he repeatedly shouted '*Coupez*', called out the right lines to Berry, and told them to do it again. Cuny, getting his big break, apologized repeatedly for what was obviously not his fault.

I was thinking how nice it would be just to be concerned with putting together a fantasy story set in another time. My shirt was drying out and I was beginning to feel warm again in the hot atmosphere. There was a sudden bang as a bulb exploded in one of the light arrays. Carné shouted 'Coupez' again and I went to move forward to replace it. Carné looked at the lighting, which didn't appear diminished by the loss of the bulb, and waved me away. Instead, he put his arm around Berry's shoulder and led him to a corner, whispering in his ear. Repeating his proper lines, I presumed. We all knew them by now.

I resumed my position by the back wall and the tedious effort of completing the scene continued. It was nearly there when Jean-Luc joined me during one of the cuts. We watched in silence until the next break when he said, 'Let's have a coffee.' We went to the canteen and I got an ersatz 'coffee' and he poured himself a glass of water.

'What's new?' he asked as we took a table near the window. The rain had stopped but the eves were dripping into the flooded flowerbed and spilling water onto the cement. The sky was still a sullen grey.

'Carné's very patient today,' I said. 'That scene should've been wrapped up an hour ago. Is he a gambling buddy of Berry's?'

'Don't know. I haven't heard that.'

We made more small talk, about the drenching we had both got that morning, my unreadable Simenon novel, now sodden from the pocket of my jacket. Then he said, 'I passed on your warning to the others.'

I nodded, noting that it was now 'my' warning. His initial hostility when I showed him the list had disappeared. I wondered if he had accepted my explanation then, or whether he had been told to cultivate me. I knew I was being sucked into dangerous games.

'They're grateful,' he added. 'Has Tillon come back to you yet?'

I shook my head. 'I haven't seen him.' I drank the dregs of the 'coffee' and took a deep breath. It was unlikely anyone had seen me in Benetti's car but it was not impossible. 'Somebody else has approached me. Pierre Benetti.'

Jean-Luc gave a sharp intake of breath. 'He's a dangerous fucker,' he said.

'You know him?'

'By reputation. What'd he want?'

'To talk about the troubled times in Ireland.'

'He knew you were involved?'

'No,' I said, deciding to turn this game a little on its head. 'You're the only one here who knows anything about that.'

'I respect that. I haven't told anyone.'

'Good. He said he hoped the French wouldn't end up like the Irish, killing one another at the behest of foreigners.'

Jean-Luc snorted. 'And who's he working for now? Hitler or Mussolini?'

'What do you know about Benetti?'

'You know there are people here who think Nice should never have been given back to France?'

I nodded. 'He's one of them?'

Jean-Luc shrugged. 'He's a fascist. The dangerous kind. Not one of the brawlers. One of the ones who tries to present himself as a reasonable man.'

'Has he been in the Sûreté a long time?'

'Yes. He's always been an enemy of the party.'

It was the first time Jean-Luc had indicated overtly to me that he was still a member of the Communist Party, although I already knew that. What I didn't know for sure, and didn't want to know, was whether he had ever really left it.

It was dark when I finished work. The sky had cleared and a fresh moon hung over the Baie des Anges. I walked along the Promenade des Anglais, for once not taking pleasure in the moonlight on the water or the lights curving around the bay and the distant casino at its eye. Instead, I kept my head down to avoid the puddles and walked fast to stay warm. It was cold but I was carrying my jacket -- it was still too damp to wear.

Mrs Mac's was crowded as if her customers had been cooped up at home all day by the rain and were looking for an excuse to get out. 'What a day,' she said, looking happy as she added another beer to the line waiting for Ange-Marie. 'Did you ever see anything like it?'

'Not since the last time,' I replied. When it rained in winter in Nice, it tended not to bother with half- measures.

'Somebody's grumpy today. Did you get wet?'

I ignored the question and asked her for some tokens for the phone and went into the booth at the end of the bar. I asked the operator for the number of O'Casey's hotel at Vichy. She told me it would take about ten minutes.

I waited by the booth, drinking my beer, and surveying the café. Henri Tillon was with some of his colleagues at the far end of the zinc. I glowered at him, waiting for him to catch my eye but he didn't look my way. The rest were mostly regulars I knew by sight, the people from the printworks next door, the old men who played cards, those of whom I knew nothing more than the fact that they came to the bar frequently.

Ange-Marie came by with a tray full of beers and wines and said, 'Mme Bonnard wants to know why you're not talking to her today?'

'I'm waiting for a phone call,' I said. 'I'll talk to her when I'm finished.'

It was closer to twenty minutes when the phone rang and I went into the booth and picked up the receiver. A woman's voice gave the name of the hotel and I asked for Monsieur O'Casey. She had trouble with my pronunciation of his name until I asked for '*le diplomat irlandais*'.

O'Casey came on the phone with a cheery 'hello', sounding like a man who had had a good dinner, or, more likely, a long lunch. His tone cooled when I identified myself but that may have been my imagination. Or the fact that the line sounded as if was carrying our voices in waves that undulated like the sea.

'How is everything?' he asked.

'Not good. Your friend is getting very impatient. She needs arrangements to move along as quickly as possible.'

There was a pause as the wave of static rose and fell. '*Cad atá tu á rá?*' He lapsed into Irish. *What are you saying?*

I grappled with the sudden change of language. My Irish was little more than rudimentary and long unused. One of our column commanders had insisted on issuing all commands in Irish and tried to teach us the conversational language. But it was very hit and miss, a distraction in the midst of a guerrilla war. I hadn't joined the fight to go back into a classroom.

'*An dtuigeann tú Gaeilge?*' he asked into my silence. Do you understand Irish?

'*Beagán.*' A little.

He ignored that limitation, rattling off something in Irish. I could tell it was a question and assumed he wanted to know what was the problem with Gertie Maher. I tried to construct a response but my Irish wasn't up to it on the spur of the moment. He repeated what he had said more slowly. I replied in English: 'She's very impatient. She wants to go home. She needs to go home as soon as possible.'

'I understand,' he said. 'Tell her I'm doing everything I can to speed up the travel permits.'

'*Ba mhaith liom dul abhaile anois,*' I said, dragging a phrase out of my memory. I want to go home now. If he presumed as well as I did that someone might be listening in to our conversation I certainly didn't want them to know that I was telling an Irish diplomat I wanted to get out of France now.

'*Tú féin*?' Yourself? He sounded surprised, even taken aback.

'*Sea*.' Yes.

'*Agus cad mar gheall ar do bhean chéile*?' I only caught the mention of a wife and presumed he was asking about Solange.

'*Sea*,' I repeated.

There was a sound like a sigh which might have been him or might have been the wave-like phone line. 'Thanks for keeping me informed,' he said. '*Bí cúramach*.'

He hung up and I replaced the receiver. That wasn't very satisfactory but his parting comment, be careful, at least indicated that he understood there were problems. That he had to get Gertie Maher out of Nice soon. And Solange and me as well. It also suggested that he knew more about what had got her into trouble than he had told me in the first place.

I finished my beer at the bar and Mrs Mac came over to me. The café was beginning to thin out, the after-work crowd drifting home. Henri Tillon was still chatting with his cronies, avoiding my eye, though I suspected he knew I was there.

'Your diplomatic friend says he's doing everything he can to hurry up the permits,' I told her in response to her 'well?'

She glanced at the phone booth as if it would confirm what I said. 'You were talking to him just now?'

I nodded.

'Something to do with your new friend?' she said, managing to make the 'friend' sound anything but friendly. 'She was in here looking for you earlier.'

'Did she say what she wanted?'

Mrs Mac paused, trying to remember the precise words. 'She said she needed more.'

'More what?' I asked automatically though I knew what the message meant as soon as she said it.

'She didn't say.'

'Are you giving her money?'

'No, of course not.'

'What does she want more of then?'

I shrugged. 'She didn't say? That's all she said? She wanted more?'

Mrs Mac raised a suspicious eye. 'You should be careful with that one.'

'Don't worry. She's not my type.'

'She's trouble. I can tell from the cut of her.'

'The cut of her,' I repeated with a laugh, trying to make light of it.

'Yes,' she said with a defiant tilt of her chin. 'If you spent as long as I have behind this bar, you'd know whom to be suspicious of too.'

'What about Henri Tillon?' The policeman had his back to me now, listening to one of his colleagues. There was a sour satisfaction in the thought that he might be avoiding me now rather than me avoiding him.

'Henri's a decent man. He was good to Lucien in the old days.'

'Really?' I was surprised. She had never mentioned anything about that before. But she didn't offer any explanation of how Tillon had helped her husband in the past. I was about to ask but she changed the subject to why she wanted to talk to me.

'Gerard won't come to Ireland with me. Not even for a holiday. Not even to meet his relations.' She was on the verge of tears.

I reached across and squeezed the fist she had formed unconsciously on the zinc. 'Maybe you should go yourself anyway. You need a holiday.'

She ignored me. 'I pleaded with him but it was no use. He said now was no time for a holiday in the midst of a war. And he had met his Irish relations before and had no interest in seeing them again. He doesn't remember any of them, of course. He was only four or five the last time we were there. Two years after Lucien died.' She looked at me and answered my suggestion. 'I can't go myself and leave him here. God knows what trouble he'd get into.'

'A holiday would do you good.' There was no point telling her that Gerard would get into trouble whether she was here or not. 'You could do with a rest. Close the place for two weeks.'

'How could I get to Ireland and back in two weeks these days?'

'Maybe you should go somewhere else for two weeks. A nice hotel on Lake Garda.'

She smiled at the thought. 'I was there a few years ago. It's so hard to go anywhere these days.'

'But not impossible.'

'Maybe so.' She managed a wan smile. 'Thanks, Marty.'

# Nine

On my way out of Solange's next morning I went down to the basement and retrieved the jewellery bag from behind the main fuse board. I thought of bringing it with me but decided against it. I did what Gertie had done, selected a ring, brooch and necklace which had distinctive designs on them. I put them in my pocket and replaced the bag.

I half-expected Pierre Benetti to be waiting outside for me again but there was no sign of him. I walked up around the Castle hill and the bay opened out below me, lifting my spirits, as it always did. It was a beautiful morning, washed clean by the previous day's rain. The sun was working its way up the sky, glistening on the water, shining on the cleansed leaves of the palm trees, and picking out the fresh red roofs of the Old Town. It held all the promise of a new beginning but the jewellery in my pocket reminded me that it was a false promise: it was just another day.

I spent the day locked in the over lit fantasy world of the Middle Ages, mostly trying to read my Simenon novel. My services were scarcely needed but I had to be on hand. The novel's pages had stuck together from yesterday's wetting and had to be prised apart carefully. They were still damp and tore easily and the print had run in places. It was hardly worth the effort but I had nothing else to read while the interminable re-takes went on and on.

During the lunch break Jean-Luc sidled onto the form at my table with his plate of flavoured rutabaga and a glass of water. We ate in silence until the man opposite finished and went away.

'I've been asking around about Benetti,' Jean-Luc said. 'He is a fascist, like I told you. But he's also a careerist, not above lining his own pockets. A vindictive bastard who doesn't like to be bested. You know the kind? Takes everything personally, bears grudges.'

'Jesus,' I sighed. Just the kind of person I didn't want to be dealing with.

Jean-Luc gave me a wan smile. 'You know Laurent Poulenc?' he added. 'The painter?'

He was one of the names on the Sûreté's list given to me by Henri Tillon but I didn't know him other than to see. A small, wiry man in his fifties. I shook my head, fearing the worst.

'He's disappeared.'

'Arrested?'

'No,' Jean-Luc said. 'Decided he wasn't going to wait around to be arrested. Gone into hiding.'

'Because of the list?'

Jean-Luc nodded.

'Shit,' I said.

Jean-Luc looked at me in surprise. 'Why do you say that?'

'Because it's my doing.'

'It's his decision. Maybe better off. He'd thank you if he could.' He paused and glanced around. 'He's trying to put together a resistance unit.'

I didn't want to know. I said nothing. Jean-Luc finished his lunch and asked me if I wanted a 'coffee'. I nodded and he went up to the counter. I sighed and squeezed my eyes. I could feel a headache coming on.

Jean-Luc returned with our drinks. He looked around and then took the seat opposite me. He leant forward and dropped his voice, even though there was nobody near us now. 'Did you get a good look at Arletty's German this morning?'

'No,' I said, surprised by this turn in the conversation. Jean-Luc wasn't one for gossip about film stars.

'You must've have seen him. He was in there watching that scene all morning.'

Now that he mentioned it, I had noticed the well-built man in a double-breasted grey suit watching the filming. I had put him down automatically as someone from Continental, the Germany production company that was funding the film. 'That's the flier?' I asked.

'I don't think he's a pilot,' Jean-Luc said. 'He's an officer in the Luftwaffe but I think he's got some desk job. Hans-Jürgen Soehring.'

I tried to remember what I had seen. Arletty had tripped over to him during one of the breaks while Carné repositioned the cameras. She had embraced him briefly, kissing him on both cheeks. That was why I assumed he was from Continental, that she was ingratiating herself with the company. Soehring, if that was him, looked to be in his early thirties, a decade younger than her. 'Are you sure? That guy is a lot younger than her.'

'Yes, he is. That's him all right.'

I sipped at the 'coffee' and wondered why I bothered drinking it. I should follow Jean-Luc's example and switch to water. He was lighting one of the fake cigarettes that I couldn't be bothered smoking. He coughed and winced as the foul smoke drifted into his eyes.

'Do you remember how to make a bomb from your days in Ireland?' he asked casually as he wiped a tear from his eye.

I froze for a moment. 'Are you out of your fucking mind?' I stared at him.

He took another drag on the cigarette and blew out the smoke without inhaling. 'It's outrageous that she can carry on like that,' he said in a calm voice.

'You want to kill her?'

He shook his head. 'Him.'

'Jesus Christ!'

'It would send a message to all the *collabos*. And it would be a very powerful message to those who think they're above retribution. Like her. You know she's a friend of Laval's daughter?' Laval was Marshal Pétain's prime minister and an even more fervent advocate of collaboration with the Nazis than the Marshal.

'You can't be serious,' I said. But I knew he was. The fact that he or someone else had been collecting information about this Soehring and Arletty's friends confirmed it. 'You know what'll happen if you try this. The Germans will take out fifty hostages and shoot them. Fifty innocent people. Maybe a hundred.'

'This isn't the occupied zone.'

'You think that'll stop them?'

He shrugged.

'You think Vichy won't do it for them?'

He gave a wintry smile. 'That would expose them finally if they did that. Lining up innocent Frenchmen and women against a wall and shooting them in reprisals for a German.' He shook his head.

'That's what you want?' I could hear my voice rising in incredulity. At the same time I had the sickening realization that I had heard this kind of logic before.

'It's a war.'

'Don't fight a fucking war unless you can win it.' I grabbed his packet of cigarettes, took one, and held out my hand for his matches. He passed the box to me, watching me closely. I lit it and inhaled the harsh smoke. Even though it burned my throat, it was somehow soothing.

'You won't help us then?' he asked.

I shook my head. 'I've no idea how to make a bomb. I've never made one. And even if I had, I wouldn't help you.'

We stared at each other, neither blinking. I wasn't altogether sure he was serious, or if he was testing me. Either way, I'd never expected to be involved in these types of discussion again. I'd got away from them for the best part of twenty years and here they were again out of the blue. My anger began to dissolve into tiredness, a bone-deep weariness that threatened to drain away my will to live.

'Another thing,' I said in a tired voice. 'Where do you think they'll look for hostages? Around here. Pick fifty people we work with every day and shoot them.'

'That's why you won't help?'

'No. It doesn't matter whether we know the innocent victims or not.'

'There's always unintended casualties in war.'

'Easily said,' I snorted. I'd heard that one before too.

We lapsed into silence. He finished his cigarette and went to get up, putting his empty glass on the cleared plate. 'Forget I said anything,' he said.

'How do I do that?'

He settled back on to the form. 'What does that mean? What are you going to do?'

'Nothing. I'm not getting involved.'

He shook his head. 'There's no room for *attentistes,* those waiting to see what happens.'

'I'm not an *attentiste,*' I said dismissively. 'I'm not waiting to see who comes out on top.'

'What then?'

'I'm not getting involved. But I'm asking you to think long and hard of the consequences before you do anything like that.'

'And if we do it?'

I thought for a moment, trying to put my position, such as it was, into words. It was non-involvement rather than neutrality. But neither non-involvement nor neutrality was ever that simple. 'I won't do anything to help them,' I said. 'I won't do anything to harm you.'

Jean-Luc considered that. 'Okay,' he said and stood up again.

As I was leaving the studio that evening, I passed Arletty and the German I now knew as her Luftwaffe lover. She was sitting in the passenger seat of his Mercedes convertible. He was raising the roof while she chattered at him in her distinctive Parisian accent. His brown hair was combed straight back from his square face and he had light blue eyes.

They drove past me at the gate to the street and it occurred to me that Jean-Luc and his friends didn't need a bomb. A hand grenade lobbed into the car when the roof was down would probably kill both of them. It was just a matter of being in the right place at the right time on a sunny day. Which left me wondering again if Jean-Luc's request for my help was a test rather than a plan.

I gave up wondering and turned my mind to Gertie Maher and the jewellery in my pocket as I walked along the Promenade. Should I go directly to her apartment to deliver it or check first if she was in the Café du Raisin? It was a nice evening, the cold north wind had died, and the moon was near full. There were few pedestrians about. I was so absorbed in my own thoughts, I didn't notice anything amiss until I became aware of somebody behind me.

Hands slid under both my arms and a voice said in my left ear, 'Come with us'. As they steered me to the left, the black Citroën appeared at the kerb. I went with them, thinking about the jewellery in my pocket. How would I explain it when they searched me? One pushed me into the back of the car and the other got into the front passenger seat. I didn't recognize any of them.

Nobody said anything as we drove along the Promenade, swung left into Boulevard Gambetta and then right into Boulevard Victor Hugo. We stopped outside the police station and one of them led me inside and into an interview room. I didn't have long to wait until Pierre Benetti appeared.

'Excuse the drama,' he said as he sat down opposite me. 'I could have offered you a lift myself, but ...' He shrugged, leaving the 'but' hanging in the air. He offered me a Gauloise Caporal and I took it. He lit both, inhaled and said, 'So?'

I gave him my best impression of a Gallic shrug.

'What do you have for me?'

'Nothing. I told you the last morning. I know nothing about these men that I'm sure you don't know already.'

'Tell me what I know already.'

'They're carpenters and painters. I know nothing about their politics. What they think of the current situation. I never discuss it with them.'

'You know they're communists.'

'I don't actually. I know Jean-Luc Lebret used to be a communist. But he gave it up.'

'He pretended to. To get himself released.'

I shrugged.

'Laurent Poulenc?' The painter Jean-Luc had told me had gone into hiding.

'He a communist too?'

'Actually, no.' Benetti said. 'He's a follower of that renegade de Gaulle.'

I had assumed Poulenc was also a Communist when Jean-Luc told me he had gone into hiding but the fact that he was a Gaullist changed things. It meant that Jean-Luc was happy to tell me about a rival *résistant*, and that I was being gently sucked into the mire of French politics.

'You didn't tell him about our interest?'

'No,' I said. 'I've never spoken to him. Except maybe once or twice in relation to work.'

'He's missing. His wife thinks he might have been kidnapped.'

'Kidnapped?'

'You're surprised?'

'Yes, Why would he be kidnapped? He's a painter, not a rich man. As far as I know.'

Benetti sat back in his chair and contemplated me. I smoked my cigarette and O'Casey's parting words on the phone came to mind, *bí cúramach*. Don't be fooled into talking too much because I'm on safe ground with Poulenc. Benetti was still treating me as a friendly accomplice but that could change at any moment. And I was aware

I had no plausible reason for the jewellery in my pocket if he chose to have me searched or detained.

'I don't believe it either,' Benetti said. 'Maybe he's run off with a younger woman.'

I laughed in spite of myself.

'You don't think so?'

'Maybe,' I said. 'Have you ever seen him?'

Benetti shook his head. 'Not exactly a Romeo?'

'I don't think so, but who knows?'

'He's part of a terrorist group,' Benetti said in the same conversational tone. 'And they're planning something.'

I took a final drag of the Gauloise and stubbed out the butt on the metal ashtray.

'These are dangerous people.' Benetti leaned forward to stub out his cigarette too. 'Dangerous times.' He stood up. 'Thanks for coming in.'

He held the door open for me and accompanied me down the corridor to the public office. 'Keep your ears open,' he said quietly as he shook hands with me, maintaining the pretence that we were colleagues in a joint enterprise.

I headed for Mrs Mac's, fearing that someone might follow me and not wanting to confirm suspicions by making any moves to thwart them. Gertie Maher wasn't there. I had one drink, an inconsequential chat with Mrs Mac, and made my way to rue Berlioz. The streets were empty. I crossed them unnecessarily and couldn't see any signs that I was being followed.

Gertie was happy to see me. 'You got my message,' she said. 'I was beginning to worry.'

I took out the three pieces of jewellery I had selected. 'I assumed this is what you wanted,' I said, placing them on her tiny table. 'More samples.'

'Actually, I wanted everything,' she replied with an apologetic look. 'I was lucky. I found the owners of the pieces I had in one of the hotels up there.' She nodded her head in the vague direction of the central station. 'Most of the people in that hotel used the same jeweller.'

'The one you robbed,' I said mildly.

'The one who robbed them,' she corrected me.

'It's just as well you want them all back,' I said. 'I can't hide them any longer. It's too dangerous. The Sûreté is taking an interest in me.'

'Why are they interested in you?' She looked at me as if she was seeing me for the first time.

'They're not really. They're interested in some people who work in the film studio. I'm being dragged into it because I work there too.'

'What are they up to, the people in the film studio?'

'Nothing that I know of.'

Gertie opened a cupboard under the sink and took out a bottle of wine. I shook my head when she offered me a glass. She poured one for herself. 'It would be good if all the people fighting the fascists joined forces,' she said after tasting a sip.

I told her I had been picked up on the Promenade the same way she had been, taken to the Sûreté building and questioned. 'If they had searched me, I was in trouble,' I said.

'But they didn't.'

'Not this time. Look, it's too dangerous for you and for me if they find anything on me'

She sipped at her wine, thinking. 'I could use your hiding place.'

'No.' That would be even worse, drawing her and whoever might follow her to Solange's building.

'What then?'

I shrugged: it wasn't my problem. 'I talked to O'Casey,' I said, switching the subject. 'Told him to get a move on. That it was imperative to get you out of here as soon as possible.'

'Did you tell him about this?' She pointed at the jewellery.

'No, but you should get out as soon as you can. It's only a matter of time before the flic find out about this. If they don't know about it already. Do you have O'Casey's number?'

She nodded.

'Call him and tell him you need to leave now.'

'I can't do that. I have things to do here.'

'Because you're a Jew?' I finally voiced my suspicion.

'Yes,' she said, her voice rising with defiance and anger. 'Do you know what it's like for Jews here? They're fleeing for their lives from the Nazis. Being hounded at every turn. Robbed of their only means to keep body and soul together. Trapped here with no way out.'

There was a brief knock at the door and it opened without a pause. A young man stepped in and stopped in surprise when he saw me. He glanced at Gertie, her face flushed from her sudden anger, and he looked back at me. Gertie said something to him in rapid German and then turned to me. 'This is Willi,' she said, pronouncing his name in the German way.

Willi was tall and thin, with a narrow face under black hair. He was wearing an ill-fitting suit of a heavy dark material that had seen better days. The jacket was too short and fraying at the cuffs and the trousers fell short of his shoes. It looked like a well-worn hand-me-down from someone shorter and older than his twenty or so years.

He noticed the jewellery on the table and he and Gertie exchanged a few sentences in German. Then he took a paper bag from his jacket pocket and left it on the table. More jewellery. Gertie looked at me. I muttered 'putain'. Fuck.

'We have nowhere to keep it,' she said to me, a note of pleading in her voice. 'Nowhere safe.'

They both watched me while I thought about the problem. I had no doubt that my hiding place was secure. The danger lay in carrying the jewellery around. And it couldn't be just hidden and forgotten about if Gertie was returning it to its original owners. They needed a system where there was minimal movement and flexible access, a halfway house that didn't compromise either of us. 'Okay,' I said. 'But we need a better arrangement.'

'Like what?'

'I don't know.' Mrs Mac's would be ideal but I dismissed it immediately. I couldn't involve her in this. 'I'll have to think about it.'

Gertie launched into German again. When she had finished, Willi held out his hand to me and I shook it. 'Thank you,' he said in heavily accented English. He said something to Gertie and left.

'What did you tell him?'

'That you would help us.' She tipped the contents of the paper bag onto the table as if the main issue had been resolved. I watched her sort quickly through the pieces, looking for inscriptions inside the rings, judging the uniqueness of the designs. She put a handful of pieces to one side, returned the rest to the paper bag, and handed it to me.

'How long has this being going on?' I asked, wondering how long it would take the police and the jewellers to realize what was happening. It wouldn't take very long if the owners of the jewellery made the mistake of re-selling them to the same person. Or the jewellers began to compare notes.

'A few months, I think.'

'It's going to get more dangerous the longer it goes on.'

'I know,' she said. 'What do you suggest?'

I gave a half-laugh. 'What do you take me for? A criminal mastermind?'

'Aren't you?' She smiled, the first time I had seen her smile. It transformed her face. 'I'm disappointed. O'Casey said you could solve any problems I had.'

'He lied. And you didn't tell him your real problems.'

She held up the wine bottle, offering me a drink, but I declined again. I took the paper bag of jewellery and put it in my pocket. 'I'll see you in the Café du Raisin tomorrow evening with the other bag,' I said.

'I met the policeman who talked to me about the poison letter today,' Solange said as we finished our dinner. 'He gave me a lift to work.'

'Really?' I said, feigning minimal interest while cursing Benetti. The bastard was toying with me, letting me know he could pick her up anytime. Just like he had had me snatched off the Promenade.

'He said they had received another denunciation but he had thrown it in the bin.'

And would take it out again if needed, I thought. If it existed.

'Drove me all the way to Signora Mancini's,' she added.

'What was he doing out there?'

'He didn't say. Said it wasn't far out of his way.'

She cut an apple into four parts as dessert. It was another of her employer's regular small gifts of things to eat.

'Did he ask you about her? Signora Mancini?'

'No. Why would he?'

I ate my first quarter of the apple. 'He's not the kind of detective who does anyone a favour for nothing. He's usually looking for something in return. For information.'

'Why do you say that? Do you know him?'

'I've heard things about him. He's dangerous.'

'Says who?'

'I don't remember. People. It's best to have nothing to do with anyone in the Sûreté.'

She gave me a quizzical look. 'You are becoming very suspicious these days.' It was becoming a refrain with her.

'These are dangerous times,' I said. 'You can't be too careful.'

She ate her second quarter of the apple while keeping her eyes on me. I took my second quarter. 'Is this one of Signora Mancini's own stock?' Her villa on Cap Ferrat had a large garden with all sorts of trees running down to the shore.

'No,' Solange said. 'Her own apples are long gone. Remember she gave us a big bag of them last autumn.'

I remembered. There was no doubt Signora Mancini had been generous with her surplus food. Where she got it I had never asked and Solange never told me. If she knew, which I assumed she did.

'Have you given any more thought to going to Ireland?' I asked.

'You're serious about that?'

'If it can be arranged. Which I'm not sure it can.'

'For how long?' She turned the questioning back on me.

'I don't know. Until the end of the war maybe.'

She fell silent and I waited. 'I wouldn't like to go away until Pierre and François come home,' she said eventually. They were her two brothers in a German prisoner of war camp.

'That will probably be at the end of the war,' I suggested gently.

'It could be before that.' She looked at me and I could see the hope in her eyes. 'If enough volunteers go to work in Germany, they could be released at any time.'

I said nothing, not wishing to throw cold water on her hopes. The Germans were offering to release a prisoner of war for every three young Frenchmen or women who volunteered to work in Germany. The offer, supported by the Vichy government, had found few volunteers so far, and there was no reason to think that would change. Indeed, there was talk that it might become compulsory for military age Frenchmen to go and work in German factories and farms if the number of volunteers continued to fall so far short of their requirements.

'Can you understand that?' she asked.

'Yes, of course. Perhaps we could go for a few months only.'

'And how would we get back afterwards?'

'That could be difficult,' I conceded. Casual travel wasn't easy, even impossible.

'Why didn't you think of this years ago? Before the war?'

'I don't know,' I lied. I'd had no incentive to return then. Not to a country which had offered me a choice between emigration and a bullet in the back of the head. And the choice wouldn't have been on offer at all if I hadn't had the luck to successfully hide my revolver before I was caught. The penalty at that time for being caught with a firearm was death. That had been my first and formative experience with secret policemen.

'Anyway,' she said, bringing me back to the present day, 'you can't go away now that they're filming in La Victorine.'

'That won't last too much longer.'

'Maybe they'll get another film after this one.'

'Maybe.'

'Or you can go back to doing very little work and be happy again.'

I laughed. 'Was I happy then?'

'I think so. I don't think these long days at work are good for you. They're making you tired and suspicious.'

'You could be right,' I said, happy to let her think so. It wasn't the work alone that was tiring me but the sleepless nights worrying about being caught in the vice between Benetti and Jean-Luc. And the knowledge that my sleep might be broken by the damned New York nightmare again. Then there was the lesser problem of Gertie Maher. Which had taken a lurch up the scale with the appearance of her associate, Willi. And the fact that his too-small jacket didn't quite conceal the butt of the revolver in his belt.

# Ten

News about the shoot-out on the rue de France reached the studios at lunchtime the next day, an hour or so after it happened.

'Two young guys shot dead robbing a jeweller's,' Jean-Luc told me during our break. I thought immediately of Willi and Gertie and my heart sank. 'Apparently it was an ambush.'

'What do you mean?'

'The flics were waiting for them. They'd taken over the place opposite and opened fire when the two emerged from the shop. Didn't give them a chance to surrender. Just cut them down.'

'Who were they?' I asked, trying to adopt a suitable level of interest while fearing the worst.

'I don't know. They were set-up, whoever they were. Somebody obviously informed on them.'

Not necessarily, I thought, but I kept the thought to myself. It didn't take a genius to stake out a few likely targets in the midst of a spate of robberies of jewellers. I had more or less warned Gertie about such an eventuality the previous evening.

I spent the afternoon in the midst of the make-believe of the filming, trying to work out the ramifications if Willi was dead. It depended on whether Pierre Benetti and his colleagues knew of Gertie's association with him. She had told me she was arrested originally because she was seen with some young man. If that was Willi, they'd be calling on her. And I'd been seen with her in Mrs Mac's by that weaselly bastard Henri Tillon and God knew who else. If Benetti could link me, even indirectly, in any way with Willi, I was in real trouble. He would then have a serious hold over me rather than his tenuous threats to Solange.

'Hey!' Marcel Carné was clicking his fingers and shouting at me. 'Wake up!'

A fuse had blown, blanking out one of the cameras. I replaced it and repaired the old one with a length of fuse wire while the filming resumed. But my mind remained on Gertie, thanking God that I hadn't brought the jewellery she wanted back with me that morning. I had thought about it but had decided to get the bag after work before meeting her in Mrs Mac's. If I was picked up with those in my pocket, I was truly fucked.

I left work and walked back towards the town along the avenue de la Californie, a block inland from the bay. I half-expected Benetti's heavies to appear at my shoulders at any moment but nobody accosted me. The avenue gave way to the rue de France and I came upon the jewellers'. It was a small shop, a window on either side of the door. The windows were boarded up, presumably shot out. The footpath was still wet where it had been washed. There was no sign of any damage on the shop opposite or on its first- floor windows. It seemed all the gunfire had been in one direction.

An old woman passing by blessed herself.

Gertie wasn't waiting for me in Mrs Mac's, an ominous sign. 'You heard the news," Mrs Mac greeted me. 'We had more drama up the street today than you had at the picture factory.'

'So I heard.'

She leaned closer across the zinc. 'One of them was a friend of Gerard's.'

'What? A Legionnaire?'

'No. One of the people in the port. Gerard's known him since they were children. They used to be great friends in school at one stage.'

I absorbed this information, turning everything I had presumed on its head. So Willi wasn't dead. Gertie wasn't in danger. The robbers were members of the gang in the port, the gang linked to the Italian mafia. It was a straightforward robbery. Or perhaps a protection racket gone wrong. They may have gone there to threaten rather than rob the jeweller.

'He was still friendly with him as far as I know,' Mrs Mac was saying, the worry lines creasing her face. She looked exhausted.

'Jesus,' I said. 'You think he's involved with them too?' It was not as unlikely as it sounded. The local mafia was deeply involved in the black market and happy to ally itself with the new political order. It wouldn't surprise me to learn that there was an overlap of members at the edges between them and the Legionnaires. They certainly shared methods.

'I don't know what to think anymore, Marty,' she said. 'That's the God's honest truth.'

'You really need to get away for a while. For your own sake.'

She gave me a don't-start-that-again shrug and looked over my shoulder. 'Your new friend has arrived,' she announced drily.

Gertie appeared at my shoulder a moment later and said 'Bonsoir' to Mrs Mac. She ordered a glass of red wine and Mrs Mac said she'd send the drinks to a table. 'You heard?' I asked when we sat down.

Gertie nodded.

'That could have been your friend,' I said. 'You have to give it up.'

'For a little while.'

'For good. It's too dangerous.'

We fell silent while Ange-Marie delivered our drinks. When she had gone, I said: 'The police are obviously staking out all jewellers.'

She checked there was no one within earshot and lowered her voice anyway. 'We knew there was someone else robbing them.'

'You know who they are now.'

She nodded. 'Criminals.'

'The mafia. You know what the mafia is?'

She nodded again and took a sip of her wine. 'Willi has a plan. To steal the jewellery back from the criminals. Some refugees have also been selling to them on the black market. They sometimes get better prices because the criminals move the stuff elsewhere. Paris, Rome.'

'So you want to take on the mafia? As well as the police? And the Vichy government?'

A hint of a smile appeared around her lips. Put like that, the idea appealed to her. She turned earnest again. 'We can't give up. The people who need help need us.'

'You won't be much help to them lying dead on the street like those young lads this morning,' I said, disliking my parental tone even as I heard it. I sounded like my father twenty years ago as he lectured me against involvement in the politics of the day.

'Have you got the jewellery?' she asked, getting back to business.

I shook my head. 'I thought it was better left where it was for the moment.'

She glanced at her watch. 'But I promised to give it back to its owners this evening.'

'You can explain to them what happened.'

'They can't afford to wait. Some of them are facing eviction from their hotel. They need to sell it again.'

I sighed. There was no point arguing with her. Besides, it would be a relief to get rid of it. 'You want both bags?' I offered, hopefully.

'Just the first one. I don't know who owns the second lot yet.'

I told her to wait. It would take me half an hour to get it and return. I went along the rue de France towards Place Massena where a small crowd was gathering outside the casino. There was a flatbed cart ready for a meeting, flaring torches at two corners. Up avenue de la Victoire there was a moving mass of torches as the Legionnaires paraded down to the rally. I cut down through the Cours Saleya to the Promenade and around the Castle Hill to the apartment building. I thought I could see light through the slats in Solange's apartment but wasn't sure.

I recovered the jewellery bag and made my way back to the café, avoiding Place Massena. Occasional cheers drifted down to the waterfront as the rally got underway. The casino on the Jetée-Promenade cast its welcoming lights like bait onto the water to entice the unwary and the desperate but nobody seemed to be biting tonight.

Gertie stood up as soon as I entered the café and led me back outside. She glanced up and down the empty street and put out her hand. 'I'll come with you,' I said. 'The Legionnaires are out in force tonight.'

'There's no need. I'll be all right.'

'What if you run into them again?'

She thought about it for a moment and said, 'Okay'.

'Where are we going?'

She named a hotel I'd never heard of as she turned up rue du Congrés in the direction of the station. Crossing boulevard Victor Hugo a small group of Legionnaires passed in front of us. Gertie slid her arm under mine and moved closer as if we were a couple. But the Legionnaires were hurrying to their rally and didn't give us a glance. She withdrew her arm.

We had passed Place Mozart and were in avenue Durante, a straight street of belle époque buildings, when it happened. I felt a bang between my shoulder blades and was pitched forward. I just had time to break my fall with my right arm but my forehead hit the ground. I heard Gertie scream and tried to struggle to my feet but a foot on my back held me down and I could feel a hand in my jacket pocket pulling out the jewellery bag. Then there were two shots in quick succession and the pressure on my back disappeared and I could hear somebody running.

I got to my feet. Gertie was leaning against the wall of a building, breathing heavily. A man was running away up the street. Then he stopped, bent down and picked up something. He turned and walked back towards us. I could see the gun in his right hand and feared the worst for a moment until I recognized Willi. In his other hand he had Gertie's handbag and the jewellery bag.

Willi put away his revolver and his arm around Gertie. She rested her head on his shoulder while they exchanged some words in German. I looked up and down the street. There was nobody in sight, but the gunshots surely had not gone unnoticed. I scanned the upper stories but there were no opened shutters or people peering from balconies. It wasn't wise to be curious those days.

'Are you all right?' Gertie asked me. There was a smear of blood on her right cheek.

My forehead was throbbing and the back of my hand was badly grazed. 'Yes,' I said. 'We should get out of here.'

The three of us walked up the street quickly until we reached a hotel. 'This is it,' Gertie said to me.

We went in and it took me a moment to realize that Willi had not followed us. Gertie asked for someone at the reception desk. As we waited, I asked her what had happened back there.

'Criminals tried to rob us,' she said. 'They must have been waiting outside the Café du Raisin and followed us.'

'And Willi saw them,' I added, realizing that he had been providing protection for her.

She nodded. 'I'm sorry,' she said. 'I told you there was no need to come with me. As you saw.'

A middle-aged woman appeared at the bend of the stairs and signaled to Gertie. We followed her up three flights of stairs and into a small bedroom cluttered with suitcases and clothes. An older man was sitting in the only chair, looking shrunken in a dark suit. Gertie and the woman talked for a few moments in German or Yiddish; I couldn't tell one from the other. Then the woman left the room and came back with a jug of water and got a facecloth from a suitcase. She cleaned the small cut on Gertie's cheek and then took my hand and washed the grit and sand from the grazes on the knuckles. She rinsed out the facecloth, folded it into a small square and pressed it against my forehead. I replaced her hand and held the flannel hard against the bruise.

Meanwhile, Gertie had emptied the jewellery onto the bed and separated and spread the items as if she was a saleswoman. She also took the samples from the second lot of jewellery out of her handbag and placed them on the pillow. A succession of women came and went, picking up their property and thanking her effusively, some with tears in their eyes. When they had finished, the samples were still there. The older man looked on without interest; he was in another world, having given up on this one.

Gertie collected her unclaimed samples and put them back in her handbag as we prepared to leave. The woman shook my hand, careful not to press on its grazed back and said, 'Merci beaucoup', as we left.

I scanned the street outside but there was no sign of Willi, although I presumed he was still nearby. 'Did Willi hit anyone,' I asked Gertie as we walked towards her apartment.

'He wasn't trying to. He just frightened them off. They were only young thugs.'

But young thugs who knew she was carrying jewellery, I thought. Who were a step ahead of her plan to rob the local mafia.

I had my story ready by the time I got home. 'Legionnaires,' I told Solange. 'Knocked me down when they heard my accent. Accused me of being an English spy.'

'Is that why you want to go away?' she asked as she wrapped a gauze bandage around my grazed knuckles.

'It's not the main reason. But every time I open my mouth I'm conscious that someone who doesn't know me suspects me.'

'But your accent isn't that noticeable.'

'Not to you maybe. You're used to it.'

Later, I lay awake trying to sort out my problems. In spite of the turn of events with Gertie Maher, my main fear was still the Sûreté and the suave Benetti. I knew that he or one of his colleagues would turn nasty very soon when I did not deliver what he wanted. A plan began to form in my mind. It wasn't a great plan but the more I thought about it, the better it seemed in the dark. I slept soundly, without dreaming.

***

The lunch break came early the next day in the studio and I put a call through to Seamus O'Casey in Vichy from the phone kiosk beside the canteen. I was waiting outside it for the connection when Jean-Luc came by and saw the multicoloured swelling on my forehead. I gave him my explanation. 'You see. You can't stay neutral, even if you want to. You coming in to lunch?'

'Waiting for a phone call first.'

'I'll keep a seat for you.'

What had seemed like a good card to play the night before didn't appear to be so good in the brightness of another sunny day. But it was the only card I could think of and there was nothing to lose in trying it. I lit a fake cigarette as I waited, trying to get my thoughts straight.

I didn't waste any time coming to the point as soon as O'Casey came on the line. 'I was assaulted by Legionnaires last night and accused of being an English spy,' I said, transmitting as much outrage as I could down the shaky line. 'I want you to make a formal protest to the French government about the treatment of Irish citizens here. We are not British. Many of our friends lost their lives to prove that and it's not good enough to have this country dismiss and ignore our neutrality.'

There was a long silence. 'Hello,' I said into it eventually, wondering if the line had broken down.

'Cad atá tu á rá anois? O'Casey's voice came back faintly. What are you saying now?

'I'm telling you that a group of Legionnaires surrounded me and asked me questions here last night. When they heard my accent, they knocked me to the ground and accused me of being an English spy. You can't allow Irish citizens to be treated like this. You have to protest to the French government. Otherwise, what was the point of our fight for independence? Or does that independence mean nothing at all?'

There was another pause until O'Casey said what I wanted to hear. 'Send me a report about it.'

'I will. But I don't want it put in a file and forgotten about. I told you about this kind of thing when we met. I haven't seen any changes since then. Things have got even worse with the harassment of Irish citizens going about their lawful activities. You should come and visit again.'

'Tuigim,' he said.

'I hope you do understand,' I repeated for the benefit of the listeners I was counting on transcribing this conversation. 'Action is what counts. It's the only way to put a stop to this carry-on. It's an insult to an independent neutral country and you shouldn't allow it happen.'

'Send me a written report,' O'Casey repeated. 'And I will consider what is appropriate.'

'I'll do that right away. Thanks.'

'Bí cúramach,' he said. Be careful. Which was becoming his standard sign-off.

'Slán go fóill,' I replied. Bye for now.

I hung up the receiver and took a deep breath. I had no idea what O'Casey made of our conversation. He probably interpreted it as a problem with Gertie Maher; perhaps that he would have to bail her out again. Fair play to him, I thought, for going along with my complaint.

What he made of it didn't actually matter since it wasn't intended for his ears. I hoped it would get back to Benetti and he would see it as an attempt to go above his head to his political masters. And that he would back off and leave me alone. There was the possibility, of course, that it would have the opposite effect on him. But that was a risk I was willing to take. I didn't have any other cards to play.

I got my plate of the daily mush and joined Jean-Luc at a table with two of his carpenter colleagues. One was in the middle of a story about two neighbours fighting over ownership of the apples from a tree that spread over the other's fence. The dispute ended with one shooting the apples off the tree on the other side, a denunciation for terrorism, and the arrest of both. When he finished his story, Jean-Luc said to his other colleague, 'Tell Martin what's on the menu today in the other dining room.' The other dining room was where the stars and production executives ate.

'Bœuf Bourgignon ou entrecôte de veau.'

'You've just ruined my lunch,' I said, continuing to fork the flavoured rutabaga into my mouth. I was too hungry to care what our betters were eating.

'You know why shooting has finishing for the day?' Jean-Luc asked when the other two had left.

I shook my head. I knew it was part of a plan. Everyone had been very efficient that morning. There had been fewer than usual takes of the planned scenes. Even the devil had known his lines.

'The lovers are going riding at a château near Vence,' Jean-Luc said. 'They want to get in a couple of hours before dark. Then they're going to dinner in the Grand Hotel in the town. They're moving there from the Negresco.'

Why was he telling me this? To show that he and his friends knew where Arletty and her German were? Or to tell me that something was about to happen?

'Someone has told them to be more discreet,' Jean-Luc was saying. 'So they're taking to the countryside.'

'I thought Soehring had gone away.' Actually, I hoped he had gone. 'I haven't seen him here for the last few days.'

'Probably been told not to come here so often.'

'I hope you've given up your crazy plan.'

Jean-Luc shrugged. 'You know Vence?'

'No.' I had been there once many years ago but didn't remember much of it. All those towns up in the hills tended to blur into one. 'Seriously,' I stared at him. 'It's madness.'

'You think we should do nothing?'

'No. But there's lots of other things you can do.'

'Like what?'

I laughed at the idea of the Communist Party seeking my advice on political agitation. 'You don't need me to tell you.'

'We need to do something that'll work. Something dramatic. That'll make it clear there's a price for collaboration. No matter who you are, how famous you are.'

Arletty was very popular, probably the best-known female film star in France. 'You can't touch Arletty. If you did, it'd rebound on you. Have the opposite effect to what you intended.'

Jean-Luc fell silent and lit a cigarette. He suddenly looked deflated. He had obviously come to the same conclusion. Killing Soehring would provoke a savage response from the Germans; killing Arletty would damage the opposition to Vichy and its Nazi overlords. A wave of relief swept over me. 'You can take less dramatic actions,' I suggested, remembering the young man who had shouted collabos at the actresses going into the Negresco hotel.

He waved the idea aside with a sweep of his cigarette. 'I have something for you to tell Benetti,' he said. 'A British submarine is going to land weapons here next week. They'll be transferred to a fishing boat off the coast and brought into the port.'

It was my turn to feel deflated. Was this another test, I wondered. Or was the party trying to set me up as some kind of intermediary with the Sûreté. Whatever it was, I certainly didn't want any part of it. 'Why are you telling me this?'

'To get Benetti off your back.'

I glared at him to see if he was joking. 'You know how this works as well as I do. If I tell Benetti anything, I'm caught. Trapped in his web. For ever.'

'You don't have to worry about getting anyone into trouble,' Jean-Luc persisted. 'It's not true.'

I laughed without humour at the ridiculousness of the idea. 'I won't tell Benetti anything. I haven't told him anything and I'm not going to tell him anything. Because I have nothing to tell him.'

'And if he arrests Solange again?'

That took me by surprise. Jean-Luc had obviously given almost as much thought to my predicament as I had. And understood my basic vulnerability. 'I'll deal with that if it happens,' I said with more confidence than my situation warranted.

'How?'

'I don't know. What I do know is that the worst thing for me would be to tell Benetti anything.'

'Okay,' he said with the air of a parent giving up on a recalcitrant child. 'I thought if you demonstrated your uselessness as an informant, he would leave you alone.'

As we left the canteen, I was wondering whether Jean-Luc could be as naïve as he sounded.

Benetti was waiting for me on a bench on the Promenade near the town centre as I walked home in the early afternoon. The sun was still hot and I watched a lone fisherman casting his line from the frothy edge of the tide. He was either a beginner or merely reserving his spot for the evening. Either way, he was unlikely to catch anything before dark. Which reminded me of going lake fishing as a child and putting worms on a hook and the way they wriggled in desperation as the point pierced their flesh. Like I was wriggling now.

I was lost in a reverie about the lake and its little perch and didn't see Benetti until I was about twenty yards from him. It was too late to turn away and cross the road to the avenue opposite. He was already watching me, his arm stretched along the back of the bench as if he was reserving my place.

I sat down and he asked what had happened my forehead. So he hadn't read the transcript of my phone conversation with O'Casey yet.

'Where did this happen?' he asked after I told him my story.

'One of the streets between Place Massena and Cours Saleya.'

'Did you recognize any of the Legionnaires?'

I shook my head. The Promenade was moderately busy along here. None of the passers-by paid us any attention but I was sure many of them recognized Benetti for what he was without knowing him. Everybody's antennae were finely tuned these days.

'Would you recognize them again?' He sounded solicitous.

'I don't think so. It was quite dark. They were in uniform. It was only a matter of seconds really. They stopped me, asked me where I was from. I told them I lived in Nice. They pushed me from one to the other, accused me of being an English spy. And one of them knocked me to the ground from behind.' I held up my right hand to show the grazes on its back.

'Have you reported it to the police?'

'No,' I said. 'It's not a police matter. It's a diplomatic matter.'

'A what?'

'A diplomatic matter. I've reported it to the Irish legation at Vichy. It's a matter for them to take up with the government. The treatment of Irish citizens in L'Ėtat Français,' I said, using the official title of the unoccupied zone. Benetti was watching me with a perplexed expression. 'Ireland has always been a friend to France. And we've always looked on France as a friend throughout the centuries of English oppression. So it's no small matter to us to be harassed as English, as an enemy, and treated like this in what we always regarded as a friendly country.' I turned to face him. 'You understand that Ireland is independent.'

He continued to watch me in silence and I held his stare. I didn't doubt that he understood the message I was delivering. With any luck, the transcript of my phone call would be on his desk soon to prove that I was not bluffing. 'You're over-reacting,' he said at last.

'There is no greater insult where I come from than to be called a spy,' I retorted. 'Especially an English spy. Not long ago that was tantamount to a death sentence in Ireland.'

'The Legionnaires are only old soldiers and young fools who've lost their uniforms and made up their own.'

'They're loyal supporters of le Maréchal,' I pointed out.

'He doesn't need or want them.'

'So why are they allowed to march around and harass people at will?'

He shrugged. 'You should report it to the police,' he said.

'All right. I have to write out a report for the Irish legation anyway.'

'And what do you have to report to me?'

I was going to pretend not to know what he meant but changed my mind. 'I wish I could make you understand that I know nothing. That I don't discuss French politics with anyone here. That I have no idea what people think of the situation beyond complaining about the rationing and the food shortages.'

He turned his attention to two young women going by. They were well dressed in matching tan-coloured belted overcoats and had contrasting hats on the sides of their well-coiffed hair. 'Off duty whores,' he remarked as they moved on.

'You know them? ... I mean professionally?'

'Who else can afford nylon stockings these days?' he asked, getting to his feet. 'There's a lot to be learned from simple observation. Keep your eyes and ears open. We will continue our conversations another day.'

He disappeared into the shifting flow of strollers and I breathed a sigh of relief. I had won that round: at least I had made the running and prevented him from pressing me too hard. But I knew he wouldn't give up that easily.

I continued along the Promenade but I suddenly felt very tired. The sleepless nights and pressures were getting to me. I found a seat facing the bay and closed my eyes, feeling the heat of the sun, and listening to the soothing shuffle of the pebbles as the breaking waves rolled them to and fro. When I woke, the temperature was dropping fast. The sun had gone cold and was disappearing in a red sky off to the west.

# Eleven

The rest of the week was uneventful. Benetti left me alone and Gertie stayed out of my way. It began to feel like old times, nothing to bother me beyond the daily demands of work and the common gripes about the effects of the distant war on our lives.

Filming was moving along smoothly too. Those who hadn't worked under him before had grown used to Marcel Carné's foibles. Everyone adjusted to Jules Berry's tendency to re-write his lines and made allowances for his nightly gambling misfortunes at the casinos. The young actors and actresses, especially the on-screen lovers Marie Déa and Alain Cuny, were no longer star-struck by their famous colleagues. Gossips wondered whether they were taking their on-screen role into their off-screen lives as well. Arletty flaunted her relationship with Hans-Jürgen Soehring, though Jean-Luc told me on the Friday that the German had left the Riviera.

'Why are you telling me about their every move?' I asked with a smile to take any antagonism out of the question.

'Don't you find it insulting?' he asked back.

'Yes.' I gave him the expected answer. I understood his feeling, but I didn't find it as insulting or upsetting as he did. I wasn't French. The benefit of living in a foreign country was to be emotionally distanced from its domestic controversies.

On the Sunday Solange was making lunch for Signora Mancini and a group of her friends and suggested I come with her to the villa on Cap Ferrat. 'There's bound to be food left over,' she said. 'It'll guarantee you one good meal for the week.'

The villa was on the brow of the peninsula with its gardens running down to the edge of Villefranche bay. The house was two stories over a basement and had a vaguely Greek theme to its design. Signor Mancini had bought it from a ruined White Russian arms dealer at the end of the 1920s when he was considering fleeing from Mussolini's Italy. Its full-time staff was now reduced to Marc, the former chauffeur who was Signora Mancini's factotum, acting as butler, gardener and general handyman.

We made our way from the entrance gates around the side path that led to the back of the house and into the kitchens in the basement. Solange opened the refrigerator and surveyed the pantry. Both were well stocked with fish, fowl, cheese, vegetables and pastries. They were like windows on another world.

'Where does all this come from?' I asked.

Solange put her finger to her lips and looked around. There was no one else in the kitchen. 'Marc organizes everything,' she said in a low voice. He obviously had extensive blackmarket contacts.

Solange went upstairs to consult with Signora Mancini about the menu and I settled at the kitchen table to read The Big Sleep, a cheap American paperback I had picked up at a second-hand bookshop that was selling off its English books at a pittance now that there were few English readers left on the coast.

Marc appeared in the doorway, a clutch of wine bottles held against his chest. He hesitated in surprise when he saw me. We had met before but never exchanged more than the usual courtesies. I didn't even know his second name; doubted if Solange knew it either. In his fifties, he was as much a part of Signora Mancini's house as the Doric columns beside the front door.

Solange arrived back as we struggled to find something to say to each other. 'We've lost two people,' she said. 'The couple from Milan can't make it.'

'So the signora told me,' Marc replied. It was always unclear to me whether he was Niçois or Italian: his accent seemed to bridge the difference.

'Down to six guests,' Solange said to me as if I were waiting for the news. It was good news; there would be plenty of spare food.

Marc began uncorking the bottles of red wine and Solange set about chopping onions and deboning chickens. Two middle-aged women arrived, taking off their coats to reveal traditional black and white waitress uniforms. I slipped out the back door and sat on a bench by the wall in the suntrap outside. I read my book, oblivious of the chatter and chopping and pounding in the kitchen. The smell of cooking spread slowly, creating a gnawing hunger in me. Finally, Solange emerged and handed me a bowl of onion soup and a silver spoon.

She called me in later and pointed to a plate of chicken marsala on a bed of linguini at the table. I sat down across from Marc who was already eating his lunch. Snatches of talk and laughter came from upstairs as the waitresses pushed through the kitchen door. Solange was preparing the dessert, whisking a bowl of cream.

I was tempted to ask Marc if he knew Gerard Bonnard. It had occurred to me that Gerard was probably involved with the gangs around the port, as his father had been; and as his friend who had been shot outside the jewellers was. They were the people who dominated the blackmarket, in spite of the Vichy government's readiness to blame the Jews. Marc must deal with these gangsters but I didn't know him well enough to ask. Besides, Solange would want to know why I was asking him about Gerard, and I didn't want to explain my suspicions. Or, even less, why I held them.

We finished our meal in silence. Marc complimented Solange. The waitresses brought back cleared plates and took a cheeseboard upstairs. 'No cheese for you two yet,' Solange said. 'But you can have your dessert first.'

We did and I went back outside into the sun and picked up my book again. It got me thinking about Los Angeles and whether I should go back. But that would not be wise. I'd never been able to really relax there. It was a long way from New York but it was still the same country. It was a long way from Chicago to San Francisco too, but Al Capone had ended up in Alcatraz. Not that I had any reason to think anyone wanted to put me in jail for what had happened in New York.

Solange arrived with a cup of real coffee and returned a few minutes later. She held out her two closed fists. I tapped the left one and she opened it. It was empty. I shrugged. She opened the other fist with a smile and I caught the stubby Gauloise Caporal that fell out.

Later, we walked home through Villefranche-sur-Mer and along the Lower Corniche. There was hardly any motorized traffic on the road and the shadows were lengthening, splitting the bay below between azure and ultramarine. We went over the edge of Mont Boron and the sun was suddenly in our faces as we descended towards Nice port.

'Are you in trouble?' Solange asked out of the blue.

'Me?' I didn't have to pretend surprise.

'That policeman said you might be.'

'He's approached you again?' I inwardly cursed Benetti. That bastard would not give up. But then I hadn't expected to shake him off so easily.

'No. Not since the morning he gave me the lift to Cap Ferrat.'

That was reassuring. 'What did he say?'

'He said he was afraid you might be in trouble. And he didn't want to see you become involved in things you mightn't understand. Being a foreigner.'

I laughed a cynical laugh. 'That's very considerate of him. But I'm not involved in anything. I'm not in any trouble.'

We walked on in silence. She was linking me and squeezed my arm tighter.

'Is that why you want to go to Ireland?' she asked after a moment, ignoring my denial.

'No.' I lied. 'It's to get away from the war. The rationing and all that.' Even as I said it, I knew it sounded implausible. Especially today, given the lunch I'd just eaten. The truth was that things were not bad for us. We had work and the rationing could be circumvented enough to make it bearable. The war was far away. We were far from any frontline. We were not under threat of air raids. We weren't refugees, especially not Jewish ones. France was oddly at peace, especially here in the unoccupied zone, as long as you weren't perceived as an enemy of le Maréchal and his government. The battles being waged were the same as those that were always waged here. Political.

'Is it to do with that Irish woman?' Solange persisted.

'No,' I said automatically but then reconsidered. 'Well yes, in a roundabout way. Meeting the diplomat who asked me to advise her got me thinking of going back to Ireland. And also made it possible to get the necessary travel permits.'

'Mme Bonnard thinks she's trouble.'

'I know. But all she needs is some advice, explaining things to her about life in Nice she mightn't understand.'

'Like what?'

'Like avoiding the black market. Being careful who you talk to. Not talking politics or mentioning the war.'

Solange came back to the subject in bed that night. She propped herself on her elbow and looked down at me, biting her lip in a nervous twitch. 'There's something else I should tell you,' she said.

My heart sank.

'Benetti said he would try and get Pierre and François released if I told him what you were doing. And he said he'd make sure nothing happens to you.'

'He's lying. How can he get them released from a German camp?'

'I know,' she said, but I could hear the hope in her voice. Or thought I could. Even the faint possibility that Benetti could bring her brothers home from the war that had ended here nearly two years ago was a temptation. 'I didn't tell him anything,' she added, searching my eyes to see if I believed her.

'There's nothing to tell.'

'But he thinks you're up to something.'

'He's wrong.'

She buried her head in my shoulder and I put my arms around her and felt her body relax slowly as she drifted off to sleep. I lay awake for a long time, cursing Benetti and how he was poisoning our relationship, creating suspicion needlessly. Like he had threatened to poison my friendship with Jean-Luc.

How had a couple of days of near normality led to me think earlier that this country was at peace? That the war and its defeat had not messed it up beyond belief.

***

Things got worse the next day. I was taking refuge in *The Big Sleep*, unable and unwilling to put it down and hoping all morning there would not be a summons from Carné or Antonioni, the Italian assistant director. None came and I was happy to remain immersed in Los Angeles. I had lunch on my own, still not wanting to be disturbed. I finished the novel by the late afternoon and realized that I hadn't seen Jean-Luc all day.

I went along to the carpenters' workshop and asked the first man I saw where Jean-Luc was. He stared at me and then spat on the floor beside my right foot, walking away without a word.

Another carpenter I knew slightly had seen what had happened. 'What was that about?' I asked him.

'Seriously?' he asked back. 'Jean-Luc's arrest?'

'I didn't know,' I said, taken aback.

'You didn't know?' he laughed. 'You were seen. On the Promenade.'

'Wait,' I called after him as he walked away. He stopped and turned back towards me. 'When was he arrested?'

'On Saturday.'

'It had nothing to do with me.'

He continued on his way, everything about his demeanour saying that he didn't believe me.

Neither did anyone else, it appeared. Once I knew about Jean-Luc's arrest, I became aware of people averting their eyes, swerving away to avoid me. A fellow electrician who did talk to me revealed that two others had been arrested at the same time: both were on the list Henri Tillon had given me. I presumed they were Communists too.

Leaving the studio that evening, I knew that my days working there were numbered. If I was going to be ostracized for informing on Jean-Luc and his comrades, it was only a matter of time before I would be forced out. I could already imagine the studio managers neither accepting nor rejecting my denials but arguing that people wouldn't work with me and so I would have to leave.

My days in France were clearly numbered. All thanks to that bastard Benetti who had deliberately put me in this position by forcing me to sit with him on the Promenade as everybody went home from La Victorine. And then following up with the arrests a few days later. He was just paying me back for refusing to play along with him.

I made my way to the Café du Raisin, oblivious of everything but my own dark thoughts. Mrs Mac poured my beer while concluding a conversation with one of her regulars. She passed it along the zinc to me and then came over when she finished her conversation. 'A message for you,' she said, reaching behind her to take a folded slip of paper from under the Maréchal's portrait.

'Can you come around with the latest news this evening at 8 please,' it said. It was signed G. Maher.

Mrs Mac gave me her disapproving look. The Maréchal glared at me over her shoulder with his pitiless blue-eyes. 'She called in earlier,' she said. 'Just left this message. Didn't even buy a coffee.'

I asked her for a token for the phone and booked a call to Vichy. I waited in the phone booth, dredging my memory for the necessary words in Irish but failing to find enough of them. And thinking about what Solange might have told Benetti about Gertie Maher in spite of her assertion that she had told him nothing. She knew little, no more than our cover story. Which would sound harmless to her. But Benetti could put two and two together if he wanted and link me through Gertie with the Jewish friend who had got her arrested in the first place. Which was probably Willi or someone like him. And Benetti could use that as extra leverage against me.

The phone rang and I asked O'Casey when he would come to Nice with the necessary papers for everyone.

'I have to go to Paris tomorrow,' he said. 'There are urgent problems there.'

*'Tá deacrachtaí anseo,'* I said. There are difficulties here. *'Tá sé tábhachtach. Go han-tábhachtach.'* It's important. Very important.

*'Tuigim,'* he sighed. I understand. But it sounded more like an automatic assurance than a genuine one. I searched for some stronger expression of urgency and had to settle for *'Níl mórán am againn.'* We don't have much time. Which was far from as forceful as I wished.

*'Tá fhios agam.'* I know.

'I don't think you realize the extent of it,' I said elliptically, breaking into English and conscious of not wanting to tip off any listeners to the urgency of my request.

'Okay,' he replied carefully. 'We're working on all aspects of the case. It's got the highest priority.'

I had to be satisfied with that. He signed off with his usual *'Bí cúramach.'*

'Well?' Mrs Mac asked when I emerged from the booth, aware of whom I had been calling.

'Very hard to get a straight answer out of these fellas. He says your permits have got the highest priority.'

She shrugged. 'It doesn't matter anyway. I can't go.'

'You've decided?'

'How can I go?'

'I think you should. Even if Gerard won't. You need a break from all this.' I waved my hand to encompass the café, although we both knew that it was from her son that she needed the break. 'And the chance mightn't come again soon if you don't take it now.'

'What do you mean?'

I took Gertie's note from my pocket and tore it into pieces. 'Because O'Casey is under pressure to get her home to Ireland and can tag you along with her. Otherwise, he is under no pressure to help you.' I dropped the pieces of paper into the ashtray. She looked at them as if I had shredded her hopes as well.

'I don't know what to do.'

'Don't make any decision until you have to. Until you have the travel permits.'

I went home to collect the remaining bag of jewellery, assuming that that was what Gertie meant by the latest news. I doubted that she had meant the latest word from O'Casey: she didn't seem to be in a hurry to get back to Ireland.

Willi was in the tiny apartment with her and I handed over the bag. Gertie put it in her handbag. 'You've found the owners?' I asked.

'Most of them anyway,' she said. 'We're bringing these back to them now.'

Gertie locked the apartment door behind us and we went down the stairs. As we stepped out onto the street, I told her that I'd spoken to O'Casey. 'He says your permits have the highest priority.'

'Okay,' she said without any evident interest.

I turned to go my own way and saw two figures step out of the shadow of an entrance across the street and one of them raise a gun. 'Get down,' I shouted and grabbed Gertie around the shoulder, pulling her roughly to the ground. We both fell awkwardly.

Two shots rang out in quick succession. One bullet zinged off the metal door handle above us. I heard the sickening thud of the other hit a body. Willi gasped as he was thrown back against the door and slid to the ground. He had pulled out his revolver and it fell from his hand and clattered to the footpath.

I reached for it and loosed off two quick rounds in the direction of the gunmen. They ran and I was on my feet running after them. My brain screamed stop. My legs kept going, fueled by anger and adrenaline. They were younger and faster than me but I kept going anyway. They rounded a corner at speed and I followed, the hammer cocked, leading with the gun, ready to fire.

One had apparently looked back as he went around the corner and had crashed into a pole. He was getting to his feet as I came upon him. He slumped back onto the ground, a look of terror on his face. I pointed the gun at his head, its sight jumping up and down with my heavy breathing. It was Gerard Bonnard.

The other youth had stopped up the street, undecided what to do. I fired a warning shot in his direction, and heard it ricochet off the road. He ran.

I turned my attention back to Gerard, automatically thumbing back the hammer for another quick shot. I could see both his hands. He didn't appear to be armed. His expression hadn't changed. His mouth was half-open and his eyes were wide with fear, making him look more boyish than his usual surly glower. We stared at each other in silence for a long moment. I didn't know what to say, so I said nothing. I raised the gun skywards and eased the hammer down, uncocking it. I walked away.

Gertie was cradling Willi in her arms back at the hall door, saying something softly in German. His face was grey and a dribble of blood ran from the side of his mouth. His dark shirt was wet but there was no movement in his chest, no sign of breathing. I felt around his neck for a pulse and found nothing.

'We have to leave,' I told Gertie.

She ignored me. 'He's gone,' I said quietly, trying to raise her by the arm. She resisted at first but then allowed me to help her to her feet. 'We have to walk away calmly,' I added, putting my left arm around her shoulder. I still had the revolver in my right hand. I checked the street in both directions. There was nobody nearby, but the police had to have been alerted by now. And I was concerned that Gerard's companion might be still around, though I doubted it. Willi was probably the target, not Gertie or me.

We walked away slowly, turning to the right to cross the Avenue de la Victoire into the side streets off the main axis. Gertie sobbed quietly as we went, letting me guide her. At first, I didn't know where we were going, just getting away from the scene of the shooting. I led her towards the old town and Place Garibaldi. Then we crossed onto rue de la Republique and I opened the doors into my small flat.

I looked at her when we got in. There were blood smears on her coat, on her cheek and her hands. She stood patiently while I unbuttoned her coat and got her to wash her hands. She sat on the bed and I wrapped a blanket around her, worried that she might go into shock. All the while tears ran down her cheeks. She paid no attention to her surroundings.

I searched the cupboard and found O'Casey's bottle of Jameson with a dribble of whiskey in the bottom. She drank it in one gulp. I checked myself in the mirror and couldn't see any sign of blood on my face or clothes. I washed my hands carefully and wiped the blood from her cheek with a facecloth. I dabbed at the blood smears on her coat with cold water.

There were a couple of dirty cups and plates in the sink, their bottoms growing fungus from the dregs of the coffee I had had here after Solange decided I should move out temporarily. I found the bag of ersatz coffee, boiled some water and made cups for both of us. I sat down on the bed beside her, encouraging her to drink it. She sipped at it dutifully every time I told her to drink.

I made more coffee and she kept drinking it whenever I asked her. Eventually her tears stopped flowing and she said something in German.

'What?'

'I've known him all my life,' she said, more to herself than to me.

'I'm sorry about Willi,' I said uselessly.

We sat like that for a long time until I told her to lie down. She did so and I got her another blanket and slipped off her shoes. She closed her eyes and I left after a little while, unsure of whether she was asleep or not.

It was close to midnight and the city was dead. I walked across the empty square, seeing nobody. The cafés under its arcades were closed. There was no traffic on the streets. I felt exhausted, all the adrenaline drained away. My brain tried to work out the implications of what had happened, of Gerard's involvement, and of Gertie's disclosure that she had known Willi all her life. Which meant she hadn't been in Vienna teaching English. Which raised the question of who she really was. What she was doing in Vienna. And what O'Casey did or didn't know about her.

But what really slowed my pace through the deserted streets was my surprise at my own reactions, at my automatic response to being shot at. I hadn't followed O'Casey's instruction, bí cúramach, or my policy of non-involvement. A different instinct had taken over and hurled me into action, chasing the gunmen, prepared to shoot. Even as I was doing it, I was telling myself to stop, you are a pacifist. Beyond being a neutral, beyond being uninvolved, you've been a pacifist above all since that day in New York. But I hadn't stopped.

I didn't know what to make of that.

# Twelve

I was back in New York, crossing the street, my eyes on the Italian's car as it glided to a stop at the pavement. But the buildings on the street were no longer New York's. They were now the ornate *belle époque* buildings of Nice. I was aware of this and wondering about it, but my focus was on the car. Two doors opened, on the pavement side. I started firing as the two men were getting out, walking steadily towards them. The one at the back door slumped sideways. The window of the door shattered, and I fired through it at the man getting out of the front seat. He turned awkwardly and got back into the car. I couldn't tell whether I had hit him or not. The man at the back door was pulled into the car. The engine revved and the car shot away. Its open doors banged shut off a parked car. I fired at a head in the back window and the glass splintered. The revolver clicked empty. I turned away and walked calmly back the way I had come. I had done my job.

I woke with my heart pounding, my breathing fast and heavy. Solange turned over but didn't wake up. I lay still, waiting for my heart to settle. I could still hear the revving of the engine, the doors banging off the parked car like two extra shots. And all the while I could also hear the shrill scream of a woman. Gertie? Had she screamed?

It was almost five o'clock and still dark. I slid my feet onto the cold floor, dressed quickly, collected some bread, milk and the remnants of the cheese that we had brought home from Signora Mancini's on Sunday evening. I checked Willi's revolver; there were three live rounds left. I put it in my hiding place in the basement on my way out.

The morning air was cold and I walked fast to rue de la Republique. Gertie was still asleep on the bed, the blankets wrapped tightly around her. She opened her eyes when I turned on a light and watched me cut the bread and slice the cheese. I put them on a plate and left them on the bedside table and made two cups of coffee.

'You need to eat something,' I said, taking a piece of bread and cheese for myself.

'What is this place?'

'My flat. But I'm not living here. You'll be safe here.'

'Where is it?'

I told her. She didn't appear to have any memory of anything that had happened after Willi was shot. She sat up and swung her feet onto the floor. She sipped at the coffee and took a tentative bite of bread.

'Are you sure he was dead?' she asked after a moment. Her eyes filled with tears but she bit her lip to hold them back.

'He wasn't breathing,' I said.

'I have to go and tell his family.'

'They're here?'

She nodded and named a shabby little hotel on the edge of the old town.

'That's not a good idea. The police will probably be there.'

'I have to,' she said.

'You should stay out of sight for the moment. Stay here. Don't go out. Is there anything you need from your flat?'

'Clothes.'

'I'll collect them later if you give me the keys.'

'I'll do it myself. I can't stay locked up here.'

I shrugged. I had already learned that there was little point in arguing with her. She drank more of the vile coffee and ate cheese and bread, visibly recovering her strength and determination. I gave her the keys to my apartment and told her I had to go to work.

'Maybe it's better if you could go to my apartment,' she said. 'If you don't mind.'

'Okay. I'll do it after work.'

'Do you still have the gun?'

'It's in a safe place.'

'Give it to me.'

'What do you want it for?' I didn't like the sound of this.

'Protection.'

Revenge was more likely. 'It won't protect you. It didn't protect Willi,' I said. It was doubtful if she had recognized Gerard: I hadn't seen him either until I chased the two assailants. 'Do you know who shot him?'

'Criminals.'

'Who?'

'I don't know who.'

That was a relief. The thought of her going after Gerard wasn't something I wanted to have to deal with. 'Black marketeers?' I prompted.

She nodded.

'Had Willi tried to rob them?'

'He'd talked about it but I don't think he'd done anything.'

'I presume Willi wasn't working on his own.'

She said nothing, which was an answer in itself. 'Okay,' I added. 'I don't want to know. I think you should give the jewellery to the people who owned it. Get rid of it before the police link you to Willi.'

'Yes.' She brightened up at the thought of something useful to do. 'That's a good idea.'

I went to work but I was distracted all day by what had happened. Nobody spoke to me. Most avoided any eye contact. A few recognized my presence with discreet nods. One of the other electricians, usually work-shy, leapt to attention whenever anything needed to be done. I had finished *The Big Sleep* but I couldn't have concentrated on a book anyway. I had plenty of time to think about Willi's death and its consequences, for myself, for Gertie, and for Gerard.

How and why was Gerard involved? Had he seen the note Gertie had left me in the café? Was it him and the shooter who had attacked us previously? Was there something other than the jewellery robberies going on? Something I knew nothing about?

And then there were the questions about Gertie; who exactly was she and what she was up to?

Nobody joined me for lunch but somebody had helpfully left *Le Petit Niçois* on the table. It was open at the sports pages and I turned it back to the front page. The main headline said 'Jewish Terrorist Shot Dead in Nice Street'. I scanned down the story quickly, then read it slowly. It named Willi as Austrian Chaim Zigelman, aged twenty, a terrorist known to police. He was also involved in the black market, it said. Police believed he had been shot by a rival gang of foreign black marketeers.

The report showed all the prejudices of the Vichy regime which liked to class all foreign Jews as terrorists and to blame the black market on them. There was nothing in it that implicated Gertie, Gerard or me.

It was a relief to leave the oppressive atmosphere of La Victorine at the end of the day. The afternoon was cloudy and the sun already hidden. A stiff breeze from the west was at my back as I headed towards the city centre, undecided where to go. I half-expected Benetti to make the decision for me at any moment, but there was no sign of him.

I ended up at the Café du Raisin, half out of habit and half out of a conscious decision to carry on as usual. It was buzzing with the after-work crowd, the smoke gathering in a haze around the ceiling lights. Ange-Marie was behind the bar, replaced as waitress by one of the women who normally came in on her day off.

'Where's herself?' I asked when I caught her attention. It was very unlike Mrs Mac not to be on hand for the busiest part of the day.

Ange-Marie gestured towards the upstairs. 'She has a headache.'

'Not Gerard, is it?' I ventured. Ange-Marie was well aware of Mrs Mac's domestic burden.

'No, no. Just a bad headache.'

I leaned on the zinc and drank my beer. I was aware of someone coming up beside me and trying to catch Ange-Marie's attention. He said in a low voice: 'Any news about Jean-Luc?'

I glanced sideways. It was the printer from next door, whom I knew slightly as a fellow regular named Claude. My first thought was that he must be another Communist. 'No,' I said.

'He asked me to do a job for him. I don't know what to do with it now.'

Ange-Marie responded to his raised hand and he ordered a beer and a glass of white wine.

'Come next door and I'll show you,' he said quietly as she went away.

'I don't know anything about a job for Jean-Luc,' I said. Neither of us looked at the other.

'Wait ten minutes and come next door. Just push the door in.'

'Why are you telling me this?' I asked neutrally.

'Jean-Luc said it was your idea.'

We said nothing more. Ange-Marie came with his drinks and he paid her. After a few moments I turned around and rested my back against the counter. Claude was at a table with a dark-haired woman who was telling him something as much with her hands as her voice. Heads you win, tails I lose, I thought. Was he a police provocateur? Or a Communist inviting me into a trap?

More likely a trap, I decided. From the way he mentioned Jean-Luc, as if he was a friend, a comrade. If it was a Communist trap, I had no illusions about what that could mean. I had read enough about the Spanish Civil War to know how ruthless they were, but it wouldn't be possible to evade them indefinitely.

I glanced around the rest of the café and saw Henri Tillon in his usual spot at the other end of the bar. He caught my eye at the same time and then looked away. When I looked back, Claude and the woman were leaving. I took my time finishing my drink and then followed them.

The door was ajar, as he had said. I pushed it in with my foot, briefly regretting that I didn't have Willi's revolver with me. But I knew it wouldn't have done me much good if this was indeed a trap. Besides, not having a gun had saved my life on one occasion in the past.

There was a small public office inside. It was dark and a light showed around a door beyond it. I pushed that one open and went into the workshop. Claude was putting away some composing sticks. I glanced around quickly: there was no one else to be seen.

'Here you are,' Claude said, reaching into one of the deep shelves under the table on which he had been working. He pulled out a parcel wrapped loosely in brown paper and held it out to me.

'What is it?' I didn't take it.

'The posters Jean-Luc was supposed to collect on Saturday.'

'They're nothing to do with me.'

'He said it was your idea,' he said again.

'I don't know anything about any posters.' I put my hands in my pockets as if to underline my refusal to take them.

He dropped the bundle on the table and pulled back the brown paper. The poster was small, simple and crude. 'No to Collaboration', it said across the top. Underneath was a photo, roughly reproduced but still identifiable, of Arletty and Hans-Jürgen Soehring, with a red X across it. So Jean-Luc had taken my advice not to shoot either of them but to try and embarrass Arletty. Which, from the little both of us had seen of her, had only a slim chance of working.

'Are you a member of the party?' I asked Claude.

'No.'

'Me neither. I don't want them. I wouldn't know what to do with them.'

'I don't want them here either. Jean-Luc promised me he'd take them away as soon as I did them on Saturday.'

'You heard he was arrested on Saturday?' But obviously he had not heard that I was the prime suspect for denouncing him.

'All the more reason I want them out of here.'

'I can understand that,' I said. 'But I can't help you. And I don't know why he said it was my idea. It wasn't and I certainly didn't know he was asking anyone to print them.'

'What am I going to do with them? Burn them?'

'Is there no one else who could stick them up on walls?'

He gave me a sly look as if everything I had said so far was an obvious lie. It occurred to me that Gertie's friends might do it. It'd be less risky than running around with guns robbing black marketeers. But what they were engaged in was on a different plane to putting up illegal posters.

I picked up the top copy and examined it more closely. It was just the right size to cover the posters of le Maréchal that appeared in rows on walls. But the closer you looked at it, the grainier the photo became. The typeface and red X weren't very sharp either. 'It's not very clear, is it?' I said.

'I didn't want it to look too professional,' Claude said with a humourless laugh. 'Wanted it to look like a home-made job. I don't want anyone knocking on my door.'

I put the poster back and made my way out. Claude pushed the parcel back into the depths of the shelf and followed me out, flicking off the lights as we went.

'Is it true about Arletty and the German?' he asked.

'Yes.'

'She has some nerve,' he said with what might have been a touch of admiration as he locked the hall door behind him.

***

I made my way to Gertie's flat, thinking that Jean-Luc's decision to have the posters printed was proof that his talk of assassinating Arletty or Soehring was just that: talk. Which made me wonder if he was really still in the party. If he was, he wasn't on its ruthless wing. Which was a relief to me, proof that our friendship hadn't been based on a miscalculation. Although such thoughts about friendship were academic now.

I took a roundabout route to rue Berlioz and went by Gertie's flat on the opposite side of the road. Nobody followed me as far as I could see. The street was quiet. The only people I saw were an elderly couple shuffling along. I went back to Gertie's building.

There was no sign of blood on the pavement outside the door or of what had happened there the previous night. I let myself in and walked upstairs to her place. Her door was still locked and the inside untouched as far as I could see. Which was a good sign: the police hadn't linked her with Willi's death.

I found a small suitcase on top of the narrow wardrobe and gathered enough clothes to fill it. I squeezed in the only pair of shoes that were there along with a toothbrush and some bottles of lotions.

I half-expected she wouldn't be in my flat when I got to the rue de la Republique but she was sitting on the bed, looking pale and drawn. I put her suitcase down beside her. 'Thanks,' she said mechanically.

'Have you eaten?' I asked.

She nodded.

'Been out?'

She nodded again. 'I went to see Willi's family. They were all gone. Taken away to a concentration camp. His father and mother. Younger brother and sister. She's only twelve.' She seemed close to tears again.

'Maybe they were just taken away for questioning,' I offered.

She shook her head. 'Everybody saw them being pushed into a police van. Driven to the railway station.' She paused. 'They've seen it before. Numerous times.'

'I'm sorry,' I said pointlessly. I had heard vague stories of foreign Jews being taken away if they got into trouble of any kind. Nobody talked about it or where exactly they were taken.

'Do you have a cigarette?' she asked.

I shook my head. I looked at what passed for the kitchen area. The bread and cheese I had left her this morning was all gone. 'You need more food.'

'I can't stay here,' she said.

I told her it was probably safe to go back to her own apartment if she wanted to.

'I might move in with some other people,' she said.

'Refugees?' She made no reply and I added: 'That's not a good idea. You don't want to be looked on as a refugee. O'Casey would not be happy about that.'

She shrugged and said nothing.

'You said last night that you had known Chaim all your life,' I said, using the name the newspaper had given Willi.

That caught her attention. 'How do you know his name was Chaim?'

'That's his real name? Chaim Zigelman?' She confirmed it with a curt nod and I told her what the newspaper report had said.

'He's not a terrorist. Wasn't.'

'You weren't teaching him English all your life,' I said quietly.

She said nothing for a long moment, resting her arms on her knees and staring at her linked hands. 'I grew up in Vienna. The Zigelmans were our next door neighbours. Chaim and I played together a lot as children. We moved to Ireland about' -- she paused to calculate – 'eight years ago. After the Nazis took over in Germany. My father saw what was coming and decided to get out.'

She looked up at me as if to gauge my reaction. Numerous questions leapt to my mind, not least what her real name was. But I curbed my curiosity. The less I knew, the better. I was already too deeply immersed in all this. 'Why did you go back?'

'To try and help some people to get out.' She closed her eyes and took a deep breath. I knew what she was thinking. She blamed herself for her childhood friend's death and his family's incarceration.

'It wasn't your fault,' I said, even though I didn't know that for a fact. For all I knew, she could have been the driving force behind the robberies and whatever else Chaim might have been involved in. 'But you've got to look after yourself now. You don't want to get caught up in any more trouble here.'

She didn't show any sign of being convinced.

'Do you want to go back to Ireland?'

She nodded.

'Then keep away from refugees. Forget about the jewellery robberies and all that. Stay here as long as you like or go back to your own place. But keep your head down. Contact O'Casey and tell him you need to get out of here urgently.'

'Don't tell him what happened. To Willi. I mean Chaim. Any of it. Please.'

'Okay,' I said after a moment. Telling him would undoubtedly make him get a move on, expedite the permits we were all waiting for. 'I won't, but you have to make him see the urgency of the situation. You don't know what the police will find out about your role in the robberies.'

'They won't bother investigating Chaim's death,' she said bitterly. 'He's only a Jew and they've taken away his whole family. That's the end of it.'

I knew deep down she was probably right. The Statuts des Juifs, the laws curbing their activities, and the constant diet of abuse in the local papers, had turned the Jews into non-persons.

# Thirteen

The axe fell when I was watching a tender love scene between the devil's agent and the beautiful young wife he had been sent to seduce and destroy. Naturally, he was the one seduced by her beauty and virtue, and Alain Cuny and Marie Déa were acting out the transformation. Most of the crew was watching to determine whether they were acting or, as the rumours had it, were simply replicating their real life relationship. I put down my new book, Eric Ambler's *A Coffin for Dimitrios,* to watch as well.

The chemistry between them was unmistakable. If they were only acting, they were very good actors. Marcel Carné called 'cut' several times but only to allow for a change of camera angles. Cuny and Déa repeated the scene perfectly each time they were asked. In between, they continued to hold hands. I saw one of the crew hold out his palm for a colleague to pay him a few francs: he thought he had won the bet that they were real-life lovers too. Unless they were just staying in character.

During the latest break a messenger boy told me I was wanted in the administration block. I made my way over there, aware of what was coming. The assistant manager, a short tubby man in his late fifties with a cigarette hanging from his mouth, took me into his office.

'We have an awkward situation here, Martin,' he said when he had positioned himself behind his desk. He didn't invite me to sit down. 'Very awkward for you as well as for us.'

So it was going to be in my own interest to fire me, I thought.

'Very awkward,' he repeated as he stubbed out his cigarette in the full ashtray. 'We have no complaints with your work, but some people say they won't work with you anymore.'

'Who won't?' I shot back.

He waved his hands in a dismissive gesture and reached for the packet of Gitanes on the desk and offered me one. I took it and bent across his desk to let him light it.

'So.' He inhaled the word with a lungful of smoke as he sat back in his chair. 'We think it would be best for everyone if you took a little time off.'

'What does that mean?'

'Just that.' He looked surprised, then added, as if he realized that I mightn't have understood the French. 'Some days, a week or two perhaps. Until the situation has been clarified.'

'Am I being fired?'

'No, no. Absolutely not.'

'Do I get paid for the time off?'

He breathed out a stream of smoke as if it was his patience. 'That's not possible. But' – he opened a drawer and took out some banknotes – 'in recognition of your good work and long service, we can give you a little cash.'

I took the money. 'I didn't denounce Jean-Luc Lebret or the others,' I said.

He nodded as if it didn't matter. Which it didn't. 'We're in the middle of filming,' he shrugged. 'You know how it is. We can't allow anything that might disrupt it.'

'So they've threatened to strike.' I didn't need to spell out who 'they' were: the Communist-controlled union.

He raised his eyebrows, stood up and held out his hand. I shook it and left.

I went back to the electricians' workshop, gathered my tools, and the few other possessions I had there. The security man at the gate nodded at me, probably for the last time.

It was the middle of the afternoon, a blustery day of scudding clouds that turned the sun dim and bright as they sped overhead, raising and lowering the temperature. I wandered along the Promenade as aimlessly as the refugees who had nowhere to go except in their dreams. There was only one place for me to go now. Home.

I hadn't used that word in relation to Ireland for a long time, not since I had been given the Hobson's choice of leaving it or a lonely execution in the Dublin mountains. But where else could I go? There was nothing for me here now, apart from Solange.

I took a seat facing the bay and wondered what I could do to persuade her to come with me. Or would I go without her? I didn't want to do that but there might be no alternative. This was a choice for both of us more fundamental than the unspoken question of marriage. The one that could break us up.

The waves piled up and crashed on the stony beach. The sun played hide and seek with the clouds, teasing with its sparkle on the water one moment and its flat light the next. The wind ruffled the swell into small white horses that chased each other across the bay. Snatches of conversation passed behind me. I paid no attention to any of it. None of it raised my spirits as the blue Baie de Anges and its lustrous light usually did. I was immersed in my own bleak thoughts, but I decided nothing.

I sat there until the sun went down and the wind revealed its underlying cold. I got up stiffly and continued towards home. I turned up boulevard Gambetta, passing shops with queues outside them, and on into Victor Hugo. At the police station I asked for Benetti and was left waiting for almost half an hour.

'At last.' He beamed at me as I was shown into his office and pointed to the chair in front of his desk. 'You have something for me?'

'Jean-Luc Lebret is not a Communist,' I said as I took the seat. 'Why have you arrested him?'

Irritation replaced his smile. 'And what business is it of yours why he was arrested?'

'I've just been fired because of it.'

He displayed neither concern nor interest in my news. 'Actually you've been on my mind. I've been meaning to ask you about your new Jewish girlfriend.'

'I don't have a new girlfriend.'

'Mlle Delmas says you do.'

'I don't.'

'Why does Mlle Delmas think you do?'

'She doesn't. You must have misunderstood her.'

'She lied to me, did she?'

I said nothing. This wasn't going the way I had expected, but I hadn't thought through why I was talking to Benetti. It had been an emotional response to my predicament and to the knowledge that Benetti was to blame for it. Clearly it was a mistake.

'Or you're lying to me,' he said, glaring at me as if he was seeing me for the first time. 'Tell me about the Jew?'

'Who are you talking about?'

'The Irish Jew you say you're not fucking.'

'She's not a Jew. There are hardly any Jews in Ireland.'

'She looked like a Jew to me.'

'Her name is Maher,' I said in a reasonable voice, trying to remain calm and extricate myself while wondering where he had seen Gertie. 'There are lots of Mahers in Ireland. They're not Jews.'

'She's not a Jew and Lebret is not a Communist,' he snapped. 'You're an expert on everyone today.'

I thought about walking out but that was probably not a good idea.

'So what are these tête-a-têtes you have with her in the Café du Raisin about?'

I shrugged. 'She's waiting for travel permits to continue on her way back to Ireland.'

'So why was she consorting with Jewish terrorists here?'

'That was just somebody she met in a café,' I said. I hoped he was referring to the reason for her arrest in Nice and not that he had linked her to Willi/Chaim. 'She didn't know who she was talking to. That was all cleared up by the man from the Irish legation.'

'You were a terrorist yourself once, weren't you?'

'I was a soldier in the army of the Irish republic.'

'The army of the republic,' he said with a sneer. 'Once a terrorist always a terrorist,'

I realized I shouldn't have used that phrase: it had as subversive a meaning in France then as it had had in Ireland two decades earlier, even if French and Irish interpretations of the republic were not that closely aligned. 'It was a civil war,' I said. 'A long time ago.'

'That was why you went to America? Into exile?'

'That was all a long time ago,' I repeated. I didn't like this direction the conversation was taking either. Benetti had clearly been looking into my background in too much detail.

'You haven't answered my question,' he said. 'What were these tête-á-têtes with the Jew about if they weren't about sex?'

'Just general conversations. Life in Nice and so on.'

'What about life in Nice?'

'Places to go. Things to do and see. While she's waiting for her permits.'

'You're a tourist guide now.'

'The Irish legation asked me to help her, answer her questions and so on while she's in transit here. I'm helping them out.'

He leaned forward suddenly and banged the flat of his hand on the desk. 'Don't give me that shit again,' he shouted. 'You're not a fucking diplomat. You're a nobody here.' He pressed a button on his phone and the door opened after a moment and a uniformed policeman came in. 'Take him downstairs.'

The policeman caught me under the arm and lifted me up. I was stunned by the sudden change in Benetti's demeanour. His anger seemed to have come from nowhere. 'Hold on,' I began but the policeman stopped me with a curt 'Shut up' and gripped my arm until it hurt.

'Wait,' Benetti ordered as we turned towards the door. He wrote something on a piece of paper and handed it to the policeman. 'Bring her in too.'

My escort called to a colleague for assistance as we went along a corridor and then down steps into the basement to the cells. They took me into an open one and emptied my pockets of my keys, lighter and wallet and took my watch. Then one grabbed my arms from behind and the other hit me a few quick jabs in the stomach and slapped me hard across the face twice. 'We don't want any trouble with you,' he said. 'Understand.'

He pushed me back against the wall and they locked the barred gate behind them. Drops of blood fell on the floor from my nose. I lay down on the plank bed and squeezed the bridge to stop it bleeding. I felt nauseous and my stomach hurt but not as much as the knowledge of my own stupidity. I should have known better than to tangle voluntarily with the likes of Benetti. What had I been thinking? Or, more accurately, not thinking? After twenty years I was back in a police cell. Back, in a sense, where my life had been set on the path that had brought me to Nice.

The night passed slowly. I dozed fitfully, unsure whether I was awake or asleep for most of the time. The naked bulb in the corridor shone in my eyes if I faced the bars that made up the door and its surrounds. I lay on my right side but the hard board and absence of a pillow soon made that uncomfortable. Somebody was snoring down the corridor and another inmate coughed periodically and breathed with a rasping breath in between his harsh barks.

The dawn came up with a milky light through the frosted glass behind the bars on the little window. Breakfast was a cup of lukewarm phoney coffee and a hunk of hard bread torn off an old baguette. Policemen came and went, bringing an array of prisoners up and down to the cells. They ignored me. I didn't recognize any of the prisoners.

My main worry was that it was Gertie whom Benetti had told his henchmen to bring in. And that he could link us both to Chaim and his murder. Not that the police were likely to go to any trouble finding Chaim's killer: their treatment of his family proved that. But they would want to know about his associates. I hoped that Gertie had not gone back to her flat and wouldn't be located immediately.

With luck, I would be released sooner rather than later. Benetti would realize he had no further use for me now that I couldn't be one of his spies in La Victorine. But my connection to Gertie added another interest in his eyes.

I was lying on my back staring at the flaking ceiling when footsteps stopped at my cell.

'My God,' Solange said when I sat up and stepped over to the bars. She looked down at my blood-stained shirt. 'Are you all right?'

'I'm fine,' I said. 'It was only a nosebleed.'

The policeman escorting her said, 'You've seen him now.' He pulled her by the arm and led her towards the stairs.

'Are you all right?' I called after her.

She looked back over her shoulder and nodded. I tried to give her a reassuring smile.

I lay back down on the plank. I didn't blame Solange for having told Benetti about my meetings with Gertie but I doubted that she thought I was having an affair with her. I had told her next to nothing about Gertie for obvious reasons. What she knew about our meetings in the Café du Raisin had probably come from Mrs Mac. She was suspicious of Gertie and I could hear her describing our meetings as tête-á-têtes, a favourite phrase of hers. And, I had to admit, my recent late-night arrivals home and early morning departures could have raised justifiable suspicions.

To my surprise, I fell asleep for most of the afternoon and it was getting dark when I awoke. Shortly afterwards, the policeman who had punched me the previous evening opened the cell gate and motioned me out. He brought me upstairs to the public office, found my possessions in a drawer behind the desk and gave them back to me. I ostentatiously counted out the ten hundred franc notes the studio manager had given me and the small change in the wallet.

'My toolbox?' I asked.

The desk sergeant indicated where it was with a kick. The box was open and somebody had rummaged through it. There was nothing compromising among the few other possessions I had added when leaving the studio.

'Is Mlle Delmas still here?' I asked the policeman.

He shook his head.

Outside it was like a time lapse. It was going home time again, twenty-four hours later. The boulevard was busy with cyclists and a few cars with gas tanks on their roofs. The pavement was less busy with pedestrians, well wrapped against the evening chill. The air felt fresh and clean.

I walked down rue Meyerbeer, past small shops and a couple of hotels, my jacket buttoned up to hide my bloodied shirt. Mrs Mac's was full of light and talk, with the usual hint of real tobacco in the smoky air. A few regulars nodded to me, taking in my unusually dishevelled state. Mrs Mac saw me when I was halfway to the bar and put down the glass she was filling from the beer dispenser. She beckoned me to the end of the counter and raised the flap. 'Solange is upstairs,' she said. It was what I had hoped to hear.

Solange heard me climbing the stairs and was waiting at the top. We embraced and held each other tightly in silence. She looked me up and down when we broke apart and asked if I was all right. I nodded and asked her the same. 'I'm fine,' she said.

'They had me in for a few hours and I demanded to see you. I didn't believe you had been arrested.'

We went into the kitchen and sat at the table. She picked up the cigarette that was burning in the ashtray. 'You're smoking now,' I said and took it from her fingers and inhaled deeply. It was a real cigarette.

'Why did they arrest you?' she asked.

'What did they tell you?'

'That you were consorting with terrorists.'

I laughed a humourless laugh and gave her back the cigarette. 'Benetti arrested me because I was being cheeky with him.'

She didn't look convinced. She got up and tossed me the pack of Gitanes from the counter. I lit one for myself. 'What did he ask you?'

'He wanted to know about the Irish Jewess.'

'What about her?'

'Why is she here? What's she doing? Who are her associates? I couldn't tell him anything. I don't know anything about her, do I?' She gave me her earnest look that demanded an explanation without asking for it.

'There's nothing to tell. She's waiting for her travel documents. And the man from the Irish legation asked me to help her out while she's here.'

She maintained her earnest look, waiting for more.

I put my cigarette in the ashtray, reached across the table and took both her hands in mine. 'I'm not having an affair with her if that's what Benetti told you.'

'I was beginning to wonder.'

I agonized for a moment about telling her more. I didn't want to involve her in any of this but she needed more reassurance. 'She got into a little trouble and I had to help her sort it out. Nothing serious,' I said, lowering my voice.

She was still waiting for more information, but I didn't want to tell her anything else. It wasn't that I didn't trust her but I had no doubt how manipulative Benetti could be. 'Listen,' I added, still holding her hands. 'She'll be on her way back to Ireland soon and this will be over.'

She was about to ask something else but let it go. 'Are you hungry? I said I'd make dinner for Mme Bonnard and Gerard.'

'Starving,' I said. 'And I want to wash up.'

'You do that and I'll get to work.' She lowered her voice and added: 'There's lots of food here.'

I went into the bathroom, took off my bloodied shirt and washed myself. I hadn't told Solange about being fired yet. I had enjoyed working in the studio, watching the make-believe take shape. It was like the Riviera itself in a way, a world of fantasies and dreams. Perhaps I was just in retreat from the real world. I would miss La Victorine more that I would miss the loss of income. There was plenty of work for an electrician; I just had to go looking for it now, instead of trying to dissuade people from asking for favours.

There was a delicious smell of cooking when I emerged from the bathroom. 'What is it?' I asked Solange.

'Porc au poivre.'

Mrs Mac arrived upstairs just as the dinner was ready as if she had a sixth sense. She called to Gerard. A look of horror crossed his face when he saw me. He hesitated in the doorway and I thought for a moment he was about to turn tail, but he came in and I smiled at him and said hello. He nodded in return.

'You really should open your own restaurant,' Mrs Mac said to Solange after complimenting her cooking.

'Maybe when the war is over,' Solange said. She and I had also had this conversation on occasions and agreed that it was too difficult with the rationing to attempt it now, although Mrs Mac and Signora Mancini never seemed to have much difficulty getting whatever supplies they required. But neither of us had any desire to become involved with the black market.

'Marty would make a wonderful maître d',' Mrs Mac gave me a smile. I wondered if she had heard about my job; she picked up all sorts of gossip from her perch behind the bar. But she would hardly think that news something to smile about.

Solange laughed. 'I don't think I'd hire him for that.'

'That's a relief,' I said, 'but I'll come and eat there every day.'

'You could wash pots in the kitchen,' Solange suggested.

Mrs Mac and Solange traded news about various people they knew. Gerard ate his dinner quickly and left without speaking a single word. Mrs Mac raised her eyes in an apology to Solange and they went back to the talk of people they knew. I listened without taking in much, thinking how normal this scene should be: dinner in a family setting, appetising food, inconsequential chat, even a recalcitrant son. But nothing was exactly normal those days.

Mrs Mac stood up to make some real coffee. 'I forgot with all that's going on,' she said to me. 'There was a young man looking for you today. An American, I think.'

'An American?' I replied in surprise. I didn't know any Americans in Nice. Indeed, there weren't many Americans left since the US had entered the war the year before, especially not young ones: they had left in a hurry, fearful of being interned as enemy aliens.

'He sounded like an American to me,' she said, handing me a letter from her pocket. 'He left this for you.'

The envelope was handwritten and addressed to M. Martin Harris. My inclination was to put it in my pocket and open it later. But Solange was watching me while Mrs Mac busied herself with the coffee pot. It was better to open it now, despite my better judgment, than appear to keep more secrets from her.

The notepaper was headed United States Mission to France and had an address at Vichy. It said: 'Mr O'Casey of the Irish Legation has asked me to check in with you during my visit to Nice. Please contact me at the Hotel Suisse before Friday.' The name at the bottom was written in capital letters: Max Linqvist, Third Secretary.

I passed the note to Solange, even though she didn't read English, to show I wasn't hiding something else from her. I told Mrs Mac in French for Solange's benefit what it said. 'It may be good news about your travel permits,' I added.

Mrs Mac raised her shoulders in resigned rejection. Solange looked at me with concern and I knew what she was thinking. That it could be news too about my own travel documents to return to Ireland. It was clear from her expression that that would neither be good nor welcome news.

# Fourteen

Next morning, I lay in bed watching the slats in the shutter brighten as the sun rose over the shoulder of Mont Boron. Solange was still asleep beside me. I had been awake for a couple of hours, trying to think through what I ought to do with the next stage of my life. It seemed obvious that the present phase was over, the phase that had begun with my arrest in Ireland and my effective expulsion from the country. The phase that had led me to New York and Hollywood and on to the Riviera. My only regret was that I hadn't pursued my initial interest in Hollywood by getting into screen directing. It was too late for that now; besides, I had just lost my toehold, such as it was, in the movie business.

Solange stirred as I was wondering what I could do if I went back to Ireland. 'What time is it?' she asked in a sleepy voice.

'Nearly eight.'

'Why are you still here?' She moved closer and reached her arm over my chest.

'I don't have to go to work this morning.'

She dozed for a little while. I felt the warmth of her body and slid my arm under her head. No, I thought. I can't go anywhere unless she comes with me. And she doesn't want to go anywhere. Not until the war is over and her brothers are released from captivity. Even then, I suspected, she wouldn't want to leave France.

'What are you thinking?' she asked.

'Nothing much. Just drifting.'

'Drifting where?'

'Where the tide will take me.'

'Out to sea.'

'And back to shore.'

'So, nowhere,' she said with a smile.

I leaned over and kissed her eyelids. She climbed on top of me and we made love. Afterwards, she washed and dressed and had a quick cup of coffee while I lay in the rumpled bed. 'Do you have to go?' I asked. 'Couldn't we take the day off?'

'Not today. And you've already made me late. There'll be nothing left in the market.'

She gave me a quick peck on the forehead and said 'Á ce soir' with a suggestive wink. The door banged as she left.

I got up, opened the shutter and the sun blazed in. Two small fishing boats were in the centre of the harbour, their white sails fluttering loose as they coasted towards their berths. A flock of gulls screeched around them.

I took my time getting dressed and having something to eat and then sauntered along the quay. The sun was well up, hot and glinting on the still water. A line of luxury yachts tied up alongside each other had a forlorn air about them. Who knew when they had been to sea last or where their owners were now? I examined them as I passed by slowly, stopping now and then to look at their dusty portholes and unscrubbed decks. I was killing time but also acting out my new unemployed status in case anyone was taking an interest in me.

In Place Garibaldi I walked around two sides of the square and suddenly took a seat at a café, facing back the way I had come. Nobody changed course or stopped or dodged behind one of the pillars of the arcade. I drank a coffee and smoked a cigarette, all the while watching the comings and goings around me. If anyone had been following me, they were too good at their task for me to spot.

In rue de la Republique I opened the door of my apartment building quickly and went upstairs to my room. Gertie wasn't there. The place had been tidied up; the bed was made and there were no dirty dishes in the sink. But her suitcase was on the floor in a corner so I presumed she was still staying there.

I made my way back to the port and continued past it around the rough cliff face of Castle Hill. The half-circle of the Baie des Anges opened out before me, the sea a soothing soft blue, white-fringed by the breaking waves. I went into the Hotel Suisse where I had also met Seamus O'Casey and asked for Monsieur Linqvist.

He came down the stairs a few minutes later. He was in his early twenties, tall and loose-limbed in the American way, and had light brown hair combed straight back over a smiling face. He was wearing light-coloured slacks and a sleeveless pullover over an open-necked shirt. He looked more like a rich young tourist than a diplomat.

'I'm Max,' he said, holding out his hand. I shook it. 'Will we take a stroll?'

He didn't wait for an answer and led the way out onto the Quai des Etat Unis. I was happy to go with him. If someone was following me, I was quite content for him to see me with an American diplomat. It would help my hints that I had friends in high places, although it was only more likely to get up Benetti's nose again.

Linqvist stopped at the edge of the Promenade and inhaled deeply, as if he had just arrived after a long journey cooped up in a third-class carriage. 'I love this place,' he said. 'So different from the mid-west where I come from. Do you know it? The American mid-west?'

'No. I passed through it once by train.' And I had had other things on my mind than the endless prairies at the time.

'Yes, Seamus told me you spent some time in America. In Hollywood.'

I nodded, becoming cautious. I hadn't expected this to be about me. We ambled along. He was getting glances from other strollers to whom he looked like a vision from a fondly remembered past.

'How did you come to be here?'

'I came with a movie crew and stayed on.'

'Good choice.' He gave me an open smile and suggested we sit down. We took a bench facing across the Promenade at the sea. He took out a packet of Lucky Strikes, shook a couple of cigarettes out of its torn top, and held it out to me.

'Seamus said to tell you he was sorry he hasn't been able to come back,' he said after he had lit both our cigarettes with a flat lighter. 'He's had to spend a lot of time in Paris. He asked me to touch base with you and check that everything was okay.'

The statement was an invitation to tell him about Gertie Maher but I didn't take it up. It was probably my general paranoia at the time but I had no proof that he was a diplomat or that O'Casey had taken him into his confidence. He was clearly an American and appeared to know O'Casey. Other than that I knew nothing about him.

'I'm surprised you still have a legation in Vichy now that America is in the war,' I said.

'Yeah. One of those odd diplomatic things. But we're not at war with France or' – he glanced around to make sure nobody could overhear us – 'what's left of it. L'Ėtat Français is not technically at war with anyone. We're at war with the Axis and France isn't actually part of that unholy alliance. Not yet, at least.' He paused. 'So how is life in Nice?'

'Difficult for a lot of people. Food shortages and so on.'

He shrugged that away as though it was a given everywhere these days.

'And the Italians? They don't interfere?' The Italians technically controlled this half of the French Riviera and had annexed Menton and a strip of land next to the border. They had an armistice control commission based in Nice.

'Not that you'd notice anyway.'

'So le Maréchal is in charge?'

'Appears to be.'

'And how's his popularity?'

'Waning since the shortages got worse.'

'Hmm. I noticed some of his posters have been defaced. And I saw an anti-collaboration one near the station.'

'With a picture of a man and woman on it?'

He nodded. 'Are they anyone in particular? The picture wasn't very clear.'

I told him about Arletty and Hans-Jürgen Soehring, happy that Claude, the printer, had found someone to take the posters and begin distributing them. Linqvist didn't know who Arletty was so I explained that she was one of France's most famous film stars and currently filming here.

'That's very interesting,' he replied. 'Were there protests at the studio?'

'No.'

'What's the movie? A propaganda film?'

I gave him a brief résumé of the plot. He dropped his cigarette butt on the ground and stamped it out with his heel. I held on to mine until it was about to burn my fingers.

'Seamus said he had some worrying phone calls from you. That something had gone wrong.'

My paranoia about him eased: the fact that he knew about my phone calls to O'Casey helped to prove that he was who he said he was. 'Has he sorted out the travel permits he promised?'

'Yes, they're on the way.'

'Good. Gertie wants to leave as soon as possible. What about the other ones? For Madame Bonnard and her son?'

Linqvist looked perplexed. 'Who are they?'

I explained briefly.

'He didn't tell me anything about them.'

'That was the agreement. That he would arrange both sets at the same time.'

'I'm sorry. I don't know anything about that.'

'I can't believe he'd renege on it.'

'I'm sure he won't. He's a man of his word. He didn't mention it to me, that's all. He was more concerned about Miss Maher.'

'Why?'

'Because she'd been arrested here once. And he was afraid she'd be picked up again.'

'Why?'

'He didn't tell me. Only asked me to check in with you and see if she was still okay. He was worried about your calls.'

He was sticking to his script. Whether he knew more or not, I couldn't tell for sure but I suspected he did. 'She's okay now,' I said. 'There was a little trouble, but I think it's been sorted out.'

'What kind of trouble?'

'She was involved with some refugees but it's okay now.'

He searched my face, willing me to elaborate but unwilling, for some reason, to ask me direct questions. I didn't volunteer anything more. He switched his attention to the bay and we sat in silence for a while. People passed by, the refugees in their heavy northern suits, the locals in overcoats. It was not as busy at this end of the Promenade as closer to the town centre. Linqvist broke the silence. 'I called to the address on rue Berlioz that Seamus gave me a couple of times,' he said. 'There was never anybody there.'

'Do you know her?' I asked, prompted by something in the way he had said that.

'Slightly.' He nodded: 'I was posted to the legation in Dublin before I came here. I met her once or twice. She's a friend of a friend.'

'She must have very important friends. She's got the Irish legation in Vichy working for her. And now the American legation.'

He laughed. 'I'm only doing a favour for Seamus. Okay, partly because I had met her in Dublin. It helps to be able to put a face to the name.'

'And you want to meet her now?'

He nodded again. We had finally arrived at the point of his note and of this meeting. He needed my help to get to Gertie. I let him wait for a bit while I decided what to do. 'There's a café in the south-east corner of Place Garibaldi,' I said. 'I don't know the name of it but I'll meet you there at seven this evening.'

'Okay.' He gave me an appraising look, reassessing his impression of me. Clearly he had come to me as a fallback, as briefed by O'Casey, expecting me to simply give him a new address for Gertie. 'Are you an American too?'

'I don't know,' I said carefully. Was that a shot in the dark or did he know more about me? 'I had a passport but it's long out of date.'

'That's easily rectified. Renewing it is only a routine matter.'

'What are you doing here? Apart from favours for O'Casey.'

'Checking on some of our citizens who've stayed on. They're mostly elderly and need reassurance that all's okay. Especially since the younger ones cleared out when Hitler declared war on us after Pearl Harbor.'

He stood up and we shook hands. 'You know where Place Garibaldi is?' I asked.

'I'll find it.' He nodded back towards his hotel. 'I've got a guidebook. See you at seven.'

I watched him wander back along the Promenade, oblivious the surprised glances he was receiving. He wouldn't have been out of place less than three years ago when the world was normal and visitors still wintered here. Now, he seemed like a ghost.

I went back to Solange's place and spent the day lounging about, escaping into the Eric Ambler story. But the escapism went only so far. I began to feel a certain affinity with his main character, an English author in search of a plot who finds himself caught up in the murky worlds of Balkan politics and crime. I, too, was being pushed about by forces outside my control and not entirely understood.

I finished the book and decided to act as normally as possible and go to Mrs Mac's. It was dark outside and the Promenade was cold and almost empty. I was close to the Café du Raisin when I saw Gerard emerge and come towards me. He didn't notice me until I stopped right in his path.

'There's something I want to ask you,' I said. 'Why did you kill the man I was with?'

'He was a Jew.'

'Nobody's going around shooting Jews because they're Jews.'

He looked over my shoulder as if he was plotting an escape and sighed when he couldn't see one. 'Because he killed a friend of mine.'

'Who?'

He gave me a name that meant nothing to me. 'What happened to him?'

'He was shot. Up the street there.'

The penny dropped. The jewellery shop robber who Mrs Mac had told me was a childhood friend of Gerard's. 'He was shot by the flic,' I pointed out.

Gerard shuffled from one foot to the other, eager to end this conversation and get away. I noticed that he was wearing his Legionnaire's uniform under his overcoat.

'I haven't told anyone yet that you were involved in the murder,' I said slowly.

'He set my friend up. Told the flic and let them ambush him. Shoot him down like a dog in the street thinking they'd got the Jew robbers.'

'Why would he do that?'

'Because,' he said with exaggerated patience, 'he had done a deal with my friends. He had stolen some stuff from them. When they caught him, he said he couldn't give it back because he'd sold it already. He said why don't you rob this place yourselves; it's got even more valuable pieces. He said he had checked it out and was planning to do it himself, but they could do it instead.'

I didn't know what to make of that. It sounded unlikely but I doubted that Gerard was quick enough to make up a story like that on the spot. Unless he had been planning for this or a similar conversation. 'Listen,' I said, changing my tone, 'you should think about going to Ireland with your mother.'

'Mind your own fucking business,' he said in English and stepped onto the road and walked around me.

I went into the café and exchanged inconsequential chat with Mrs Mac. As I was leaving after one drink, Claude the printer gave me a faint smile and I nodded to him.

My apartment in the rue de la Republique was still empty; there was no sign that Gertie had been back there since my morning visit. I sat at the table and waited.

She turned up when I was about to leave to meet Linqvist. 'There's a man here from the American legation who wants to meet you,' I told her. 'Max Linqvist. Says he knows you.'

That stopped her in her tracks. 'Max is here?' she replied, taken aback. I couldn't tell whether she was happy or the opposite at the news. But it certainly surprised her.

'Waiting in Place Garibaldi to meet you in ten minutes.'

'What did he say?'

'That he's doing a favour for Seamus O'Casey. Checking that you're okay.'

'Did you tell him about Chaim?'

I shook my head. 'I said there had been a problem but that it had been sorted out. Speaking of Chaim,' I added, "had he come to some kind of deal with the black marketeers he had taken jewellery from?'

She stared at me for a long moment, a lot of things clearly going through her mind. I took her hesitation as a broad confirmation of Gerard's story. 'I don't know about that,' she said at last. 'Where's Max?'

'I'll show you.'

'You don't need to come.'

'It's no trouble,' I said, being deliberately obtuse. 'It's on my way home.'

We walked in silence to Place Garibaldi and under its arcade to the café I had described to Linqvist. It was full of men inside and we had a quick look around. He wasn't there and I checked my watch. It was a minute to seven. We took a table outside and waited in the cold.

'Any news about Chaim's family?' I asked Gertie.

'They're gone,' she said with an air of finality. She tightened her coat around her and folded her arms over her stomach, wrapping herself up against more than the cold. The prospect of meeting Linqvist had not filled her with joy, I decided.

I saw him crossing the road and approaching. 'Gertie,' he said as he came up to us, 'good to see you again.'

'Max,' she said, taking his outstretched hand and giving it a limp shake. 'This is a surprise.'

'Yes,' he said. 'They sent me to Vichy. Must think I'd absorbed enough conservative Catholicism in Ireland to understand this place.' He turned to me, 'No offence, Martin.'

I shook my head, not sure what I might have taken offence at. 'Would you like a drink?'

'Not for me,' Linqvist said. He glanced at Gertie and she shook her head. 'Thank you for arranging this,' he said to me.

It was a clear dismissal. I stood up and left with the sense that looking after Gertie was no longer my function. Which would be a weight off my shoulders if it were true. She had got me involved in a murder and on the periphery of God knew what else. But I had come through it unscathed. And she was now somebody else's responsibility. But I knew, too, that my scheme to get Mrs Mac and Gerard travelling permits to Ireland had also fallen through. As well as my own chances of getting back there.

I walked home, preparing to face my next problem: telling Solange that I had lost my job.

# Fifteen

Solange took my loss of pay as philosophically as I did but she recognised what an emotional break the loss of the job was. Mrs Mac saw it the other way around.

'It's time you got a real job anyway,' she declared. 'Instead of working with those people in that make-believe place.'

I didn't ask what she meant by 'those people'. As a regular cinemagoer and a lover of gossip about its stars, her attitude was a surprise. She disapproved of them all at heart, it appeared; or else she was disappointed in them on my behalf.

'I'm afraid there's no word about your travel permits,' I said, changing the subject. 'I hoped the American would have good news from O'Casey but he hadn't.'

'Ah, it was useless anyway,' she sighed. 'He won't go.'

I had had a vague notion that I could use Chaim's murder to pressure Gerard into going to Ireland with her but that evaporated with his blunt response to the subject. Short of threatening to denounce him to Benetti or Tillon, I couldn't see any other way of encouraging him to leave the country. And I had no desire to have any more dealings with either of them.

'You should still go on your own. For a holiday.'

Mrs Mac shook her head decisively and changed the subject. 'I'll put the word out that you're available for work. You'll take on any electrical work, I suppose.'

Her influence was impressive. The next day I was approached by one of her other regulars who was afraid that the wiring in his place was going to set the building on fire. 'The sockets keep sparking and blowing fuses,' he said.

I told him I'd be happy to rewire it if he could provide the wire. That was the flaw in my new plan; finding supplies when I didn't have the studio stores to pilfer, especially now that they were well-stocked again.

'Where am I going to find copper wire these days?' he asked plaintively.

He knew the answer as well as I did but he didn't seem keen to go to the black market. I wasn't keen to go there either, but I promised I'd try and find some.

I told Mrs Mac I'd talk to Gerard about going to Ireland. She said I was wasting my time but she lifted the flap on the counter and I went upstairs and knocked on his door.

I went in when I heard a grunt. He was lying on the bed reading a mimeographed document. If I hadn't known better, I would have presumed it was an underground anti-Vichy tract. Perhaps it was, given the poster of Adolf Hitler tacked to the wall. It showed Hitler facing a rally with his half-hearted own salute and had a slogan in German along the top. Le Maréchal wasn't right wing enough for Gerard.

'I need some electrical wire,' I said without preliminaries. 'Could your shooter friend find some for me?'

He lowered his document and studied me, deciding whether to tell me what to do with myself. 'It'll cost you,' he said, opting to be businesslike.

'I know that.'

'How much do you want?'

I didn't know the size of the customer's home but reckoned a hundred metres would probably suffice.

'I'll see what I can do.' Gerard raised his document and pretended to read it again.

'You should think again about going to Ireland with your mother,' I said in case she asked him what I wanted.

He ignored me. I added, 'I need the wire as soon as possible,' and left the room.

'You were right,' I told Mrs Mac downstairs. 'It was a waste of time.'

'Your friend is back for another tête-à-tête,' she said coldly.

I turned and saw Gertie at the window table. There was an untouched glass of red wine in front of her.

'I told Max how helpful you have been,' she said as soon as I sat down opposite her.

'Everything?' I asked.

She nodded.

'Including Chaim?' I added, my mind quickly rearranging all I thought I knew about her. 'You're an American?'

'Well.' She gave a slight smile. 'Yes and no. Like you.'

'What does that mean?'

'Max says you're an American too. As well as Irish.'

I drank some beer, staring at her. She held my gaze, a touch of amusement on her lips as she watched me putting two and two together. 'So you're really working for the Americans,' I said at last. 'Spying.'

The word turned her amusement into a passing smile as if the idea was ridiculous, something she couldn't quite believe herself. But she nodded confirmation at the same time.

'That's what you were doing in Vienna,' I added. 'Not teaching English or anything like that.'

'I was doing both,' she said.

'And you're working for the Americans here too. That's why you got involved with Chaim and the refugees.'

She shook her head. 'No. That's personal. What I told you about Chaim and his family is true. They were our neighbours in Vienna.' She sighed heavily and picked up her glass of wine for the first time.

'What does Max think of that?'

'He doesn't approve.'

'He wants you to go back to Ireland? Or America?'

She nodded. 'He also wants to meet you tonight. He's leaving in the morning.'

'What for?'

'He wants to thank you in person. For helping me.'

That sounded unlikely but I didn't voice my scepticism.

'That's why I levelled with you,' she added. 'So you'll understand why he's thanking you. He probably won't explain anything and you'd be left wondering why he cared and why he was grateful.'

I took that as her roundabout way of expressing her own thanks to me. 'When are you leaving?' I asked.

'In a few days.'

'You've got all your travel papers?'

'Yes.'

So O'Casey had reneged on our agreement, I thought. Gertie had her papers but there was no sign of Mrs Mac's. The fact that she wouldn't use them didn't excuse his bad faith. 'Does Seamus O'Casey know all this?' I asked.

'I don't know for sure, but I don't think so. He just thinks there's someone in Ireland using political pull to get me home safely.'

I smiled inwardly at her expression for political influence: she was as Irish as Mrs Mac and I no matter what her other allegiances. The thought made me glance back at the bar. Mrs Mac was watching us with a look of unmistakable disapproval. I automatically sat back in my chair before realizing that it probably looked to her like a guilty gesture. We had been leaning across the table close to each other, talking quietly as if it was an intimate conversation.

'There's one other thing,' Gertie said, wrapping up all loose ends. 'Can you give me back Chaim's property?'

'What do you want it for?' I leaned forward again. I wasn't keen to give her back the gun, worried about what she might do with it before her departure. Like shoot Gerard if she had recognized him that night, though I was pretty certain she hadn't and I hadn't told her about him.

'It's not for me. It's for his friends.'

'It didn't do Chaim any good,' I said. 'It won't do them any good either.'

Gertie sighed. 'You don't understand. The one thing I learned for sure in Vienna is that the Nazis are set on killing all Jews.' She saw the scepticism on my face and leaned further across the table. 'Max doesn't believe it either but I am telling you it's true. No Jew sent to a camp from Vienna has ever been seen or heard of again. They are being murdered wholesale. It's true. I know you think I'm exaggerating but I'm not. Everybody thinks we're exaggerating but we're not. Chaim's family is probably dead already.' Her eyes began to fill with tears and she searched in her handbag for a handkerchief. She blew her nose and blinked back the tears. 'They will never be seen or heard of again.'

I didn't doubt her sincerity but it did sound like exaggeration. It was hard to believe that anyone in the middle of the twentieth century in Europe would set out on such a path. And whatever about the Nazis, it was harder to believe that the Maréchal would countenance such a thing in his Etat Français. Although I knew as everyone did how wide the strain of anti-semitism was in France. A lot of it was aimed at refugees but the Statuts des Juifs didn't just apply to them. And you only had to watch Gerard and his Legionnaires to see it in action nightly.

'I'm sorry,' Gertie was saying, sniffling and putting away her handkerchief. 'But we can't leave them defenceless, to be rounded up like cattle.'

'Okay. I'll bring it round later. Where will you be?'

'Can I stay in your apartment?'

'Sure,' I agreed. It was a good idea if it kept her out of sight and out of trouble until she departed.

We left together and walked in silence, lost in our own thoughts. We parted in Place Massena where I offered a few words about being careful and she responded with a few routine nods. The night was still young but there were not many people about. The casino seemed almost deserted. The doormen glanced at me as I went by but made no effort to entice me inside. I wasn't an obvious customer. I cut through the Cours Saleya where most of the buildings were in darkness and the skeletons of market stalls emerged from the gloom.

Max Linqvist was in the sitting room in the Hotel Suisse. He looked more like a diplomat this time, wearing a dark three-piece suit with a watch chain visible on the waistcoat. Actually, he looked like a young person trying to appear a lot older and more authoritative than he was. But he just about managed to pull it off, avoiding looking ridiculous.

'Thanks for dropping by,' he said as I took the armchair next to him. 'You met Gertie then.'

'If that's her name,' I shot back. I didn't know if Gertrude was a likely name for a Jewish girl in Austria but Maher certainly wasn't.

That took him by surprise. 'Um ... yeah,' he said. It wasn't clear whether his response was confirming her name or my doubts. He covered it up by reaching for his cigarettes on the table.

'I wanted to thank you for taking care of her,' he said when we had settled back with our smokes. 'It probably involved more than you bargained for but we're all the more grateful. She's very thankful too, although she might not have told you so.'

'Not in so many words.'

'Well she told me. She couldn't have got by without your help.'

'You got her into some dangerous situations.'

'Not me, not us,' he said quickly. 'We wanted to get her out of Vienna. It was too dangerous for her now that America is in the war. She was supposed to come back immediately. But she stopped off here and became involved with some old friends.'

'You believe what she says about the Germans murdering Jews?'

'I don't know. She's not the only one bringing back those stories. But I don't know the extent of the reports or how reliable they are.'

Spoken like a true diplomat, I thought. 'Are you really a diplomat?' I asked.

'For the moment,' he said easily, 'but part of my job is planning for the future. And that's the other reason I wanted to talk to you before I left.'

I could see what was coming and didn't do anything to dissuade him from continuing. But I was beginning to wonder why everyone wanted me as an informant.

'We need to have people on the spot here to help us understand what's really happening. What the French are thinking. How they see the Vichy government. The Italians. The war in general.'

'Spy for you,' I said.

He laughed and I thought that this was probably the same conversation he had had with Gertie at some time in the past when he recruited her to whatever organisation he worked for. 'It's not as dramatic as that. Just general information-gathering. So that we have an accurate picture of what's going on in this country.' He paused to stub out his cigarette. 'At some point we're going to have to boot the Germans and the Italians out of France and we need to know whether the people of France will be with us or against us.'

'With you surely.'

'Some of them certainly. Most of them probably. But what about the Maréchal and his supporters? And the ones who don't think he's friendly enough with the Germans? You have to remember how deep the bad feeling is towards the British after their success at escaping from Dunkirk and all the French sailors they killed at Mers-el-Kébir.'

I understood the events he mentioned. I had heard them debated in many ways and from many angles for most of the last two years. And there was no doubt that Dunkirk and the British attack on the French navy at Mers-el-Kébir had left sour feelings. But attitudes had also changed in the nearly two years since those events had occurred. Disillusionment with le Maréchal was growing; the saviour of 1940 was becoming the problem of 1942. But I was no political analyst, as I told Linqvist.

'You don't need to be. We can do the analysis ourselves, but we need reliable information from people living here day by day on which to base it. Individuals who can tell which way the wind is blowing.'

Did I want to become involved? Or was that a rhetorical question by now? Minding my own business had not kept me out of trouble. And Gertie's attempt to do something for her friends was a reproach even if it had backfired and left her former neighbours in a worse place. What right did I have to sit on the sidelines now because I had had some disillusioning experiences in my younger days?

'You also know how to handle yourself in a tight situation,' Linqvist added. 'You have military training which could come in useful.'

O'Casey must have told him something of my background. 'I wouldn't call it military training,' I gave half a laugh at the thought. 'That's a gross exaggeration. It was more haphazard than that.'

'But you know how to handle a gun if necessary. How to react under fire.' He made it sound like a compliment, even an incentive, promising me action that I didn't want. Which suggested that he was a deskman himself, had never been under fire; and had a deskman's mixture of personal inferiority and strategic superiority towards those at the sharp end.

I said nothing and he added after a moment: 'Think about it for a while if you want, but it would be helpful to know now. I don't know when I'll be back here. And I don't know when the President will change his mind about being nice to the Maréchal.'

'He's being nice to him?' I asked, to gain thinking time as well as out of curiosity.

'He doesn't like General de Gaulle in London but he could change his mind about the Maréchal and pull us out of here at any time. Break off diplomatic relations.'

'And who would I report to then?'

'That's why I'd like a decision now. I can set you up with a local contact before I leave.'

'Okay.'

'You'll do it?'

I nodded.

'That's great,' he said with a big smile. 'Uncle Sam will be grateful. If you want to go back to the States there won't be any problem with a passport. After the war.'

The niggling thought at the back of my mind that he knew why I had fled from New York returned. My paranoia perhaps. But it was not impossible that somebody like O'Casey had heard of it and shared it with Linqvist. I couldn't rule it out completely. 'Why should there be a problem?' I asked.

'You said you weren't sure whether you were still an American citizen. If there's any doubt you'll get the benefit of it for helping us out.'

A passing thought that Solange might be more willing to go to Los Angeles than to Ireland suggested itself. But that was academic unless I could go now and Linqvist wasn't offering that. After the war, he had said pointedly. There might not be any reason to leave Nice then. Who knew what would happen or when or how it would end?

Linqvist launched into instructions about the man I was to contact, when and how. He repeated them to make sure I had understood all the arrangements, the passwords so we could identify each other the first time, and how to schedule meetings. My contact was someone I would know as Charles: I would be Vincent.

'And there's one last thing with Gertie,' he added. 'Well, two things actually. Don't tell her you're working with us. And make sure she gets on a train to Barcelona.'

'How will I do that? She's not going to take instructions from me.'

'Tell her it's an instruction from me.'

'Haven't you told her yourself?'

Linqvist nodded. 'You know what she's like. Try and persuade her to leave as soon as possible. While she's still in the clear.'

'Did you recruit her in Ireland?'

He was about to tell me that it was none of my business or I didn't need to know, but he changed his mind. 'She got into trouble there and had to be rescued. She can be a little hot-headed at times, as you know. We need to get her out of here before something else happens.'

'I'll do my best,' I agreed but I knew that wouldn't be of much use against Gertie's determination.

We shook hands formally before I left. I wasn't entirely sure what I had signed up to but I knew I had stepped over a line.

Gertie was waiting in my apartment, sitting patiently at the table. I gave her the revolver and she dropped it into the handbag by her foot. 'There's only three live rounds in it,' I pointed out in case she was planning a rampage. 'You should get rid of it as soon as you can.'

'Right away,' she agreed.

I sat down opposite her. 'Max wants you to leave for Spain tomorrow.'

'I can't leave tomorrow. I've a couple of things to do.'

'Like what?'

'People to say goodbye to.'

'When are you planning to leave?'

'Two or three days at most. Don't worry,' she added with a wintry smile. 'I'll be out of your hair soon.'

'You should move on while you still can.'

'Are you one of us now?' Her smile turned impish, as if this was all a game to her, although I knew it wasn't. Not her concern for the Jewish refugees at any rate.

'Who are "us"?'

'Max didn't tell you?'

I shook my head. So much for his instruction not to tell Gertie that he had recruited me too.

'It's called the OSS,' she said. She thought for a moment to remember what the initials stood for. 'The Organisation for Strategic Services.'

That didn't mean anything to me but maybe that was the point: it wasn't meant to mean anything much to anyone.

'How did he recruit you?'

She propped her head on her hand and rubbed her forehead as if she was developing a headache. 'He didn't tell you that either?'

'He didn't tell me anything.'

'I killed a Nazi in Dublin.'

I made no attempt to hide my surprise. 'A German? In Dublin?'

'He wasn't German. He was actually English but he was a Nazi supporter.'

She watched me as I digested this information, not entirely sure that I believed her. But I couldn't see any reason why she was lying. I didn't think she was trying to impress me. So her involvement in Chaim's activities was not a flash in the pan.

'Max helped me get out of Ireland,' she added.

'To Vienna?'

'To New York. I joined the OSS, and they sent me to Vienna.'

'What do they do?'

She shrugged. 'Spying. Cause trouble for the Nazis and their friends. They say they're planning undercover warfare, but they won't allow it at the moment. They say the time's not ripe yet.'

That tied in with what Linqvist had hinted at. That my experience of guerilla warfare could come in useful at some point, although I didn't see myself ever going back to lying in wet ditches in ambush sites. I was too old for that sort of activity now. Besides, I had serious doubts about its usefulness. It certainly hadn't achieved anything other than grief in my experience.

'Have you ever killed anyone?' she asked out of the blue.

'No,' I lied automatically.

'Max said you were involved in the Irish civil war,' she added by way of explanation for the question. 'On the republican side.'

I nodded. 'I shot at Free Staters in a couple of engagements but I never knew whether I hit anyone or not. It's best not to know.'

That was a lie too. I could still see the spurt of blood from the young face of a Free State soldier and his cap flying over the side of the open-backed lorry we ambushed. We killed four of them that day, wounded a few more. I avoided the newspapers for the next few days, not wanting to know the name of my target. I wouldn't have been able to tell which of the four dead he was from their names but I was afraid they would publish photographs too. But I didn't have nightmares about him. That was war.

We lapsed into silence for a while. Then I asked her if she had any more friends from Vienna among the refugees in Nice. She shook her head.

'Then there's nothing to detain you,' I pointed out. 'There's nothing more you can do here,'

She ignored that. 'Max won't supply them with weapons. He says his bosses won't allow it.'

'What would that achieve? They'd all be massacred.'

'They're going to be massacred anyway. It would be better if they died fighting.'

'Isn't that a decision for them?'

'Yes, but we have to give them the option.'

'How is you staying here going to help them with one revolver and three bullets?' I asked brutally.

'I have other ideas,' she said defiantly. 'Are you spying on me now? Reporting back to Max?'

I denied it and, after a moment, she reached down into her handbag and took out a sheaf of papers and her green passport. She spread the papers on the table so that I could see what they were: her permits for leaving France to Barcelona and on to Madrid and Lisbon. 'Do you know any forgers?' she asked.

I shook my head.

'Printers?'

I thought of Claude. He had seemed nervous about printing the *collabo* poster, but he had done it for Jean-Luc. And found someone to circulate them. But I didn't know what his relationship with Jean-Luc had been and why he had agreed to print them. It could be personal or political or something else. Either way, there was no reason for him to do me any more favours.

'You do!' She seized on my hesitation, her dark eyes coming alive. 'You do know someone.'

'Possibly.' I admitted. 'But I don't know if he'd do it. And I don't know if I can ask him. It would put him at risk.'

'He could print the blank forms and we'd get someone else to fill in the individual details and stamps and signatures.' She gave me her earnest look. 'The right pieces of paper can save a whole lot of people. No guns. We can save them with pieces of paper!'

The 'we' did not escape my attention. Not just fellow members of this OSS but joint operators in our own private campaign. Saving people from Nazism and its French collaborators. People could be saved with pieces of paper. It was a practical proposition, hard to say no to. And much more attractive than fighting for amorphous ideas of freedom or someone else's pet solution to the world's problems.

I gathered up her transit papers, folded them, and put them in my inside pocket.

# Sixteen

The next morning I dropped into the printers beside Mrs Mac's café. An old man was behind the tiny counter and he nodded at the inside door when I asked for Claude. I went through and found Claude and a youngster working on a machine. He didn't look very happy to see me.

He finished giving the youngster instructions and then led me into the back yard. 'I see you got the posters into circulation,' I said. 'Well done.'

He looked at me with suspicion, knowing that I was going to make more demands. I showed him the transit permits and asked him if he could print these forms. He took them from me with a sigh, felt the different paper they were on, and held it up to the light. 'I don't have the paper for the French one,' he said at last, handing them back to me. 'And I don't have the typefaces for the others.'

'If I could get you the paper for the French one ...' I left the thought hanging in the air.

He nodded, as if it was against his better judgment; it was a feeling I knew all too well.

'And the typefaces?' I added. 'Where could I find them?'

'You'd have to find a printer who did work for Spaniards and Portuguese.'

'Do you know any one?'

He shook his head. 'And I'm not going to ask around. Too risky.'

'Okay,' I said. 'I'll try and get you the paper.' He took back the French permit. 'And you'll forget the details on this,' I added. It had Gertie's photograph on it and her description: height, hair colour, born in Cork, Ireland, 13/6/1921. Which I now knew for sure to be a lie. I had wondered if O'Casey knew that too.

'Listen,' he said, averting his gaze. 'I don't want to be involved in any more of this. That's my son in there. And my father. The whole family. I can't put them in danger.'

'I understand. I won't come near you again for anything else.'

He held out his hand as if we were sealing an agreement and I shook it.

I almost bumped into Gerard as I left Claude's. He was coming out of the café, in a hurry as usual, and I hoped he hadn't seen me emerge. I didn't think he had.

He stopped in front of me and said, 'I've got the wire. Have you got the money?'

'How much?'

'Two thousand francs.'

I laughed.

'All right,' he retorted. 'I'll tell him to sell it to someone else. There's no shortage of buyers.'

'Okay,' I said. 'I'll take it.' It would mean I'd have to reduce my profit on the rewiring job but without the wire, I'd have no job. I hoped that Solange could lend me some of the money to buy it.

Gerard gave me a smug look. 'He'll be at the Cours Saleya between eight and half past in the morning. His name's Jacques and he'll have a red cart. He'll want to see the money first.'

'He's a farmer?'

Gerard gave a snorting laugh and walked off before I could ask him about the paper Claude had described to me before I left. It was just as well, I thought, to see how the wire transaction went first.

I spent the rest of the day on the Promenade, reading a Dorothy L. Sayers novel I'd picked up from the secondhand bookseller who was getting rid of his English language stock for centimes. Most of the chairs on the sea side of the walkway faced inland but I chose one facing the water, preferring to turn my back on the world and its problems. It was another of those days that had made the Riviera a winter magnet for the old and the weary. The bright sun was warm and sparkled on the bay with vitality. The sea tumbled onto the shore, pulling and probing the rolling stones. There were few people on the beach, nobody in the water, and two sailing boats far out towards the horizon.

But the world's problems, or at least my infinitesimal part of them, kept intruding on the story of cocaine dealing among London's posh young people during the days of peace. I found it hard to concentrate, listening to the shuffle of feet behind me and the snatches of conversation, some in unrecognisable languages, in between the crashing of the waves on the beach. I gave up reading after a while and dozed in the sun's warmth.

It was still warm when I left and strolled back to Solange's place. The nap and walk had refreshed me and I settled at the kitchen table and read some more of the novel. The daylight was beginning to falter and I stood up to put on the light and close the window. The harbour was in shadow but the setting sun was still brightening the top of Mont Boron. I was about to close the window when I heard a car glide to a halt and tick over outside the building. I looked down on the roof of a black Citroën traction avant. My heart sank, expecting Benetti or his henchmen to emerge.

The front passenger door opened back. Solange stepped out, closed it behind her, and the car moved off.

I stood where I was, no longer seeing the sun on the hilltop. Perhaps Signora Mancini's factotum, Marc, had driven her home. She had a Fiat but maybe she had changed cars. But I knew in my heart that wasn't so: nobody changed cars with ease these days and nobody had the petrol to give people casual lifts. And the only cars without gas tanks on the roofs were official ones of one kind or another.

Solange's key in the door jolted me out of my shock. I closed the window and was sitting at the table with my book when she came in.

'Look at you,' she said brightly. 'The gentleman of leisure.' She put her shopping bag on the counter and took her handbag from it.

'You're home early,' I prompted, hoping for an innocent explanation.

'Signora Mancini's going out to dinner. Which means we're in luck.' She took a parcel wrapped in greaseproof paper from her shopping bag and opened it for inspection. It was a small bird, plucked, and split in two.

'What is it?'

'Un pigeonneau,' she said, taking some vegetables from the bag and setting them out on the counter.

I gave her a sharp look; pigeonneau was a young pigeon but I had also heard it used to refer to a stupid or foolish young man. I wasn't entirely sure of its slang meaning but her demeanour didn't suggest anything other than the straightforward interpretation.

She got herself a glass of water and sat down at the table opposite me. 'What have you been doing all day?' she asked.

'Reading. Sat on the Promenade for a couple of hours.'

She turned my novel around to read its English title aloud with a heavy accent, Murder Must Advertise. 'More murder,' she said, shaking her head. 'Don't you ever get tired of them?'

'And you?' I ignored her question. My mind was still in turmoil, but I couldn't bring myself to ask her directly why she had just arrived home in Benetti's car. 'Anything interesting today?'

She sighed. 'Signora Mancini was in one of her petulant moods. She's tired of chicken. The flowers are very late to bloom this year. Marc is becoming lazy and even insolent. It was a relief to hear she was going out to dinner.'

'Her arthritis again?'

'I suppose so.' She finished her glass of water and stood up. 'I'm going to make a marinade for the pigeonneau. I've got peas and onions to go with it. Do you want rutabaga as well?'

'Of course.' I said automatically: it was another of her standing complaints about my need for quantity over quality.

She raised her eyes to heaven but leaned across the table and kissed me.

I watched her busy herself at the counter, chopping cloves of garlic and mixing them with olive oil, cumin and black pepper. She put the pigeon halves into a bowl with the mixture and turned them over several times. When she had finished, she washed her hands and came back to the table.

'I need to leave it for an hour or so,' she said.

I was on the point of asking her about the car but changed my mind: she seemed to be in such good form despite her complaints about Signora Mancini. Don't make mountains out of molehills, I told myself. Instead, I told her I'd managed to find some wire on the black market for the re-wiring job I'd been offered, hoping she didn't ask how. I didn't want to add to Mrs Mac's worries about Gerard by revealing his black market connections to Solange although his mother probably knew already. 'But it's going to cost more than I expected.'

'How much?'

'Two thousand.'

She gave a pained grimace.

'Could you lend me some of it?' I asked.

'How much?'

'Half.'

'Of course.'

'I'll give it back to you when the job is done.'

'No hurry.' She reached over and patted my hand. 'When do you need it?'

'First thing tomorrow morning.'

Solange was in an amorous mood after dinner and we went to bed early. She took the initiative as we made love and I lay awake for a long time afterwards, trying to allay my suspicions. There was no doubt in my mind that she had been with Benetti but why? I couldn't see why he needed her to spy on me at this stage. I was of no possible use to him unless he knew about Gertie's activities.

Which was doubtful. If he had known, neither she nor I would still be free. And the Vichy bureaucracy surely would not be facilitating her departure for Ireland.

That meant his interest was probably personal. And Solange's? I could understand her desire to keep in his good books in the hope that he could get her brothers released from their POW camps. I didn't believe he could or would but that was neither here nor there; she wanted to believe him. How far would she go to meet his demands? The only thing I was sure of was that Benetti wouldn't do anything for nothing.

We left the apartment together shortly after seven thirty. The sun was just clearing Mont Boron, casting its light on our side of the port, and the morning air was fresh and clear. We kissed briefly on the footpath as we parted and I went around by Castle Hill to the Cours Saleya.

The market was already busy. It was farm produce this morning and there was a feeling of desperation about it as shoppers hurried from stall to stall in the hope of finding what they wanted. I made my way to the back, near the prefecture, where the farmers' carts and animals were clustered. There was no shortage of faded red carts and I was beginning to think Gerard had sent me on a wild goose chase. I had approached three cart minders asking if they were Jacques before a burly, red-faced man nodded.

'You have something for me?' I asked.

He put his hand under the straw covering the cart's floor and pulled out the edge of a coil of rubber-covered wire. 'You have something for me?' he asked.

I was taking the money out of my inside pocket when we both heard a commotion behind us and looked back. A horse was neighing and rearing up while its owner tried to settle it. People around it were pushing out of the way, and the cart park was suddenly becoming a mass of moving animals and people as fear spread among both. Jacques muttered a curse and said, 'Take it quickly.'

I looked around again to see what had prompted his sudden urgency. There was a line of policemen moving forward as the would-be customers of the black marketeers tried to scatter between the congested carts and animals.

'The money,' Jacques demanded with his hand out, flapping his fingers. 'The money.'

I was about to give it to him when some instinct stopped me. I moved away, joining the rush for the other side of the park. We ran into another loose police cordon. People around me dropped contraband of various kinds on the ground -- bottles, vegetables, chunks of meat -- as the police examined everyone fleeing. I raised my hands to show I had nothing as I went through the line. The policeman who eyed me quickly turned his attention to a woman behind me with a shopping bag and shouted at her to open it.

Once through the cordon, I stopped. In the narrow street behind me people were gathering from the slum of the old town and beginning to shout abuse at the police, adding to the general clamour. A couple of missiles went over my head. I tried to pick out Jacques in the midst of the chaos but couldn't see him. Then I saw a policeman raise a coil of electric wire in the air like he had won a treasure hunt.

Young men and children were racing through the tight streets of the old town, attracted to the commotion like moths to a light. I had to shoulder my way against them to make any headway in the opposite direction. It was gloomy here, the sun excluded by the high buildings and the washing overhanging the narrow passageways. The farther away I got from the Cours Saleya, the more the crowd eased, and I emerged eventually into Place Garibaldi.

I sat on a bench under its arcade and wondered about what had happened. The police occasionally raided likely blackmarket areas like the Cours Saleya. Raids were rare, despite the official rhetoric against the black market; it was a safety valve which helped to maintain public stability. But the vision of the flic holding the coil of electric wire aloft suggested that this was not a routine raid. They were after me.

That's ridiculous, I thought. There were twenty or thirty policemen there: they wouldn't have to involve that many just to catch me. If they knew about my transaction, all they would have had to do was follow me. Stop being paranoid, I told myself. It wasn't about you, it was a general operation. At least I'd saved our two thousand francs, which I could have lost easily if I'd found Jacques five minutes earlier and had had to dump the wire.

Buoyed by that thought, I left the bench and walked across the square towards the rue de la Republique to see if Gertie was in my apartment. I hadn't gone far down the street when I noticed a group of people gathered on the footpath opposite a couple of cars. I cursed, hoping against hope the cars weren't outside my building. As I got closer, I realized that they were. Then I hoped against hope that it was someone else in the building.

I joined the back of the group of onlookers and asked an elderly woman what was happening. She looked me up and down cautiously and then replied, 'I don't know, monsieur.'

There were two cars, drivers sitting in both. People drifted away from the group, bored because nothing was happening. Fortunately, others stopped to replenish the numbers, which were just about enough to provide cover. Eventually two men emerged, followed by Benetti holding Gertie by the arm, and two others. Gertie's face was pale and I knew immediately that she hadn't got rid of the gun. She didn't look left or right. Benetti guided her into the back seat of the second car and got in after her. Car doors slammed and the small convoy drove away.

The crowd of onlookers dissolved and I strolled down to the end of the long street and came back slowly on the other side. There was no sign that Benetti's men had left anyone behind. I went into the building and unlocked my door. The apartment was in a mess; drawers had been pulled out and upturned, the mattress stood on its edge, and cupboards had been emptied onto the floor. I shuffled through the wreckage but there was nothing to see, nothing to learn. They had found anything that Gertie might have hidden but I suspected Chaim's gun was still in her handbag where she had put it the night before. There was an outside chance that she had got rid of it after I'd left or earlier this morning, but it was a slim chance.

I hurried back towards the town centre, hurrying because I needed to be doing something, even though there was little I could do that was useful. In the rue de France I was about to go into the printers' when one of Mrs Mac's regulars came out of the café. We greeted each other and I continued into the café.

'Marty,' Mrs Mac greeted me. 'Not used to seeing you this time of the day.'

'Have to get myself moving early these days. I need to make a phone call.'

She gave me a token for the call box and I asked the operator for Seamus O'Casey's number in Vichy. I went back to the counter while I waited for the call to be put through.

'Come upstairs if you want some proper breakfast,' Mrs Mac said, meaning if I wanted some real coffee.

I could do with real coffee and a real cigarette but I told her I had to wait for the call first.

'When you're finished.'

'Is Gerard there?'

'In the bed. You won't see him for hours yet.'

She made me a fake coffee and I took it into the phone box to give myself time to put together some sentences in Irish that would alert O'Casey to the seriousness of what had happened. Letting him know was a risk; it would make Benetti's friends wonder how I'd known about Gertie's arrest so quickly. But time was of the essence. O'Casey had to move fast to have any hope of success. Even better if Linqvist and his American friends became involved directly as quickly as possible; they would carry more clout with the Maréchal and his minions than the Irish ever could. But it would take days to make contact with Linqvist's local man through the elaborate arrangements the American had given me.

'*Dia dhuit*,' I greeted O'Casey as soon as he came on the line, hoping to put him on notice by the Irish greeting that this was going to be a sensitive conversation.

'*Conas atá tú*? he asked carefully. I thought I detected a note of extra caution in his query about how I was but it may have been wishful thinking.

'*Níl sí go maith*,' I said, emphasising the 'she' in she's not well.

'*Cén fáth*?' Why?

'*Tá sí leis na póilíní arís*.' I said in pidgin Irish. She's with the police again.

'*Cén fáth*?' he repeated.

'*Tá sí i dtrioblóid mhór*.' My limited Irish was falling apart. The only Irish world I knew for gun sounded too like the English and I didn't want to use it. So I was reduced to trying to say she was in big trouble.

There was a pause while O'Casey tried to decipher my message.

*'Triobłóid an-mhór,'* I said into the silence. Very big trouble. *'An dtuigeann tú?'*

*'Tuigim,'* he said with a touch of hesitancy. I understand. After a moment he added: *'Ba coir liom caint le daoine annseo.'* I better talk to people here.

*'Sea, sea,'* I replied with encouragement. Yes. *'Agus daoine annseo.'* And people here. I tried to think of some word for urgently, but no construction came to me.

*'Ceart go leor.'* Okay, he said. He ended the conversation without his usual exhortation, *bí cúramach*, but perhaps he realized that the situation had gone beyond being careful. At least I hoped he did.

Mrs Mac was waiting for me when I emerged from the phone box. 'That friend of yours from the picture factory was in last night,' she said. 'Looking for you.'

'Which friend?'

'I can't remember his name and he didn't remind me. He's been in here with you a few times before but not for a good while.'

I searched my memory for who it might be. I had rarely seen people from the studios in here. 'Jean-Luc,' I said. 'But it can't be him.'

'Yes, that's him,' she nodded. 'Said he'd just been released.'

'Are you sure?' I stared at her.

'Sure I'm sure. It was very busy at the time and I was a bit distracted, another row with Gerard. But I'm sure.'

'Jean-Luc?' I couldn't allow myself to believe her.

'Yes. Definitely. Are you in trouble, Marty?'

'Me? No.'

'Why was he arrested?'

'It was nothing to do with me. What did he say?'

'Said to tell you that he'd been released.' She searched my eyes, not convinced that I wasn't in trouble.

'That was it?'

'That's all.' She gave me her suspicious look. 'What was he in jail for?'

'He wasn't in jail,' I said, resisting a temptation to tell her to ask Henri Tillon. 'Not as such. They thought he was a communist but he's not.'

'Are you sure?'

'You know I keep out of politics.'

'OK,' she sighed. 'Come upstairs and I'll put together some proper breakfast.'

Mrs Mac made conversation while we had breakfast of real coffee and croissants. She produced a packet of Gauloise *bleu* and we smoked in silence. There was no sign of Gerard, which was just as well. I wouldn't have known what to say to him. He seemed to have kept his part of the bargain, found the wire and arranged the payment. But I hadn't entirely discounted my initial belief that the *flics* were trying to catch me with contraband.

But that issue was inconsequential compared to the other bad and good news of the morning; Gertie's arrest and Jean-Luc's release. Gertie's life hung on a thread if she'd been found with the gun; she'd be branded a terrorist and executed. Her foreign nationality would not save her, especially if the Sûreté confirmed her real identity and discovered that she was a Jew from the greater Reich. The best that O'Casey or Linqvist could do might be to have her life spared as long as her real identity did not emerge. They were her only hope of survival. I couldn't see how she could talk her way out of her predicament. Unless… .

I could feel the sweat break out on my forehead.

'Are you all right?' Mrs Mac reached across the kitchen table for the back of my hand.

'Yes.' I tried to smile. 'I'm got a chill or something. All these cold nights.'

She released my hand and patted it. 'Go home to bed.'

I nodded and got up. 'Thanks for breakfast.'

She waved away my thanks. 'Do you want me to phone that Italian woman and let Solange know you're sick?'

'No, no,' I said. 'I'll be all right. I'll go home and lie down for a bit. It's nothing, A bit of a chill.'

I didn't go home. I sat on the Promenade, trying to dampen down my fears and figure out how to navigate a way through what was happening. The sun was hot and the sea the colour of heaven in a medieval painting but I was oblivious of them, overwhelmed by the morning's events. I forced myself to concentrate on them one by one; there was no reason to think they were connected.

The least of the problems was Gerard and whether he had tried to set me up for arrest. It was unlikely but I couldn't rule it out. He was the only person who knew I'd be there to meet a black marketeer. Apart from Solange, but she didn't know about it until after her meeting with Benetti. Which was the one can of worms I didn't want to open right now.

Then there was Jean-Luc and his sudden release. Which, to put it mildly, was a surprise. In spite of my denials, I knew he was a communist and Benetti knew it too, though not from me. So why had he been released a few weeks after his detention? His arrest had cost me my job; his release wasn't going to get it back. I was happy for him, but I realized when I thought about it that his release was not a problem for me. I struck it off my list.

The real problem was Gertie. A matter of life and death, literally, for her. But also potentially for me, depending on where they had found the gun. What if she had hidden it somewhere in my flat and denied any knowledge of it? Then it would be mine. And my fingerprints were on it, to prove it. But so too were hers, probably. Which meant that it would be a matter of life and death for both of us.

Slow down, I told myself. You don't know that they've found the gun on her or in the flat. You don't know that she'd try to pass the blame onto you if it was found in the flat and not in her handbag.

I stayed where I was, half-expecting Benetti's hand on my shoulder at any moment, wondering how this whole mess had come about after years of living peacefully in this paradise. The war, I thought. Like every war it dripped its poison into daily life far far away from any frontline. But I couldn't flee my fate this time. I was trapped here. There was no easy escape route. I couldn't just get on a train, like I had in New York and have it take me two and a half thousand miles away to a new life.

# Seventeen

There was no place to hide, so I went back to Solange's apartment to pick up my toolbox. I was leaving with it when Mme Lecroix, our neighbour from above, came down the stairs on her way out. She stopped to greet me. I hadn't seen her since I'd repaired her cooker and I asked her if it was still okay.

'Oh, yes,' she said. 'It's perfect. And how is Solange? I haven't seen her for an age.'

'She's very well, thank you. Working hard.'

Mme Lecroix glanced around to make sure there was no one else in the stairwell. 'I hope there's been no more of those horrible notices,' she whispered.

'No,' I said. 'That's all over.'

'I'm very happy to hear that.'

She went on down the stairs, leaving me wondering if indeed there had been more poison pen letters. Solange hadn't mentioned any. She certainly wasn't concerned about them after the abortion denunciation and Benetti had put her mind at rest, but it seemed odd that they would stop suddenly. Unless somebody had taken some action. Benetti, I thought, my suspicious mind ready to see him behind everything.

I walked back towards the Promenade and sat on the bench that Linqvist and I had occupied near the Hotel Suisse. I opened my toolbox, took out a stub of chalk, and draped my arm over the back of the seat. I checked behind that there was no one watching and drew a vertical line on the back of the second plank. In accordance with Linqvist's instructions.

I had been tempted to laugh when he had laid out the elaborate plans for meeting his man Charles. It had all sounded too Hollywood even for me, but that was the only way I could meet Charles and impress on him the urgency of the American legation trying to save its own agent. Unfortunately, this method of communication could take days.

My next move was going to be higher risk, but I calculated that there was no point trying to avoid Benetti. Hiding from him was pointless, if not impossible; confronting him might just allay whatever suspicions he had. It was a gamble, but I didn't have any other options. And it might be that I had a hidden ace.

Claude gave a heavy sigh when I arrived in his print shop.

'It's all right,' I said. 'I just need to take back what I gave you.'

'I haven't done anything with it yet.'

'The person who owns it needs it.'

He rooted into the back of his drawer and took out Gertie's French travel pass.

I thanked him and turned to go but stopped. 'I hear Jean-Luc has been released.'

'Yes,' he said, brightening up. 'I saw him next door last night.'

'How did he get out?'

He shrugged. 'Persuaded them that he had left the party in '39.'

'Good,' I said.

I was tempted to go into Mrs Mac's for a quick drink but resisted it. There was no point putting off what had to be done.

The sergeant at the desk in the Sûreté office left me waiting on a bench for more than an hour. Then a young detective appeared, trying hard to look more fearsome than his years, and barked at me to follow him. He stopped after a few steps and demanded to know what was in the box.

'Tools,' I told him. 'I'm an electrician.'

He gestured to me to open it. I left it back on the bench and did as I was told. He rifled through the phase testers, wire strippers, fuses, bits of fuse wire, plugs and sockets, and took out the largest screwdriver. He examined it like it was a weapon and said, 'Leave the box with him.'

The sergeant gave both of us a bland look as I hefted it onto his counter. He didn't touch it as we left.

Benetti was sitting back in his chair as I entered. His desk was untidy: a pen lay on top of some papers; smoke from a cigarette in an ashtray climbed upwards and wavered. He didn't invite me to sit down on the chair opposite his desk. He said nothing.

'I understand you've arrested Gertie Maher,' I said, taking her travel document from my pocket. 'I think you should have this.' I held it out to him but he made no move to take it. I placed it on the desk in front of him. 'It's her permit to leave France.'

He didn't glance at it. 'Are you still pretending to be a diplomat?'

'No.'

'Where did you get it?'

'She left it behind her by accident. In a café where we'd had a drink. She told me she was leaving today or tomorrow.'

'You know she's a terrorist?'

'No, she's not.'

He opened the drawer on his desk and took out Chaim's revolver. 'Ever seen this before?'

'No.' I shook my head.

'You're sure?'

'Yes.'

He spun the chamber. 'Know how many live rounds are in it?'

I just stared at him.

'Like to play Russian roulette?' He pointed the gun at me.

I said nothing. Above his head I could see the cold blue eyes of le Maréchal watching me from his portrait.

Benetti spun the chamber again and put the gun back in the drawer.

'She'll be out of France in a day or two,' I said. 'On her way home to Ireland. It's all arranged.'

'Didn't you hear what I said? She's a terrorist.'

'She'll be gone in a day or two. She's not going to cause any trouble in France.'

'And why was she carrying a gun?'

'I don't know. Perhaps she found it.'

He gave me a crooked smile. 'Don't disappoint me now. You can do better than that.'

'I don't know where it came from.'

'Maybe you gave it to her yourself?'

'I don't have a gun. Why would I give her a gun?'

'For protection.'

'Against what?' He was playing with me, yet I had no choice but to go along with the game.

'Who knows? Against rival suitors?'

I dropped my head, happy to encourage the fiction that my only interest in Gertie was sexual.

'Or against other dangerous people who'd been using your apartment.'

'Nobody else was using my apartment.'

'Glad to hear that. Why did you let her use it?'

I gave him my best Gallic shrug, a man-to-man thing.

He shook his head at me as if I was stupid beyond belief.

'Please let her go. Put her on a train to the Spanish border and let her go home. She has all the necessary papers. Please.'

'And the gun?' He pointed at the drawer.

'You have it. It can't cause any trouble.'

He stared at me as if he was considering what I had said. I held his gaze, pleading. Then he shook his head.

'Can I see her at least?'

'Touching,' he said, picking up the permit and looking at Gertie's staid photo. 'What do you see in her? Especially when you're living in sin with the much lovelier Mlle Delmas.'

'Just five minutes.'

He sat forward, tossed Gertie's travel permit onto a pile of papers at the side of his desk, and picked up his pen. 'She's gone,' he said, without looking at me. 'On a train to the Occupied Zone. The Gestapo likes to meet confirmed terrorists in person.'

I took a deep breath as I stepped out onto Boulevard Victor Hugo. I had half-expected to end up in a cell again but, instead, had emerged without anything to worry about personally. It was clear Benetti no longer had any official interest in me, not even in pressuring me over the arrest of an armed woman in my flat. He had surprised me once more, although I knew in my heart the real reason I was still free. It was because of Solange and whatever was going on between her and Benetti.

I didn't know what to think about that yet. And any relief at walking out of Benetti's office was removed by the thought of Gertie in the hands of the Gestapo. Her chances of survival were slim. Linqvist couldn't help her there. O'Casey was her only hope because Ireland still had diplomatic relations with Germany but his prospects of securing her release were minimal. I shouldn't have given her the gun; I should have ignored her demands. I had known she was too impetuous for her own good and it would now lead to her execution.

I went back to the Café du Raisin and put through another call to O'Casey. There was no need to cover up what I was talking about this time, so we spoke in English. I told him Gertie had been arrested; the police claimed she had had a gun; and she had been sent to the Occupied Zone.

'Where?' he demanded.

'I don't know. I presumed Paris but I don't know.'

'That's not much help,' he said in an exasperated tone.

'M. Benetti at the Sûreté office in Nice can tell you.'

There was what sounded like a 'humph' but it might have been a distortion on the phone line. '*Cad in ainm Dé a bhí á dhéanamh léi*?' What, in the name of God, was she doing?

'*Níl fhios agam*,' I pretended ignorance. I considered telling him to talk to Linqvist but that might only muddy the already muddy waters if O'Casey didn't know she was an American agent. He might simply wash his hands of her case then.

Mrs Mac poured me a beer when I finished the call and I stood at the zinc staring into the glass and discouraging conversation. I couldn't see what else I could do for Gertie: she was beyond my help at this stage. I should try and alert her Jewish friends to her arrest but I didn't know any of them or how to contact them. The only people I had met her with were the ones to whom she had returned jewellery in the hotel near the station.

Mrs Mac put another glass in front of me when I had finished the first one. She shook her head at me. 'You have to talk to Solange,' she said, folding her arms on her stomach in a gesture that brooked no dispute.

'Ah, Jesus,' I muttered. 'Not now.'

'Yes, now,' she insisted. 'You can't string her along for ever. You have to do the decent thing.'

I glowered at her and she glowered back. 'She can't wait for ever,' she added.

'Now's not the time,' I said. 'I don't even have a job.'

'Now might be your last chance,' she snapped back.

'What do you mean?'

She paused, undecided. 'You're both running out of time.'

I shook my head, indicating that I knew that that wasn't really what she was thinking. It was clear that Solange had been talking to her again and I doubted that the subject was the ticking biological clock. Or, at least, not that alone.

'Listen,' she said in a more conspiratorial tone. 'I'm sorry your lady friend has been arrested.'

'How did you know that?' I shot back in surprise.

'Marty,' she said with exaggerated patience, 'didn't I ever tell you a café is a news exchange?'

'She's not my lady friend in the way you mean it.'

She raised a placatory hand. 'I didn't mean anything.'

I calmed down, giving her credit for not reminding me that she had told me Gertie was trouble. I drained my glass and went to pay her but she waved away the money. 'I'll get you another time,' she said. 'When you're rich again.'

I thanked her and told her I'd be back in a little while.

I went up to the hotel near the station to which Gertie had taken me with the jewellery they had stolen back from some shop. I knocked on the top floor door we had visited and an elderly woman I didn't recognize answered. I asked her if she knew the Irishwoman called Gertie or her friend Chaim. She didn't know what I was talking about. I wasn't sure she even understood my French. And I realized that I didn't know what name Gertie had been using with the refugees. Or even what her real name was. I apologized to the woman and left.

Bad news probably spread as rapidly among the refugees as it did through Mrs Mac's café, I told myself as I headed back there.

Jean-Luc was waiting for me in the café and threw his arms around me in a bear hug. 'Thank you,' he muttered in my ear.

'For what?' I asked when he released me.

He ignored my question. 'What'll you have to drink?'

We got two beers and sat down at the table by the window. 'Thank you for not denouncing me,' he explained.

'For fuck's sake. You thought I'd denounced you?'

'I know you didn't. I wouldn't be here if you had.'

I shook my head in disgust at the idea that he had even considered me as an informer. 'I mean,' he added, 'if you'd told that Benetti bastard any of my loose talk about assassinating people I'd never have been released. Could have been shot. It doesn't take much these days.'

'I can't believe you thought I'd had you arrested.'

'I didn't,' he said earnestly. 'That's what I'm trying to tell you.'

'It sounds the other way around. That you thought I did and then realized I didn't when they didn't accuse you of plotting to assassinate a Luftwaffe major or whatever he is.'

He leaned back in his chair and studied me from the greater distance. 'Why are you trying to twist what I'm telling you?'

'I've been having a difficult day,' I said. His experience and casual reference to being shot jarred with what I feared faced Gertie. I knew that he didn't know anything about her and I wasn't about to tell him. But it wasn't fair to take out my frustrations on him. 'Did they give you a hard time?' I added by way of apology.

'For the first couple of days. After that they left me alone until the bruises faded and then they threw me out.'

'Where did they keep you?' I wondered if they might have taken Gertie to the same place, despite what Benetti had said about the Occupied Zone.

'A camp near Toulon.'

'Did they have women there too?'

'No. Why?'

I gave a dismissive shrug. The café was beginning to fill up with the after-work crowd. Henri Tillon and his acolytes had come in without my noticing and were at their end of the bar. Claude, the printer from next door, passed by, ignoring us as though he had never seen either of us before. Jean-Luc offered me a fake cigarette and I shook my head. He lit it and the rancid smoke drifted across the table. 'I'm sorry about what happened at the studio,' he said. 'That's been sorted out now. You can come back to work tomorrow.'

'Thanks,' I said without enthusiasm. Or, more accurately, with mixed feelings. I hadn't expected to be reinstated and I wasn't sure I wanted to be in the circumstances.

'You've got another job?' he asked, picking up on my misgiving.

I shook my head but I wasn't going to explain my lack of enthusiasm to him. My job was being handed back to me at the grace and favour of the communist-controlled union. And I didn't want to be beholden to the party or to anyone else.

'Then come back to work,' he said as if it was a straightforward offer.

'I'll think about it.'

'What's there to think about? I thought you liked working there?'

'I did, but I didn't like the way I was thrown out. Being boycotted and shunned by my workmates like I was some kind of pariah. For something I didn't do.'

'I know, but it's been put right now. I've put it right.'

'Thanks,' I said with more enthusiasm, recognizing that I had to make some concession if our friendship was to survive this episode. 'I appreciate it. I really do.'

'Good. I'll wait for you at the gate at six in the morning. We'll go back to work together.'

It was late when I got home, slightly drunk. 'You're lucky your dinner isn't entirely ruined,' Solange said. 'It's *bouillaibaisse*. Or what has to pass for it these days.'

She took a covered plate from the oven and placed it on the table and lifted the cover off with an oven cloth. Steam rose in a spicy swirl and I realized how hungry I was. 'Smells great,' I said.

'There are no mussels and only one type of fish,' she said in the upset tone of a thwarted perfectionist as she sat down opposite me. 'And no Pernod, of course. Or lots of other ingredients.'

She watched as I ate. I made appreciative noises and told her about Jean-Luc's offer that I could have my job back. I had agreed to meet him at the studio the next morning but Solange's face darkened when I spelled out my reservations about going along.

'What is the matter with you?'

'What do you mean? You don't see my point?'

'No, I don't.'

'If I go back now, I'll owe them my livelihood and be seen as one of them. Which means they can demand anything they like of me. And they will. That's the way they work. I've seen it before in Hollywood. The writers who were pressured to have their scripts approved first by the party.'

'You're not a writer,' she pointed out. 'Jean-Luc's doing you a favour. As a friend.'

'Even if he is, the party won't see it like that.'

'So what will they make you do? Cause bulbs to blow?'

I laughed as if I agreed with what she thought was the ridiculousness of her suggestion. But sabotage wasn't beyond the party if it suited its agenda. And there were many other demands it could make. 'Anyway,' I said, 'I've agreed to go back.'

I finished my dinner and she topped up our wine glasses. 'Why have you become so suspicious?' she asked.

'These are suspicious times. Dangerous times.'

'You didn't use to be until recently.'

'Things are getting worse.'

'It's that Irish woman, isn't it?' It was an accusation rather than a question.

I shook my head.

'Are you in love with her?'

'What? Don't be ridiculous,' I snapped back, surprised but not altogether surprised after what Mrs Mac had said. And that she might think so after all my late nights recently.

'Why was she living in your flat?'

'She had nowhere else to go. I told you the man from the Irish legation asked me to look after her while she was waiting to go back to Ireland.'

'Did he tell you she was a terrorist?'

'Who told you that? Benetti?'

She didn't say anything, but her silence was confirmation in itself. 'Are you in love with him?'

She looked as shocked as if I had slapped her. Her face crumpled and tears began to run silently down her cheeks.

'I'm sorry,' I said. 'I just don't know what's going on at the moment.'

'I don't either.' She tried to wipe away the tears with her fingers but they kept coming.

'There's nothing between Gertie Maher and me, other than what I told you.'

'She's a terrorist.'

'No, she's not. Benetti is a liar.'

'Then why did she have a gun?'

'It wasn't hers. It belonged to a refugee she was helping.'

'Why does a refugee have a gun? And how was she helping him?'

I sighed but part of me urged caution, aware that anything I said might find its way back to Benetti. 'It's what I said. These are suspicious times. Everybody is becoming more and more suspicious. And jumping to conclusions.' A thought struck me and I tried to divert the conversation away from Gertie. 'Like your poison letters. Have you had any more of them?'

'One,' she said.

'What did it say?'

'Same as before.' She shrugged. 'That I'm an immoral whore. A disgrace to my religion and country.'

'I'm sorry.'

'You should be.' She attempted a smile. Her tears had stopped but her cheeks still glistened with their tracks. 'That is *your* fault.'

'Why didn't you tell me about it?'

'What's the point? It doesn't matter. I won't be getting any more.'

'How do you know?'

She hesitated. 'I told Benetti about it and he insisted I give it to him. He sent someone around to collect a writing sample from everyone in the building.' She paused again. 'I didn't know he was going to do that. I wouldn't have given it to him if I'd known.'

'What did he find?'

'I don't know. If he found out who it was, he didn't say. All he said was that they wouldn't bother me again.'

Typical Benetti, I thought. The kind of thing he probably loved. He didn't have to go to the trouble of comparing the handwriting, of actually doing anything. The culprit would now be living in fear of an early morning knock on the door and unlikely to send another poison letter.

'Is he still promising to get your brothers freed?' I asked, assuming that was Benetti's hold on her. 'You know it's another of his lies. He couldn't do it even if he really wanted to. You think the Germans pay any attention to a Vichy secret policeman?'

A tear ran down her left cheek and she swept it away with her finger. I hoped she wasn't going to start crying again. 'He says he's in love with me,' she said.

It was my turn to feel like I'd been slapped in the face. It was what I had feared, although I didn't think for a moment that love had anything to do with Benetti's motivation. But it was still a shock to hear Solange confirm it.

'He says he's obsessed with me. Can't stop thinking about me,' she went on. 'He keeps turning up outside Signora Mancini's villa and insisting on driving me home.'

I gave a hollow laugh at the man's transparent cynicism. 'Is he married? With children?'

'Why should that bother me?' she retorted with a touch of bitterness. 'I'm an immoral whore, a disgrace to my country.'

'For fuck's sake,' I muttered and went around the table and knelt by her side and put my arms around her. 'I didn't mean you should feel guilty but that he should.' Even as I said it, I knew that the idea of people like Benetti feeling guilty was risible.

She rested her head on my shoulder and began to sob quietly. We stayed like that for a while until her sobs stopped and my knees began to hurt. I suggested we should lie down. We went into the bedroom, undressed quickly, and lay down holding each other. We remained silent, each lost in our own thoughts. My mind was in turmoil but I tried to calm it down, stop it simply cursing Benetti, and tried to sift calmly through what was going on.

It wasn't the prospect of freeing her brothers that Benetti was using as leverage but my freedom. It was clear to me now that the only reason I was at liberty was Benetti's desire to seduce Solange. The painful question was whether my liberty indicated that he had already done so, or whether it meant that he was still trying. Her tears made me fear the worst. Either way, he had put her in a terrible position; it could only be a matter of time before she succumbed or he took his revenge on me. The bastard had turned the tables on us. He had tried at first to use her to get me to spy on

Jean-Luc and others at La Victorine. Now he was using my freedom to force Solange to have sex with him.

# Eighteen

Solange woke me early the next morning and we swapped the declarations of love we should have made the night before. We followed them with the physical act itself, which further eased the tensions between us. 'You'd better get up,' she said as I dozed afterwards. 'You'll be late.'

'I think I prefer unemployment.'

'Go.' She pushed me out of the warmth.

I dressed quickly, cleared my dirty plate from the kitchen table, and had a quick cup of fake coffee. It was still dark outside, with no sign yet of the new day, as I walked around Castle Hill. The roads were empty and the town was dark as I came over the brow of the hill. The streetlights were all out and the Jetée-Promenade stood in the water like an elaborate sandcastle that had defied the incoming tide. I passed the Hotel Suisse and wandered casually along the edge of the footpath as if I was about to cross the road into the Cours Saleya. There was nobody around but I wasn't taking any chances of being spotted walking around the bench to check for a response from the American agent.

There was a horizontal chalk mark across my vertical one, which meant that the rendezvous was agreed for the next Monday or Thursday. And today was Thursday. Jean-Luc would have to go to work without me.

I crossed into the Cours Saleya where there were more signs of life. Early traders were preparing their stalls, setting out bric-a-brac from barrows and carts. I meandered among them, wasting time looking at the tired remnants of other lives. I found a spot among the stall-owners at the zinc of the first of the square's cafés to open and had another fake coffee with a piece of bread and jam. Eventually it was time for the morning bus to Monaco and I made my way to the terminus and joined the queue.

There were few buses to Monaco or anywhere else these days and the bus was packed. Although I had been there in plenty of time, I had to stand as it climbed the edge of Mont Boron and swerved its way around the twists and turns of the Basse Corniche. The driver preferred speed over stability and there was little traffic to slow him down. The sun was well up by now and glistened off the blue sea like a peacetime postcard. After Beaulieu-sur-Mer I began to look out for the stop at La Petite Afrique.

It was a relief to get off the bus. I stood by the cliff edge inhaling the clean air to settle my queasiness and admiring the view. Nothing broke the surface of the water as far as the horizon and there was a pleasant whiff of some flower or shrub I didn't know in the stillness. The cliff continued up on the other side of the road, dotted by the red roofs of mansions settled back amongst the outcrops of rocks and green foliage.

I was too early for the rendezvous and strolled along the road. A bicycle passed by but there was no traffic otherwise. The peacefulness would have been perfect but for my thoughts. I was still thinking through the implications of all that had occurred during the previous days and, more importantly, trying to work out what to do next. I had to go back to work at the studio in spite of my reservations. That was the easy decision. Self-employment had not been an instant success, especially given the difficulty of finding materials nowadays. Which brought me on to Gerard and the police raid on the traders and black marketeers at the Cours Saleya. It was probably paranoia to think that that was aimed at me; it would have been simpler for the police to let me collect the wire and then arrest me. But still, there was an uneasy thought that it was personal. Which raised questions about Gerard and his activities. He obviously had black market connections but was he a police informer as well?

Then there was Gertie. The thought of her made my heart sink. There was nothing I could do for her, other than what I was here to do now, send a message to Linqvist through his local agent. I didn't think he could do anything to save her either but I would have exhausted all my possible courses of actions. Unless … .

No, I shook my head involuntarily. That was a totally crazy idea. I couldn't ask Solange to plead Gertie's case with Benetti. For one thing, that would confirm her suspicions. For another, I knew the price he would exact for going along with it. For a third, it was probably beyond his powers to save Gertie if he had handed her to the Gestapo.

Which brought me to my main dilemma of the moment: Solange. Yes, I loved her. No, I didn't want to lose her. But could we overcome our mutual suspicions and the manipulations of others? Marriage was an option, but would it deter Benetti? Unlikely. Even if it did, and he abandoned his pursuit of Solange, what revenge would be then take on me, on us? Everything I knew and had heard about him told me he was vindictive as well as manipulative, not someone to accept defeat graciously. He would react violently to being thwarted, however it was done.

The obvious answer to all my troubles was to get out of Nice and take Solange with me. She didn't want to go to Ireland, even if O'Casey's offer to provide me with the necessary documents still stood, which was questionable. She might be tempted by the bright lights of America but Linqvist had made it clear that was not on offer until after the war. If it ever ended. And there was no knowing what shape the world would be in by then. Either way, time was not on our side.

I stopped and leaned on the wall and closed my eyes. I felt the sun on my face and heard the chirping of birds and smelt the flowers. All the components of peace, but peace had never seemed so far away.

The sound of a car engine dispelled the peace. I feared for a moment I had missed my contact but the car came from the direction of Nice. I checked my watch; I was still early but I hurried back to the bus stop and crossed the road to the rendezvous, the bus stop heading back towards Nice. I sat against a large rock which had been chipped away to create a space for the stop and waited.

At exactly 12.15 a black Rover with a Monaco licence plate came around the corner and coasted to a halt. The driver leaned across and wound down the passenger window. I could see a round face becoming a little jowly under a receding hairline.

'You could be waiting there a long time,' he said in English with an American accent.

'I was told there's a bus due at 12.20,' I said.

'That one's been cancelled this week.'

I opened the door and sat in. He held out his hand to shake hands. 'Good to meet you, Vincent,' he said, pronouncing the name the French way.

'And you, Charles.' I did likewise.

He let out the clutch and the car moved off. 'No matter how many times I drive it, I'm always impressed by the beauty of this road,' he said.

'You come to Nice often?' I wondered what his cover story was. He presumably lived in Monaco, which was a tiny dot of peace, unoccupied by any of the warring factions, and home to people from all of them. Rich people.

'Now and then,' he said non-committedly. 'What have you got for us?' We had clearly exhausted the small talk.

I told him about Gertie's arrest. He asked a few questions and appeared to know of her but not what had happened or anything of her activities.

'Can you let Max Linqvist know as soon as possible?' I concluded.

'Sure, but I don't know what he can do if she's in the Gestapo's hands.'

'I'm not convinced that she is. Why would Vichy hand her over to the Germans?'

'They're trying to ingratiate themselves more and more with the Nazis.'

'Still, it's worth checking it out with Vichy. Or their people here.'

'Agreed. I'll tell Max.'

We drove in silence through Beaulieu. He asked me what I thought about the mood of people in Nice. I told him they were becoming more impatient with the shortages that made daily life more difficult, and that the Maréchal's lustre as the saviour of France was fading fast.

'My local bookshop has the usual portrait of Pétain in his window above a row of books for sale,' I said. 'But the holder beneath it is empty but for a strip of paper saying '*vendu*'.

Charles laughed.

'I asked him what was the book that was sold out. He smiled and said it was a French matter.'

'I've heard of another place where they've surrounded the usual portrait with copies of *Les Miserables*,' Charles said. 'I'm told they were prosecuted.'

'Jokes are dangerous these days.'

He nodded as if this was all new to him, which it wasn't if he was paying even cursory attention to what was going on outside the enclave of Monaco.

'Anything else?' he asked.

'I need a weapon.'

He raised a surprised eyebrow at that. 'For what?'

'Protection.'

'Protection from what?'

I shrugged as if it was obvious. 'Just in case.'

He took his eyes off the road to appraise me. 'I hope you've not been watching too many movies,' he said.

'I don't go to many movies. Can I get a gun?'

'It's not time for that yet,' he said, repeating what Linqvist had told me.

'But if I need one urgently?'

'I can't imagine any circumstance in which you'd need one urgently. You're keeping your eyes and ears open. Nothing more.'

'But if I do?'

'We'll cross that bridge if we come to it.'

As we drove down into Nice, I emphasised again the importance of alerting the American legation at Vichy to Gertie's fate. He said he understood but I wasn't sure he did. I didn't mention Gertie's membership of the OSS. I doubted that he was one of them, though my doubt was based on nothing more than the fact that he was a decade or more older than me. I imagined the OSS as a young organisation in every sense.

'Is there a quicker way of getting in contact with you?' I asked as he brought the car to a stop near Place Massena in the centre of Nice.

'The present arrangement is fine. It worked well.'

'But if I need to contact you urgently?'

'There shouldn't be any emergencies.' He held out his hand for me to shake. 'A pleasure meeting you.'

I shook his hand and got out of the car. He did a u-turn and drove back the way we had come.

It was mid-afternoon by the time I reached the studio. Everyone was friendly, acting as if I'd been away on a planned holiday. 'You missed the champagne roll,' one of Jean-Luc's carpenter colleagues said, referring to the usual celebration that had taken place the week before when a certain point in the shooting had been passed. 'But it wasn't real champagne, of course.'

I found Jean-Luc at the back of the sound stage during a break in filming and apologised for not turning up that morning. 'Something came up,' I said without further explanation.

'Let's go for a walk before they start again,' he suggested.

We strolled around the lot in the sunshine, making small talk. I mentioned that we'd both missed the champagne roll. He said that the shoot was beginning to wind down. Marcel Carné was now concentrating on re-shooting scenes he was less than happy with. His assistant director, the young Italian, Antonioni, had taken a crew up to Tourrettes-sur-Loup to get some more exterior shots. There was talk of the wrap party to celebrate the end of filming being held in the Grand Hotel in Vence. I assumed that the purpose of our stroll was to demonstrate Jean-Luc's belief in my innocence to anyone who had doubts or hadn't already heard that I'd been cleared of informing.

A black Mercedes with the roof down stood outside the stars' dressings rooms. 'He's back,' I said. 'Arletty's German.'

'Been back for the past week, I'm told,' Jean-Luc said. 'By the way, the flic raided the print shop here last week looking for your poster.'

'My poster?'

He grinned. 'Your idea. Just as well I didn't ask the lads here to do it.'

'Did you tell Claude about the raid?'

'God, no. No need to give him sleepless nights.'

I was about to ask if Claude was a member of the party but held my tongue. I didn't want to know. And I certainly didn't want to give Jean-Luc, or anyone else, the impression that I was one of them now.

Benetti picked up Solange outside Signora Mancini's again that evening and she was upset when she came home. 'What am I going to do?' she asked as we embraced. I felt a surge of relief; she had answered the question I didn't want to ask. It was obvious from her reaction that she had not succumbed to his demands and did not intend to.

'Tell him to fuck off,' I said.

'And then he'll arrest you.'

'Maybe. Maybe not. He might be bluffing.'

'He says he has enough evidence to arrest you for helping that Irish terrorist.'

I let her description of Gertie pass without challenge this time. What Benetti said was undoubtedly true; the revolver with my fingerprints on it was in the drawer of his desk. But he could not prove that I knew what Gertie had been up to, though such legal niceties would not hold much water these days, especially not where terrorism was involved. 'If he does, he does,' I said with more fortitude than I felt. 'I'll tell him to fuck off for you.'

She stepped back and held me at arm's length and looked at me with a wan smile. 'Where's this tough guy coming from all of a sudden? Being back at La Victorine? Reading your novels?'

'That must be it,' I smiled, thinking of Charles' accusation about the movies earlier. Twice in one day I'd been told I was living in a fantasy world. Which was true. I had been living in my own fantasy world, not the one Solange or Charles thought, but the twilight one from which Gertie and Willi had woken me.

'Why don't you go and stay with your parents for a week or two?' I suggested, becoming serious again. 'Tell him your father is sick.'

'He won't believe that.'

'Doesn't matter. It'll make it clear to him you're going away. Getting away from him.'

'Then he'll arrest you.'

'I don't think so,' I lied. 'Once he does that, he's lost his hold on you. You'll never come back.'

'And be stuck on the farm for ever.' She gave me another wan grin. 'And I'd lose my job if I went away,' she added. 'Signora Mancini would find someone else to cook for her.'

'She can't fire you because your father is sick.'

'She has to eat.'

'She can find a temporary replacement. If the worst comes to the worst, what does it matter? I have a job again.'

'But you'll be in prison.' She gave me her earnest look and raised another fear. 'Or gone to Ireland.'

'I'm not going to Ireland without you.'

'Do you really want me to go?'

'Only if you want to.' She said nothing, clearly torn. She didn't want to go but it could solve her problem with Benetti. 'Besides,' I added, giving her an out, 'I'm not sure that offer of help still holds since I failed to do what the legation asked.'

She didn't display any signs of relief but I was sure she felt it. We went on debating the problem intermittently over dinner and afterwards, all the time ignoring the question that was at the heart of it. Marriage. At least, I was ignoring it and Solange never mentioned it either. It didn't seem to be the right time to raise it but I knew that was an excuse; it was never the right time for me. I wondered if that was part of my old life of drifting, of being on the run, of avoiding commitments. But was it part of my new life that was beginning to take shape?

I was thinking of Mrs Mac's latest lecture about doing the decent thing when I asked Solange if she had told Mrs Mac about Benetti.

'I didn't need to,' she said. 'Henri had told her about him.'

'Henri?' I repeated, momentarily confused.

'Henri Tillon. He says Benetti is making no secret of his interest, talking to his colleagues about me.'

'Jesus!' I said, taken aback. 'What did Mrs Mac say?'

Solange sighed. 'She blames you. Says it's all your fault.'

I restrained myself from cursing aloud.

'I don't blame you,' Solange added. 'I don't think it would make any difference to him if we were married.'

I gave her a grateful hug but my mind was elsewhere. Tillon's revelation explained the anger behind Mrs Mac's latest lecture. And it also added to the danger of our situation. If Benetti was making his sexual desires public, it would be all the more difficult to get him to back off. He would retaliate viciously to a public humiliation if he failed in his quest.

'Henri says he's married with two children but has had a string of affairs,' Solange was saying. 'His wife knows about them but doesn't care because they never last for very long.'

Great, I thought. He just wants to seduce her and dump her. One of those guys who wants to show off his prowess and his power. There was no shortage of them in the movie business but there they didn't have the power to take away someone's freedom, only careers and livelihoods.

'This is all Tillon's fault, you know,' I said. 'He's the one who got us into this mess. Using my request for help over the abortion letter to pressure me to inform on my colleagues.'

Solange shook her head, disbelieving. 'Henri wouldn't do that.'

'He did. He told Benetti about it and the next thing he presented me with a list of people to spy on or else you would be investigated for having an abortion.'

She stared at me, absorbing this information. 'I can't believe Henri did that.'

'It's true.'

'But he's Madame Bonnard's lover,' she said.

'Tillon? Mrs Mac's lover?' I didn't believe I had heard her correctly.

'You knew that.'

I shook my head.

'Martin,' she said, shaking her head, 'are you blind?'

'Obviously,' I muttered bitterly. I had known Mrs Mac nearly as long as I'd been in Nice and come to see her almost as a mother figure. Maybe that was why I had never looked on her as someone having an affair. My mind flicked back over numerous encounters with the two of them; nothing gave any hint of an intimate relationship. She treated Tillon as a regular customer; he treated her formally as the café owner, Mme Bonnard. 'How long has this been going on?' I asked.

'Years,' Solange said. 'Since shortly after Lucien died, I think. Henri was first on the scene of the accident and had to tell her about it. He was very helpful to her afterwards. He's always watched out for Gerard. Kept him out of trouble.'

'How long have you known about it?'

'A few years. Some time after we got together and I got to know Mrs Mac.'

'And you never told me?'

'I ...' She looked confused. 'I thought you knew. Knew before I did.'

I felt like a fool. How could I not have known? But Solange partly answered my unspoken question. 'They are very discreet,' she said. 'I found out by accident one morning when I went back with her after early Mass and he was in the kitchen, half-dressed. Mrs Mac swore me to secrecy. She doesn't want any gossip.'

And never reveals all she probably knows, I thought bitterly.

# Nineteen

I threw myself into work over the next few days, checking everything unnecessarily, tidying up stores, and responding quickly to every beck and call. The shoot was running smoothly now that the end was in sight. Everyone had accommodated each other's foibles. The younger actors were no longer overawed by their famous elders. The screen lovers, Alain Cuny and Marie Déa, were still in love off-screen but the old hands declared that it wouldn't last beyond the wrap party. Arletty had become almost indulgent with Jules Berry's approximations of his lines. Berry himself was in high good humour after a winning streak at the casinos. And everyone had learned how to live with Marcel Carné's moods and perfectionism.

I picked up a Dashiell Hammett novel from my second-hand book dealer but I couldn't concentrate on it. My own plotting kept intruding. Benetti left Solange alone. She hoped he had given up his pursuit but I suspected he was busy pursuing some unfortunate in connection with his work. I kept my conversations with Mrs

Mac light and casual, telling her the gossip from the set, and resisting the feeling that she had somehow betrayed me.

She was happy that I had got my job back but my attitude towards her had turned to mistrust. Her relationship with Tillon raised all sorts of questions. Had she known from the start that he was pressuring me to become a police spy? Had Gerard told Tillon about my attempt to buy black market wiring? Was he behind the cack-handed raid on the traders in the Cours Saleya? Was he – or, even worse, was she -- the one who had caused Gertie to be arrested?

That question had been nagging me for days: how had Benetti known that Gertie was in my apartment? Nobody knew she was there, as far as I was aware. Of course, somebody could have seen us, or at least her, entering it. More likely, somebody followed us there. But few people knew about my connection with Gertie. Mrs Mac and Gerard were prominent among them. But I couldn't bring myself to believe that she had set Benetti on Gertie's trail through Henri Tillon. She had made no secret of her dislike and distrust of Gertie, but I found it difficult to accept that she would have gone to such lengths even if she thought she was protecting Solange.

Tête-à-têtes, I thought. That was how she referred to my meetings with Gertie. And that was how Benetti had referred to them when he questioned me. Was it a phrase passed on to him by Tillon who had heard it from Mrs Mac? Or was I seeing conspiracies where only coincidences existed? I didn't want to believe in this particular conspiracy.

Gerard was another matter. I could well believe that he had followed us to the rue de la Republique and tipped off Tillon and Benetti.

'Solange tells me you know about Benetti,' I said to Mrs Mac on one of the evenings I dropped in after work. The café was busy and

Tillon at the zinc with his colleagues. I had just told the man who had asked me to rewire his apartment that I couldn't get the necessary materials.

'He's a dangerous piece of work,' she replied. Which was all the more reason it was unlikely that she had told him about Gertie.

'But what can we do about him?'

'Amn't I blue in the face telling you what you should do?' she retorted.

'I don't think being married would stop him.' I forbore from pointing out that Tillon was married with children too. But that was different, Solange had explained when she told me. Tillon's relationship with Mrs Mac was a serious long-term affair.

'Just because another man has put his eye on her isn't a good reason for you not to do the right thing.'

'That doesn't help our immediate problem,' I muttered.

'I agree with you,' Mrs Mac said. 'She should go off to her parents for a while. Out of sight will be out of mind.'

'But she won't.' I was taken aback that Solange had told Mrs Mac about our conversation. Did she tell her everything? Was I the only one who didn't know what was happening around me?

'And you know why? Because she's afraid you'll be gone when she returns.'

'She said that?'

'Not in so many words.'

'So she didn't say that.'

'Don't you ever listen to what I tell you?' Mrs Mac raised her eyes to heaven. 'She's afraid you'll pack up and go back to Ireland as soon as her back is turned.'

'I don't know where she got that idea.'

'Because,' Mrs Mac sighed, 'you won't do the decent thing.'

'I can't do that now. It'd look like I was only responding to Benetti. And it wouldn't deter him.'

'He's only a flash in the pan.'

'You just told me he's a dangerous piece of work.'

She sighed again. 'Well, he's that too.' She paused. 'You're becoming as contrary as Gerard.'

'Speaking of him,' I said, changing the subject, 'have you decided on a holiday in Ireland?'

'I told you already. He won't come and I won't go without him.'

'He'd be all right on his own here. He has someone to look after him.'

She gave me a sharp eye, wondering was I referring to Tillon, which I was.

'Doesn't he have friends among the Legionnaires?' I added rhetorically to confuse her.

'That's what I'm afraid of.' She gave me another suspicious look and stepped away to tend to another customer.

I ran in to Gerard on the rue Massena the next afternoon. Instead of walking by and ignoring me as usual, he stopped and said: 'Jacques wants to be paid for that wire.'

'I didn't get any wire from him.'

'He's at a loss because of you.'

'Not because of me,' I said. 'Because of your friends in the *flics*.'

I noted his surprise at the accusation. He glanced around to see if anyone had overheard us. 'You have to pay him,' he said quietly in English. 'He's demanding the money from me.'

This was a different Gerard, no longer the arrogant Legionnaire, more a nervous youngster. I wondered what he had got himself into. 'It's not your fault either,' I replied. 'Unless you had something to do with the police raid. Tell him it's an occupational hazard of being a black marketeer.'

'You don't understand.' There was an edge of pleading in his voice now. 'He's in one of the gangs.'

Of course he was. But I hadn't given a moment's thought previously to Jacques and his probable friends. Now I could expect a visit from some heavy-handed gangsters. 'Not your father's old friends?'

He shook his head.

'Won't they protect you?'

'Yes,' he agreed. 'That's why he wants you to pay up.'

'You told Henri Tillon about it, didn't you?'

He looked away and said nothing, confirming my suspicion. Passers-by circled around us, ignoring us.

'Why?' I demanded.

'He asked me to tell him what you were up to,' he said, still without looking at me.

'And you told him where Gertie Maher was staying?'

He went silent again, staring at the footpath.

'And did you tell him you were an accomplice to a murder?'

He squirmed and I thought he was about to walk off but he stayed put. 'Don't tell my mother,' he pleaded.

'Which bit?' I snapped back. 'That you're a murderer? A police informer? A black marketeer? A want-to-be gangster? Or a total idiot?'

'I didn't know that woman was a terrorist,' he said in a whiny voice.

'She wasn't, isn't, a fucking terrorist.'

'She had a gun.'

'And so had you. And your shooter friend. Are you terrorists too?'

'But we're on the side ---'

'Listen, you need to cop yourself on. Do what your mother tells you for once in your stupid life. Go to Ireland with her until all this sorts itself out.'

He looked like he was about to argue but then changed his mind. I was the one who had had enough of this conversation and moved off. 'What about the wire?' he asked after me, switching back to French to avoid drawing attention to us.

'Fuck the wire,' I said back over my shoulder but then turned back with a question. 'Who are Jacques' friends?'

'They operate above the station,' he said and added hopefully, 'You'll deal with it?'

I went on towards home wondering if Mrs Mac knew that her lover was using her son as a spy rather than looking out for him. I doubted it, but it was not impossible. She was caught in a terrible position with a man who was using her for his own ends whether she knew it or not. And even if she knew it, could she ditch him and risk her son losing whatever protection Tillon provided?

And now I could expect a visit from some gangsters as well as my other problems.

Solange's respite from Benetti's attentions was short-lived. I could tell the moment I got home that he was back. She looked like she had been crying. Her face was puffy and distraught. I held her in my arms. Neither of us said anything. There was nothing to say.

'He told me you're leaving the country,' she said later. 'You've been talking to the man from the Irish legation again.'

I gave a short laugh, surprised at his brazenness; he didn't mind me knowing that he'd been monitoring my phone conversations. It was what I had suspected, had even hoped, but I hadn't expected him to confirm it openly or to use it against me in this way. 'Yes,' I said, 'I've been talking to O'Casey about Gertie Maher's arrest. That's all. And I'm not sure he would help me go back to Ireland now even if I asked him.'

She looked at me, from eye to eye, as if she they were giving conflicting signals and she wasn't sure which one to believe.

'I'm not going anywhere without you,' I told her once again. 'But it would solve the problem if we could leave the country. Go somewhere else for a while. Ireland is the only option at the moment and even that's doubtful. America is another possibility but not till the war's over.'

'Why not?' The mention of America had created a flicker of interest.

'It's very difficult to get there now.'

'There are a lot of people trying.'

'Exactly,' I said, as if that explained the difficulty. She knew nothing of my relationship, such as it was, with Max Linqvist. And I wasn't going to tell her about it. 'If we could get to Ireland, we wouldn't have to stay there. We could move on to America.'

'Is that possible? Is it easier to get there from Ireland?'

I hesitated, unwilling to make a false promise. 'I don't know. But after the war, it should be.' I paused, trying to think this through. 'What I'm saying is that Ireland wouldn't be our final destination, just somewhere to escape to at the moment. We could move anywhere afterwards. We could even come back here.'

She didn't say no and I pressed on sensing a chink in her usual defences at the idea of leaving France, her family, and her POW brothers in Germany. 'We could go to Los Angeles. There's bound to be some of the old crowd in Hollywood who'd give me a job. I could teach you English while we're in Ireland and you'd be ready for a job too when we got to America. They'd love your accent as much as your cooking.'

A smile animated her pale face. 'Thanks,' she said as she put her arms around my neck and kissed me briefly. She knew as well as I did that this was a pipe dream. Or was it? The more I thought about it, the more feasible it seemed. I put to one side the risk involved in returning to America. That was all a long time ago now.

But my subconscious didn't think so: the dream came back that night. I was crossing the street in New York, walking towards the Italians, cocking the revolver by my side, opening fire as two of them began to get out of their car, still firing as one was pulled back in, they driving off, doors flapping against parked cars, me turning away satisfied at a job well done, and then hearing the shrill screams of a woman.

The screams woke me, my heart racing. There was no confusion in my mind about who she was this time. It was dark and Solange was breathing easily, still asleep. My first thought was to wonder that the screams hadn't woken her. But I hadn't paid any attention to them at the time either. I had heard them but ignored them, assuming the screamer was just a shocked witness. I was happy as I had walked away, happy that I had done my job.

But I hadn't really done my job of protecting the undercover offices of the Irish Hospital Sweepstakes. I had thwarted the Italians' robbery but the police followed the shooting with their own raid and bagged $100,000 and half-a-dozen people involved in the illegal lottery. Next day I was on a train, ordered to leave town immediately, and not stop until I got to the west coast.

And a headline on another passenger's newspaper as we steamed out of Grand Central explained the woman's screams: Girl, 4, Dead in Rival Mobs Shootout.

# Twenty

I had lunch in the canteen the next day with Jean-Luc and some of the regulars at La Victorine. The talk was about the wrap party and what might take the place of the film now near completion. Nobody relished the prospect of going back only to the weekly newsreels about the Maréchal's visits to villages and rural craftsmen, promoting the conservative values of *la France profonde*.

'Our poster girl,' somebody sneered, using the English phrase.

'Haven't you heard?' another asked. 'Pétain's dead.'

'Since when?'

'Three months ago. But nobody's told him yet.'

There was a general laugh. I was back in the fold, although some of those arrested with Jean-Luc were still detained and, by all accounts, not about to be freed in the foreseeable future. But Jean-Luc's support had cleared me of suspicion and confirmed for me his status in the party. I waited until the others had drifted away to ask him if he knew anything about a black market gang operating north of the main railway station.

He shook his head. 'Why?'

I told him of the wire saga, leaving out Gerard's involvement.

'I'll see what I can find out,' he said, aware that I was calling in a favour in repayment for my unfair punishment.

We were sitting by the window and Arletty and Hans-Jürgen Soehring sauntered by arm in arm in the sunshine as if they were boulevardiers parading down the Champs-Élysées. She had changed back into her medieval costume without the high headdress after lunch and he had on a double-breasted grey suit. They weren't talking but looked totally at ease in each other's company.

'You were right,' I said when they had gone out of sight. 'It really is outrageous that she can get away with such blatant collaboration.'

Jean-Luc shrugged and tapped ash off his cigarette into the ashtray.

'Posters aren't enough,' I added. 'Why don't you have him banned from the studio. Refuse to work with him hanging around.'

'And what about the other Germans here? The ones from Continental who are bank rolling this film?'

'Refuse to work with Arletty if he's here,' I suggested.

'You said it yourself before,' he sighed. 'She's too popular. It would only rebound on us.' He glanced around to make sure we weren't being overheard. 'We thought about strike action but it was turned down. We can't be seen to target her and we don't want to close down the film.'

'So you're doing nothing.'

'What do you suggest? A bigger poster?'

I shook my head. We stared at each other, both thinking the same thought, neither putting it into words.

***

To my surprise, Seamus O'Casey turned up in Nice the next day. He had left a message in Mrs Mac's saying that he was at the Hotel Suisse and wanted to talk to me.

'Did you talk to him yourself?' I asked Mrs Mac as she passed it on.

'I told him I wouldn't be going to Ireland after all.'

'Have you checked with Gerard again? Maybe he's changed his mind.' It was a forlorn hope but my last conversation with him might have had some effect.

She sighed, looking defeated. 'I have to face reality, Marty.'

I cut down the rue du Congrés to the Promenade in the dark. A cold wind from the west hurried me along the deserted esplanade. In front of me a small group of people crossed the road and headed into the casino on the Jetée-Promenade. I recognized Jules Berry and a few others from the set. One nodded to me and I returned a 'bonne chance'.

O'Casey was in the same small residents' lounge where I had met him before. He had two glasses on the table before him, one half full of whiskey, the other empty. His naturally cheerful face looked strained and tired. I took the seat opposite him and he produced a Jameson bottle from his briefcase and poured me a drink before passing over the water jug. I topped up the whiskey with a splash.

'What I don't understand,' he began, 'is why you haven't been arrested.'

That took me by surprise, raising all sorts of uncomfortable questions. For one thing it implied that I was a police informer who had shopped Gertie, perhaps even set her up for arrest. Here we go again, I thought, but decided to ignore the implications for the moment. 'What about her?' I demanded instead. 'Have you found her?'

He reached for his glass and took his time sipping some whiskey before replacing the glass. 'She's in a Vichy detention centre, awaiting trial,' he said at last.

That was a relief. Benetti had lied about the Gestapo but the important thing was that she could be freed; pressure could be put on the Maréchal's government, especially by the Americans. 'So you can get her out?'

'She's awaiting trial,' he repeated as if I hadn't heard him the first time. 'On serious charges. Why aren't you awaiting trial with her? The police say she was in your flat and she had your gun.'

'It wasn't my gun. And I don't live there,' I explained. 'I let her stay there because it was safer. You were the one who asked me to look after her. Remember?'

'I didn't mean for you and her to go on a crime rampage.'

'What are you talking about?'

'The gun,' he said. 'The police say it was used in at least one robbery and possibly others and God knows what else.'

'I didn't know that,' I said, not entirely truthfully. What I didn't know was that Chaim had fired a shot or shots during one or more of his robberies. Or that he may have shot someone. And that his gun could be linked to a specific crime or crimes. The gun that had my fingerprints as well as Gertie's on it. But if all it was linked to was the robbery of a jewellery store, that was almost a relief. Even these days that could hardly be classed as terrorism; just ordinary crime.

'Where did it come from?' O'Casey asked.

'She was minding it for some refugees she was trying to help.'

'Jesus Christ! You were supposed to stop her from doing things like that.'

'How was I to know she was doing things like that? You made it sound like I was to be her personal tourist guide, recommending things to do, places to see while she whiled away a week or two here.'

'What did she tell you?'

'About what?'

'What she was doing in France?'

'Nothing.' O'Casey knew very little about Gertie, I realized, certainly not that she was an American agent. He had been kept in the dark by his own bosses who, presumably, knew what she was. Or maybe not. 'You told me she was on her way home from Vienna. She met some Austrian refugees here she had known there,' I added, keeping to her cover story to try and draw him out.

'And?'

'And one of them asked her to mind that gun. I knew she was getting involved with these people and that wasn't a good idea. I tried to tell you that on the phone. That's why I suggested she move to a safe house where they wouldn't be able to reach her.'

'What's her real name?'

I tried to look surprised. 'What do you mean? Her real name? It isn't Gertie Maher?'

O'Casey gave me a disappointed look, knocked back the remainder of his whiskey and poured himself another one.

'Why do you think she has another name?' I asked while he added a careful amount of water.

He held out the whiskey bottle. I finished my drink and he poured me another. 'What are you up to here?' he asked while concentrating on my glass.

'Me? Nothing. You keep forgetting that you involved me in this, whatever it is. Not the other way around.'

'What did Max Linqvist tell you?'

'About what?'

'About her.'

'Nothing.'

'Or why he was interested in her?'

'Because she's an American citizen too. He's a diplomat same as you, looking after his citizens.'

'No he's not.' O'Casey sniffed. He was clearly disgruntled at being kept in the dark and ordered to do things without being given full explanations.

'What is he then?'

O'Casey shrugged. 'She's his problem now. I'm having nothing more to do with her.'

'Can he get her out?'

'I doubt it. She's going to jail. They say they have a cast iron case against her.'

'Have you talked to Pierre Benetti in the Sûreté here?'

He shook his head. 'Why should I? I've talked to the police chief.'

'Benetti's in charge of the case.'

'He's your contact here?'

The question was loaded with all sorts of implications but I responded to its face value. 'No. He's caused me a lot of trouble.'

'But he hasn't arrested you for harbouring a criminal,' O'Casey said, going back to his opening comment. 'At the very least.'

I cursed myself for walking into the trap and considered telling him the reason. I could tell him to mind his own business and walk out but I might need his help at some stage. It probably wasn't wise to burn this bridge to the outside world, however shaky it might be. 'Because he's trying to seduce my wife,' I said.

O'Casey looked like he thought I was pulling his leg, but he saw my face and realized I was serious. 'Surely that'd be another reason to arrest you. Get you out of the way.'

'It's the other way around. He's using my freedom to blackmail her.'

'Jesus.' He took another sip of his whiskey, staring at me while he absorbed that information. 'It's all a murky business,' he said at last. 'I'm sorry for getting you involved. I had no idea what was really going on.'

I accepted his apology with a nod. I wasn't going to tell him that he and Gertie Maher had nothing to do with my initial involvement with Benetti. Indeed, I could barely remember how this whole tangled affair had begun in the first place. 'Who is Gertie Maher?' I asked.

'She's a Jewish refugee whose family came to Ireland a few years ago and settled in Cork. Unfortunately, she's allowed herself to be manipulated by the Americans to do some dirty work for them.'

I doubted that Gertie allowed herself to be manipulated by anyone to do anything against her wishes. 'What dirty work?' I asked, eager to keep him talking now that he appeared ready to tell me something.

'I don't know exactly. And they're trying to use our good offices as genuine neutrals to help them with it. And Dublin goes along with it to try and stay on their good side.' The edge of bitterness to his voice made it clear that he didn't approve of the infringement of Ireland's strict neutrality or the instructions he was receiving from his headquarters.

I decided to strike while the iron was hot. 'Can you help me get back to Ireland if I need to go in a hurry?'

'Just yourself or you and your …? You're not married, are you?' There was no mistaking the disapproval in his voice. He probably supported Vichy's conservative travail, famille, patrie policies.

'No. But we could regularize that quickly.'

'You're afraid you're going to be arrested?'

'Yes. Because of Gertie Maher.'

'Something could be arranged. But it might not be that quick.'

'And for Madame Bonnard and her son?'

'She told me she no longer wants to go.'

'She'll change her mind if her son changes his.'

'Ah,' he sighed. 'That could a problem. Her son is French as well and of military age.'

'But there is no French army now; no conscription.'

'There's talk of the Germans pressuring Vichy to conscript young men into work battalions to be sent to Germany's factories and farms. The voluntary system isn't working, so they want to make it compulsory.'

A thought occurred to me. 'Do they know that Gertie is Jewish?'

'I don't think so. That wouldn't help her case.'

'How long do you think she'll get in jail?'

'I've no idea. A good few years, I'd imagine. It'd probably help if she pleaded guilty.'

'Can you get in to see her?'

'I've washed my hands of her now. It's up to the Americans to take care of her since they got her into trouble in the first place.'

And you got me into this trouble, I thought, but I saw from his face that he realized that, and I didn't need to spell it out.

I stepped out of the hotel and was hit by the cold wind sweeping along the bay. I was closing my jacket and tying my scarf as a figure stepped forward from the hotel's wall and said 'Mister" in English. He was about twenty and reminded me immediately of Chaim. 'I see you with Gerda,' he continued in English.

'I don't know any Gerda,' I replied but I knew whom he meant. So that was Gertie's other name. Whether it was her real one or not was anyone's guess.

'We need your help.'

My first instinct was to ignore him and walk away. That's what the old, and maybe wiser, Marty would have done. 'Where are you from?'

'Wien,' he said and then in French. 'Autriche.'

'Like Chaim.'

A smile of relief turned his face handsome and he relaxed visibly. 'Yes, yes.'

'How can I help you?'

'Guns.'

I shook my head. 'I don't have any guns.' I could have added that a gun had got Chaim killed and Gerda arrested but I doubted that he would understand my French or English. He seemed to have practised his opening lines in English much as I had practiced my phone conversations in Irish with O'Casey.

'Chaim's gun,' he said. So he was one of Chaim's associates, probably a fellow jewellery robber.

'The police have it. Gerda was arrested with it.' I wasn't sure he understood.

'They kill us,' he said and added something in agitated German that I didn't understand. I raised my hands to stop him. He took a deep breath and closed his eyes, searching for the right words. 'Rafle,' he said in French.

'A round-up,' I repeated in English. 'You think they're going to round you up?'

'Kill us.' He nodded repeatedly.

I didn't see how I could help him. The Americans weren't prepared to hand out guns. Maybe the British were. And there had to be a lot of French arms about after the disarray of their army. I remembered Jean-Luc's story about a British submarine landing arms. He said it wasn't true at the time but maybe there was something to it.

'How can I contact you?' I asked. He looked blankly at me and I tried again. 'Where you live?'

'Pension Mimosa, rue de Belgique.' He pointed at himself and said Aviv.

I repeated his name and he put out his hand and shook mine. 'Thank you, thank you,' he said with a smile.

'*De rien*,' I muttered to myself as he strode away into the old town.

Solange was packing her suitcase when I got home. She had been crying and I asked her what had happened.

'I'm going home,' she said.

'What happened?'

'Nothing.' She was folding a pullover and didn't look up.

'Tell me.'

'Nothing.' She took a skirt from the pile of clothes on the bed and began folding it. She still didn't look at me. 'I've had enough of it, that's all.'

I didn't believe her. Something had clearly happened to upset her even more than usual. I put my arms around her from behind, pinioning her arms and stopping her folding. 'Tell me.'

She dropped the skirt on the bed and turned within my arms and buried her face in my shoulder. 'I can't take it any more,' she said, barely audible. 'I don't want to leave the house in the morning. I don't want to leave Signora Mancini's after work. I spend the whole day dreading the sight of his car at the gate. And then his pretence that we're going out together. Talking like we are a couple. And,' she hesitated, 'pawing me.'

I held her tighter.

She took a deep breath. 'He said he's found a place for us to go. He didn't want us to go to one of those cinq-à-sept hotels. He wanted somewhere nice and he's found it now.' She began to sob quietly into my shoulder.

'You're right to go home,' I said.

'I'm sorry.' She straightened up and looked at me. 'He'll arrest you now.'

'No, he won't,' I said with more bravado than I felt. I thought of going with her but quickly realized that that would not work; it would give Benetti an official reason to pursue both of us to Provence. 'That's all a bluff.'

'You really think so?'

'I'm sure of it. That's the kind of bully he is.' But I knew that he was really the type of vindictive bully who was likely to carry out his threats. The odds were that I would be arrested. With a bit of luck the worst that would happen was that I would be charged with aiding an armed robber and spend a few years in jail. That is, if O'Casey was right about what was facing Gertie Maher. Prison would not be the worst place to be while this war worked itself out one way or another. Anyway, it was the least of what I deserved and had been running from for years. 'Don't worry.' I smiled. 'You're doing the right thing. Have you told Signora Mancini?'

'No. Can you do that for me?'

'Of course.'

We maintained our brave faces the next morning as I saw Solange off at Nice Ville station. She said she'd be back in a month or less. We promised to write and she insisted I stay in her apartment and I said I would. I wondered as the train puffed and clanked out of the station if I would ever see her again. Not that I doubted her return, but I was far from certain I'd be at liberty when she came back.

The stench of the dirty coal smoke was still in my nostrils as I left the station and crossed rue de Belgique on my way back to Mrs Mac's. I looked up and down the street but couldn't see the Pension Mimosa where Aviv had said he was staying. Anyway I didn't need to know where it was until I had something to tell him.

'It's probably for the best,' Mrs Mac said when I told her that Solange had gone to her parents'. I didn't need to spell out the real reason but I emphasized that everybody was to be told her father was ill. Benetti wouldn't believe it but he couldn't be certain that it wasn't true.

'It's outrageous the way that fellow's allowed to carry on,' I added, hoping to plant a thought in her head. 'Someone should report him to his superiors for abusing his position.'

'Indeed, it is,' she agreed. With a bit of luck, Henri Tillon would get a lecture from her later. And he might even act on it, though I doubted it.

'I have to phone Signora Mancini to tell her,' I said.

'Do you want me to do that? I know someone who could stand in for Solange.'

'Thanks. That would be better.'

I left her to make the call and headed for the Hotel Suisse to see O'Casey. The fact that he had talked to the local police chief about Gertie suggested that he might be able to put a spoke in Benetti's wheel, if I could persuade him to complain about Benetti's behaviour. I wasn't sure O'Casey would do me any favours but his apology for involving me in this mess was a hopeful sign. However, the receptionist said he had already checked out with his luggage.

At the studio I found Jean-Luc sitting in the open on a bench by a stage wall. I sat down beside him and neither of us said anything. The sun was hot and I closed my eyes and felt it on my face. A gentle breeze kept the temperature pleasant.

'You shouldn't have any problems with that criminal gang,' Jean-Luc said after a minute. 'They've been warned off.'

'Thanks,' I replied without opening my eyes. 'That's a relief.'

'They're not well entrenched yet. Not like the one in the port.'

We lapsed into silence again. I wondered why Gerard had used them but then dismissed the speculation. I had enough problems to worry without trying to work out what he might have been up to. I opened my eyes and straightened up on the bench. 'Do you have any contacts among the refugees? The Jewish refugees?'

A look of irritation flitted across Jean-Luc's face. 'Are you looking for another favour?'

I ignored the question. 'One of them approached me, looking for weapons.'

'Why'd he approach you?'

'A friend of mine was helping them.'

'The woman who was arrested in your flat,' Jean-Luc said, happy to surprise me with his knowledge of something I hadn't told him about.

'Yes.' It was a relief not to have to explain Gertie to him. 'You mentioned a British submarine landing arms on the coast.'

He gave a short laugh. 'Wishful thinking.'

'It hasn't happened?'

'Not that I know of. Even if it did, I doubt they'd be giving weapons to us. Maybe to de Gaulle's crowd.'

'The refugees are worried about a round-up,' I said. 'Want to be able to fight back.'

Jean-Luc lit one of his make-believe cigarettes. Two of his fellow carpenters went by carrying a trestle table. 'Some people have to do all the work around here,' one of them shouted at us in a good-natured tone.

'There are some comrades among the refugees,' Jean-Luc said quietly when they had passed by. 'They're right to be worried. But a few guns won't be of much use to him. Only get them killed.'

'Perhaps they'd prefer that than going quietly. Their decision.'

He turned sideways to look at me full-on. 'What's happened to you? You were a pacifist a few weeks ago. Or was that just a cover?'

'I'm tired sitting on the fence. Simple as that.'

'That doesn't sound simple at all.'

Nor was it, but I didn't intend to go into that with him. 'What are you going to do for your comrades among the refugees?'

'We're discussing that.' He turned away to rest his back against the wall.

'Do they want guns too?'

He shrugged, avoiding the direct question. 'We're trying to find places to hide them,' he said after a pause. 'Perhaps that's what you should do for your friends too.'

'Where would I find a place to hide them? I tried that recently and it didn't work out well.'

We lapsed into silence again. Jean-Luc leant forward to drop the butt of his cigarette on the gravel between his legs. He rubbed it into pieces and buried them with his heel.

'You seem to have turned into the pacifist now,' I remarked.

'What makes you say that?'

'You sound like an accommodation officer. Discussing where to hide your comrades.'

He glanced sideways at me with the hint of a smile and then straightened himself up on the bench and looked around. 'Are you serious about Soehring?' he demanded.

I nodded.

'And what about your previous qualms? That the Germans will execute innocent hostages?'

'It's a risk,' I said. 'But they can't do it here unless they take over this area from Vichy and the Italians. And I doubt they'll do that.'

'And Vichy can't take reprisals against innocent Frenchmen. But that won't stop them rounding up people and interning them.'

'Better than shooting innocent people randomly.'

'And losing the Maréchal more support,' he said, satisfying himself that it was a worthwhile move, forcing the enemy to retaliate and over-react, illustrating the depth of their collaboration with the invader. 'How would you do it?'

'Toss a grenade into the front of his car if the roof was down.' I said, matter-of-factly. 'Or walk up to him in the street and shoot him in the head.'

'He'd have to be on his own. Especially in the car. ... Without her.'

'Agreed.'

'Would you do it here? On the lot?'

'The easiest place to do it.'

'But not the best,' he said after a moment's thought. 'We'd all be rounded up. You'd never get away. I take it you're not planning a suicide mission?'

I noted his assumption that I'd be the shooter or bomber and the way he was distancing himself from what had originally been his idea. But I didn't blame him for that. It would be a high risk operation and the prospects of getting away with it were slim. 'No,' I replied.

'They'd probably close down the studio if we did it here.'

'And we'd all be out of a job.'

'That'd be the least of our worries.' He paused. 'You're not serious about this, are you?'

'Yes, I am. Deadly serious.'

'And you're willing to do it?' He searched my face, trying to determine how genuine I was.

'Yes,' I said. 'I'll do it.'

# Twenty-One

I woke up in the dark and turned on the light to see my watch: it was just after four o'clock. I clicked the light off again and lay there wondering if Jean-Luc was also having a sleepless night. It wouldn't surprise me if he was agonizing about my offer, worrying that I was an agent provocateur enticing him and his comrades into a conspiracy that could land them all in front of a firing squad. If I was him, that's what my suspicious mind would be thinking: that his arrest, release, and my change of heart were all part of a trap masterminded by Benetti.

It wouldn't surprise me if he distanced himself from the plot. It wouldn't surprise me either if it came to nothing. There was every chance that Benetti would implement his threat to lock me up as soon as he realized that Solange had fled. Which wasn't the worst prospect, as long as O'Casey was correct and Gertie faced prosecution only for a robbery and not for terrorism. In which case the worst they could bring against me was a charge of helping her.

I shook off these night-time thoughts, opened the window and folded back the shutters, half-expecting to see a black Citroën on the quay outside. It was cold and the tide was out, leaving the boats in the harbour lolling loosely at their moorings.

I had a quick breakfast and left the apartment. The streets were dark and empty with hardly any traffic. I braced myself at the sound of the few vehicles out, waiting for each one to slow and stop to pick me up but none did.

The dawn was beginning to seep through the dark as I arrived at the studios. Work began with the young Italian, Antonioni, shooting some linking scenes. I cut and rejoined a cable on an arc lamp that had been pulled and pushed to breaking point. Marcel Carné turned up to re-shoot a few scenes he wasn't happy with. In the first one Arletty was remonstrating with the devil, Berry, swirling around him with the intense physical delivery of her lines that made her screen presence so powerful. The cameraman said something to Carné who shouted 'Cut'. Arletty stopped in mid-flow and returned an outraged 'Quoi?' at him. 'You're too close to the edge of the frame,' he told her. She threw up her hands but returned to her starting position while Berry risked a patronising smirk.

Jean-Luc looked in as the mid-morning break began and indicated to me to follow him outside. 'You still serious about this?' he asked as we strolled towards the canteen.

'Yes,' I said.

'There's not much time.'

'Is he still here? I haven't seen him this morning.'

'I think so. I saw him yesterday evening leaving with her.'

We reached the canteen and joined the queue for the simulated coffee. We took seats at a table with some of the other permanent crew. 'Back to boredom next week,' one of them said. 'The wrap party's on Friday night.'

Jean-Luc gave me a significant glance. There certainly wasn't much time; today was Tuesday. Presumably all the principals would be leaving Nice over the weekend.

'They're having it in Vence. At the Grand Hotel.'

'That's stupid,' someone else said. 'Why's it up there?'

'They're afraid of protests,' the previous speaker explained. 'There's been a few incidents outside the Negresco. Somebody was waving a collabo poster as the actresses staying there arrived the other evening.'

This was the first I'd heard of it. I hadn't seen anything amiss there for weeks, but then I hadn't been passing by as Arletty or the others arrived or left the hotel. Neither had I seen any of Claude's collabo posters anywhere but they had clearly had had some effect.

'Still,' the other man said. 'It's stupid going up to Vence even if some of them are staying in the Grand.'

We waited behind as the others drifted away. 'Any thoughts on how best to do it?' Jean-Luc asked me.

'Explosives or grenades are out if we don't want to hurt her. Unless we can get him on his own.'

'No,' Jean-Luc said. 'She should be there when it happens. To make the message as clear as possible. Anyway, it'll be easier to keep track of her movements than his on his own.'

I nodded. 'Where is this place they go riding?'

'I'm not sure. Somewhere up the hills. I'll find out.'

'What arms can you get?'

'Anything you want,' Jean-Luc said. This was a different Jean-Luc, less cautious that he had been even the day before. He appeared to have made up his mind to trust me, that this was not a trap. And the impossible had become possible.

'A rifle, if they were out in the country. Out riding.'

'You a marksman?'

'Used to be. What about you?'

'I was the laughing stock of the marksman course when I was in the army. The instructor told me to throw stones at the enemy. I presume it's something you don't lose.'

'I don't know,' I lied. It was something that was lost without practice. But I preferred the idea of a precision shot with as few people around as possible. I had no intention of doing it any other way; I was certainly not going to become involved again in scattergun tactics on busy streets.

He shook his head. 'I don't like the idea of the countryside with no witnesses on hand apart from Arletty. It'd be too easy for them to cover it up. Say he'd been fatally injured in a riding accident.'

'Why would they do that?'

'To avoid the repercussions.'

I looked at Jean-Luc with new eyes, seeing the revolutionary behind the easy-going exterior. He wanted the assassination to have a major impact, so Arletty had to be there, and it had to be public enough to force Vichy into retaliatory acts that would further undermine its support and legitimacy. We were clearly learning things about each other that neither had hitherto suspected. Whether our casual friendship survived all this was a moot point. We were now bound together by a conspiracy.

The shadows were lengthening across the Promenade as I walked home. It seemed like a long time ago since I had seen the unknown woman's arrest on a similar evening. A lot had happened, none of it good, but it had shaken me out of my inertia, opened my eyes to what was around me, and forced me to stop running away. Not that my new approach was likely to end well. I knew there was every probability that it wouldn't.

'Any news?' Mrs Mac greeted me when I arrived at her place, meaning about Solange.

I shook my head. The café was filling up but I kept to myself, nursing my beer at the zinc.

Mrs Mac came back, giving me a worried look. 'Everything all right?'

'As all right as it can be in the circumstances.'

'How's work?' she asked, giving me the opening I had been hoping for.

'Nearly finished. They've having the wrap party on Friday night.'

'That's something to look forward to.'

'I doubt I'll be going. It's in Vence.'

She asked me why they were going up there and I told her the powers that be were worried about protests. She dropped her voice: 'Because of Arletty's fancy man?'

'Yes. There've been some protests at the Negresco. They're very worried there'll be a big one for the last party. There'll be reporters around, trying to talk to the stars. Which would be a good chance to make the protest even more public.'

'So they're going to Vence instead?' Mrs Mac asked in a conspiratorial whisper.

I nodded. 'But it's not going to work. A lot of people at the studio are angry about Arletty flaunting her German all the time she's been here. They'll definitely do something, no matter where the party is.'

'Like what?'

'I don't know. There's talk of something big. But it could be all talk, of course.'

'In Vence,' she nodded to herself. 'How will they get there?' Vence wasn't much more than twenty kilometres but travel was no longer easy.

'Where there's a will, there's a way. It'll be Arletty's last public appearance around here. The last chance for people to let her know that they don't approve of her blatant collaboration with the Germans.' I drained my glass and nodded towards the portrait behind the bar. 'Accepting le Maréchal is one thing but cosying up to the enemy is another.'

She nodded, taking the point.

'The wrap party,' I told Jean-Luc the next day. 'That's where we'll do it.'

'At the party?' He gave me an incredulous look. 'That's an even worse idea than doing it here.'

I told him the plan I had worked out the previous night and he calmed down. We went through it, detail by detail. He asked questions and I explained the whys and wherefores.

'What if he doesn't turn up there?' he asked about Soehring.

'There's nothing we can do about that,' I said, 'but the odds are that he will. He's with her every day at the moment.'

Jean-Luc nodded. It was a gamble but a reasonable one.

'Can you make the arrangements and get the information and the equipment I need?' I asked.

'Yes, that's not a problem.' He seemed suddenly nervous now that we had a specific plan.

'I need to fire the rifle myself beforehand. Make sure it's accurate.'

'That might be difficult. Where can you do that?'

'I don't know. But I'm not going in with a weapon I can't rely on.'

'Don't worry. I'll make sure everything's in good working order.'

'That's not enough. I have to be certain of its accuracy.'

'All right,' he sighed. 'I'll work something out.'

The filming dwindled away over the next few days. Arletty no longer appeared on the set and we feared that she and Soehring might have left the Riviera already. But the gossip said they were now staying with their unknown host up the hills and going riding every day. They were still expected to turn up at the wrap party at the Grand Hotel.

I carried on as normal, going to work, dropping into the Café du Raisin on my way home, making sure I did nothing out of the ordinary. Jean-Luc and I had our coffees and lunches together, usually with other crew members. He kept me up to date with each stage of the planning, appearing nervous at times, which helped me to become calmer. I had decided to do what I was going to do and what happened next was a matter for other people and fate. It was up to Jean-Luc to get the right equipment and make the details come true. It was up to Benetti to leave me alone. It was up to Mrs Mac to play her unconscious part by passing on to Tillon her information about the big protest planned for Vence. It was up to Soehring to come to the wrap party.

I fully expected a knock on the door in the early hours of every morning or a sudden arrest on the street, but nothing happened. On Thursday evening I ran into Henri Tillon as he was emerging from the toilet in the café and I was going in. 'Bastard,' I muttered as we passed.

'What'd you say?' He stopped and pushed me against the wall of the narrow passageway.

'You heard me,' I retorted.

'You know why you're not in jail?' he hissed into my face. 'Because your woman has had to open her legs to keep you free. You have turned her into a whore. You're nothing more than a pimp.'

The venom in his voice as much as his words took me aback. Anger welled up and I tried to push him away but he was leaning his weight against me and I couldn't get any purchase in the confined space.

'He knows her father's not sick,' he said, 'but he's used to waiting. And he's not going to give you the satisfaction of locking you up. You can keep on walking the streets for now. Pimp.'

'You told him that, did you? Like you tell him everything. Why's that?'

'Don't think you're going to get away with what you've been up to. You'll get what's coming to you. And for dragging Solange into the middle of it.'

He walked away and I went into the toilet and leaned against the wall. My brain couldn't stop whirling. His mention of Solange was what had really stung. Yes, it was true, I had involved her in all this but he was the one who had made that happen. Stay calm and focused, I told myself. Yes, it's all a mess. And how will what you are about to do make any of it better? I took deep breaths to calm myself and ignored the question.

Mrs Mac watched me with apprehension when I came back towards the bar. Tillon had obviously said something to her about what had happened. He was back at the far end of the bar with his colleagues now, facing away from us. 'What is it?' She looked upset.

'Your friend Henri just called Solange a whore and me a pimp.'

She closed her eyes and her shoulders slouched as she exhaled heavily. 'He's very upset and angry about the whole business. He lashes out when he's upset.'

'What's he upset about?'

'We had a bit of a row,' she said, averting her eyes and acknowledging that I knew about her relationship with Tillon.

'I don't see what he's angry about.'

'I told him he should be man enough to report that fellow's treatment of Solange to his superiors.'

'Ah,' I said, feeling a little guilty that I had planted that suggestion in her mind. 'I'm sorry you've become embroiled in this.'

'He's been very good to us,' she said. 'Got Gerard out of trouble a couple of times over the years. I don't know what I'd have done without him.'

'I hope this won't change that.'

'I don't know.' The worry in her eyes suggested that the row between them over Benetti had been serious enough to threaten their relationship.

'You shouldn't let it do that,' I added, feeling even more guilty for using her again, but I really needed her to pass on the warning about Vence to Tillon or my plan would be pointless. 'I'll apologise to him,' I offered.

'For what?'

'I started it. Called him a bastard.'

'It's nothing to do with you. I said things I shouldn't have. It got a bit out of hand with everything that's going on.'

'Seriously,' I took her hand, telling myself I was more concerned about her than about the plan. 'Don't let my troubles come between you two.'

She gave me a wan smile. 'It's not all about you, Marty.'

I returned her smile. 'I hope not.'

Back in the apartment I wrote to Solange, keeping it short and simple, hoping she was all right and telling her I missed her and loved her. I didn't mention the end of the filming, the wrap party, my encounter with Tillon, or Mrs Mac's row with him. I kept it to the essentials, a sort of farewell letter in case things went wrong.

I lay in bed, going through each detail of the plan, thinking of all the things that might not go as we hoped. No combat plan survived the first shot, it was said, and my limited experience suggested that was true enough. But the changes could as easily to be to our benefit as against us. All we needed was a little luck and things to fall in our favour.

Besides, the first shot would be the last shot in this case. Unlike the movies, there would be no second take.

# Twenty-Two

I surprised myself by sleeping late. It was bright when I woke up, an overcast day with the sun trying to glower through an unbroken cover of grey cloud. I tidied the apartment, washed the dishes I had allowed to accumulate since Solange's departure, and put them away. On the way to the studio I posted my letter to her.

La Victorine had already sunk into a despondent air. There was nobody from Les Visiteurs du Soir to be seen; the actors, directors and producers had all left. The editing and post-production would be done in Paris. Sets and other equipment were being put into storage. Nobody knew when we'd have another feature film. It was back to newsreels and informational or propaganda shorts which, with luck, would keep us employed but lacked the excitement and interest of a feature film.

I spent the morning checking the electrical appliances, making necessary repairs, and putting them away for future use. 'All set?' I asked Jean-Luc as we crossed paths on the sound stage. He nodded and kept going.

We had lunch together with a group of others as usual. Few were going to the wrap party: Vence was just that little too far and too much of a climb for most to make the journey by bicycle. The studio wasn't laying on any transport for us, its regulars.

The day dragged on. The cloud broke up and the sun eventually emerged as it was already dipping towards the west and casting long shadows. 'Back of the canteen in half an hour,' Jean-Luc muttered to me as he passed by.

There was a van standing there when I arrived. A man emerged from the kitchens and indicated to me to get in through its open back doors. Jean-Luc was already inside, sitting on the floor with his back to the partition. Along the sides were crates of bottles and closed cartons. I caught sight of some brand names as I got in and sat beside Jean-Luc: caviar, champagne, cigarettes, cheeses. It was a black marketeer's dream: supplies from the stars' restaurant to supplement the Grand Hotel's own rations.

'We won't go hungry if it turns out to be a long journey,' Jean-Luc muttered quietly.

'You have a tin opener?' I nudged a carton of caviar with my foot.

He laughed as the driver put in two more cartons, gave us a thumbs-up, and closed the doors. We were cast into gloom.

The journey felt much longer than the expected half-hour. We felt every dip and hole in the road and every sharp twist and turn as the van climbed into the hills. The boxes and crates shifted and slid, threatening to fall on our legs. I raised my knees to keep two crates of bottles pinned to the sidewall as we swung around another corner.

The van slowed at last with a crunch of gravel and it stopped. The driver opened the door and said 'quickly' and we slid out and got to our feet. We were at the entrance to what looked like a path into a forest. The driver hurried back into his cab, pulled the van back onto the road, and continued his journey.

I took several deep breaths, clearing the nausea that had been building up with the tossing and turning. The daylight was beginning to fade and the air was fresh, heavy with the scent of pine resin.

We walked along the track, turned a corner and there was a young man sitting on a motorbike waiting for us.

'All clear?' Jean-Luc asked him.

He nodded. 'They have a checkpoint just below Vence.'

'And in the town?'

'There's extra flics there. There're just waiting around, no checks that I saw.' He pointed to a barely visible path among the trees. 'They're waiting for you up there.'

I followed Jean-Luc through the trees. The path rose steeply and we brushed aside low branches that stretched across it. Gusts of wind shook the tops of the trees but the air was still. We came into a semi-clearing where the ground levelled out and the trees were farther apart. Two men were sitting on the ground, resting their backs against the largest tree. We shook hands but no names were exchanged. More party members, I assumed.

One of the men handed a canvas rucksack to Jean-Luc. He opened it and passed me a revolver and took out one for himself. I broke it and saw it was fully loaded. The other man reached around the trunk of the tree and produced a rifle in a canvas case.

I stuck the revolver in my belt and took the rifle from him, opened it, and slipped the gun out.

'It's the latest army rifle,' he said with a touch of pride. 'The MAS 36. Have you used it before?'

I shook my head and examined it. It was in good condition, smelling of oil, and clearly well-cared for. The bolt was an oddly bent shape and I pushed it forward and backwards a couple of times. It moved smoothly. I balanced it on one hand and then looked through the telescopic sight.

'It's sighted in for fifty metres,' the man who had given it to me said.

'Is that the distance?' I asked. 'Fifty?'

The two men looked at each other. 'Maybe a little more,' the rifle man admitted. 'Fifty to sixty.'

Fuck, I thought. This is where the plan falls apart. It required precision and this wasn't precision.

'Yes,' the other man nodded. 'Sixty metres.'

'I need to change that then.'

The two men began protesting at once. One stopped and the other said, 'You can't fire it here. Someone will hear.'

I gave Jean-Luc a dirty look; clearly he hadn't told them of my insistence on firing the gun beforehand. 'Just one or two quick shots,' he said to them and turned to me. 'How many do you need?'

'Depends how accurate it is.'

The two men looked at each other again and the rifle's owner shrugged. 'The trees will keep down the noise,' he said, convincing himself.

I picked a firing point at the edge of the clearing and the second man opened his canvas rucksack and took out one of a clutch of our collabo posters. I paced out what I thought was sixty metres, making a rough calculation that that was about sixty-five yards – I still thought in inches and yards – and propped the poster on the ground against a tree trunk.

The rifle owner handed me a fistful of bullets and I fed five into the breech and leaned against a tree. I sighted the scope on the centre of the red X across the smudgy photo of Arletty and Soehring and fired two rounds. Both went a couple of inches to the right and down an inch. I adjusted the scope a few clicks to the left and another up and fired another two rounds. They were now almost at the correct height but still to the right and I made another adjustment. I fed a second bullet into the breech and the rifle owner said, 'That's all the ammo you have, you know.'

I told him that was okay and fired another two rounds. They went where I wanted them to go.

The other man retrieved the poster and I slipped the rifle into its cover and the four of us set off up the hill through the forest at a fast pace. Our guides seemed keen to get away from there as quickly as possible.

It took more than an hour to make it up the steep hill to the edge of the town perched on its high rock. The rifle had got heavier and heavier as we climbed but I had insisted on carrying it myself. I didn't want it to knock against any trees and have its scope jarred out of position. I was covered in sweat and breathing heavily as we emerged into the edge of the town. It occurred to me that I was too old for this sort of action.

A woman was waiting for us and our two guides disappeared without a word. She led us through several lanes and into the back of a building and up two flights of stone stairs and into an apartment. It took a few moments to adjust to the darkness and realize that the apartment was empty of furniture. We went into the kitchen which was also empty but for a cooker and sink.

It was brighter in here; a little light from outside came through the gaps in the shutters from missing slats. The woman pointed at the right-hand shutter and I realized that the missing slats had been removed deliberately to create a firing point. She shook both our hands and wished us luck in a serious voice.

I laid the rifle on the floor and opened the window, kneeling on one knee to look through the firing point. The window overlooked a large rectangular place surrounded by well-spaced trees. To my left, along the bottom of the square, was the Grand Hotel, its ground floor all lit up, and a carpet running the short distance from its entrance to the road. I assumed the carpet was red.

'What do you think?' Jean-Luc asked. He was peering through a gap at head height in the left-hand shutter.

'Looks good,' I said. Whoever had picked the position had chosen well. There was a clear view between the spindly bare branches of the trees to the hotel entrance and the short path from it to the road.

I unpacked the rifle and rested the front end of its wooden stock on the bottom of the shutter and looked through the scope. The glass doors of the hotel came into clearer view and I could make out some figures just inside them. To the left of the doors a newsreel camera was set up in front of an unlit arc lamp. A couple of men were standing behind it, smoking. I scanned across the door to the other side where another arc lamp was positioned. Two policemen stood on the road in front of the hotel. On this side of the road, in the square, a group of children were running about, playing some game, watched over by a couple of women.

All appeared to be as you'd expect it to be an hour before the party.

I took a quick scan through the scope of as much of the square as I could see without pushing the rifle's barrel more than a few inches from the shutter. There was nothing out of the ordinary. The square was deserted but for the people near the hotel. There was no sign of extra police on standby.

'Nice and quiet out there,' Jean-Luc said, stepping back from the window and turning around to light a cigarette.

'Yes,' I said, withdrawing the rifle slowly and propping it against the wall.

'They're not expecting anything,' he added with satisfaction. 'Which means the shock will be all the greater.'

I grunted what sounded like agreement. But I didn't agree. I would have been happier to see a stronger police presence, an indication that they were expecting trouble. It appeared that my indirect efforts to warn them through Mrs Mac and Henri Tillon had not succeeded.

I tried to rest, sitting on the floor against the wall, relaxing my breathing, and emptying my head of all thoughts. Which wasn't easy. The children playing in front of the hotel worried me. As did the lack of policemen to corral them and other onlookers and keep them out of the way. Another fuck-up like New York didn't bear thinking about. I was determined not to fire unless I had a clear shot and a safe backstop.

Jean-Luc alternated between watching from the window and pacing around the kitchen smoking. I resisted the occasional urge to tell him he was making me nervous. It was useful to have something else to concentrate on rather than my own fears.

'There's a few hundred people there now,' Jean-Luc announced from the window as the time ticked closer to the official start.

'Any more flics?'

'Ten or so.'

A while later he announced that the arc lights were on. I positioned the rifle through the shutter and looked through the scope. The lights lit up the red carpet and the roadway in front of it like a stage and cast the hotel doors into darkness. The crowd in the square was increasing all the time, mainly women and children, but they were out of the way, held in place by a thin line of policemen.

'Someone coming at last,' Jean-Luc said.

I swung the rifle around and saw the car driving down the opposite side of the square. It wasn't Soehring's Mercedes.

It stopped at the red carpet and the assistant directors got out and walked into the hotel without looking back. Then a steady stream of cars began to arrive, one every few minutes. Marcel Carné and his script writer Jacques Prévert emerged from one and hurried up the carpet. Someone told them to stop and wave to the crowd. They turned and waved, Prévert with the inevitable cigarette in his raised hand, Carné making a grimace of a smile. The director didn't like being directed. The crowd returned a feeble cheer, not knowing or caring who they were.

A proper cheer greeted some of the young actresses as they emerged from their cars in party dresses and bare shoulders. They managed to avoid shivering in the cold night air as they smiled and waved. Someone is directing all this, I thought. The studios or Vichy's propaganda ministry or both. Trying to show normal life continuing amid the abnormal. Maintaining the Côte d'Azur's reputation for glamour and warmth in spite of the dark and cold. I could almost hear the excited newsreel commentary in my head.

The main actors and actresses arrived individually except for Alain Cuny and Marie Déa who came together, holding hands. The crowd responded to their roles without knowing anything of the film's story and waved enthusiastically.

'The Mercedes,' Jean-Luc said in an excited voice. 'He's coming.'

I kept the scope trained on the road in front of the hotel and inhaled several deep breaths to calm myself and keep my heart rate steady.

'Definitely his car,' Jean-Luc added.

The Mercedes edged into my view and stopped. The driver's door opened and Soehring stepped out as another man stepped forward to take over as driver. The crowd began to cheer as they recognised Arletty in the passenger seat. Soehring smiled at them and crossed in front of the car to open her door. Among the cheers the first sounds of a chant began and grew stronger and clearer as the cheers dwindled away. À bas les collabos! À bas les collabos! Down with collaborators. I could see the back of Claude's posters being waved in the air.

Suddenly policemen were swarming in front of the crowd from both sides of the hotel. I kept the scope centred on Soehring who had paused and then continued on around the car. He reached the passenger door and Benetti appeared beside him from the hotel, saying something to him as he bent down to pull the handle.

Soehring straightened up and I squeezed the trigger.

The crack of the shot in the confined space deafened me and I couldn't hear anything for a few moments. The scene before me turned into a silent movie, everything still for a fraction of a second. Then people were running back up the square and Soehring's Mercedes was taking off at speed. Someone doused the arc lights and darkened everything. Sounds began to return and I could hear shouts and screams as people rushed away.

I scrabbled around on the floor looking for the ejected casing. The woman who had brought us to the room reappeared, took the rifle and slipped it into its cover. 'Wipe it,' I snapped at her.

'Later,' she said. 'Get out.'

Another woman appeared and disappeared with the gun. I was still on my knees, running my hand over the floor where the casing should be. The first woman told me again to get out quickly as she replaced the slats in the shutter. My hand brushed against the copper casing and I put it in my pocket and followed Jean-Luc out the door.

Outside, the woman with the rifle had disappeared and the young man from the motorbike was waiting. He guided us back out of the town, into the woods and down the treacherous hill where his motorbike was still parked. We paused there for a few moments, getting our breaths back. I took the empty shell from my pocked, wiped it clean and tossed it as far as I could among the trees.

'You missed,' Jean-Luc said, the first words he had spoken since the shooting.

I said nothing, resting my hands on my knees, still breathing heavily. I hadn't missed. Benetti was down.

We sped back to Nice on the motorbike, me as the pillion passenger. He weaved his way through the city, keeping off the main roads, and dropped me near Place Garibaldi.

'See you at work on Monday,' I said as I dismounted.

He gave me a look of disappointment as if I had failed to live up to his expectations and roared off. The cafés and bars around the square were busy with chatter and light. It was still early in the evening, though it felt to me as if it should be the middle of the night. I walked home wondering if Jean-Luc's disappointment was because I had missed Soehring or based on the realization that I had used him and his comrades for a personal vendetta. I would find out on Monday. If we were still at liberty.

At Solange's apartment building I went down to the basement and opened my hidey-hole behind the electricity meter. I wiped the revolver I still had in my belt with the tail of my shirt and put it away. I would give it to Aviv and his friends in a few days. If Jean-Luc looked for it back, I'd tell him I had tossed it into the harbour in case I was picked up.

I went upstairs and cleaned up my clothes as best I could, getting rid of any signs that I had been in a forest. There was nothing to eat except half a hard baguette, which I dipped in ersatz coffee to soften it.

I lay on the bed feeling exhausted. I thought of writing to Solange again, telling her to come home. But I knew that would be unwise. Perhaps I could send her a copy of tomorrow's *Le Petit Niçois* but even that would be foolish. I'd just have to wait for her to hear the news about Benetti's death from someone else.

I had no doubt he was dead or at least seriously injured. I had seen the bullet strike. He would not bother her again.

The Vichy government would crack down heavily on its enemies in Nice. Which meant that the communists and suspected communists would be rounded up along with known supporters of de Gaulle. But they couldn't execute innocent French people in reprisals, as the Germans would have done in response to Soehring's death. My hope was that everyone would believe, as Jean-Luc had believed initially, that Benetti was the unfortunate victim of a plot that had gone wrong.

Whether I got away with it or not was a secondary consideration and depended on people and things outside my control. What mattered was that Solange was free. A great weight was lifted off my shoulders.

# Twenty-Three

Solange came home a week later. She made no mention of Benetti's death. Neither did I. I knew better than to claim credit for it, however obliquely. We settled back into life as if nothing had happened.

I went to work every day, half-expecting to be swept up in a mass arrest of the communists and Gaullists at the studio. To all our surprise, there were no arrests. Some of Jean-Luc's comrades didn't turn up for work, or what little there was of it. I presumed they had gone into hiding but they drifted back after a few days when it appeared that none of us were suspects.

What was happening became apparent as the newspapers changed their story. Initial coverage suggested that it was a plot to assassinate Hans-Jürgen Soehring that had gone wrong. After a day or two the story changed. Benetti was the target and the suspects were black marketeers whom he had been investigating. Reading between the lines, it appeared that Vichy had decided it was not politic to admit to an anti-German attack. Better to make it a local criminal matter.

Mrs Mac gave no hint of realizing what had really happened. She added some detail to the official theory, no doubt gleaned from Henri Tillon. The black marketeers in question were her husband's old gangster friends.

'I have my knees worn out praying for Gerard,' she said after telling me that more of the gang had been rounded up. 'I hope they don't come for him too.'

'But he's not involved with them, is he?' I asked innocently.

'God's honest truth, I don't know whether he is or he isn't. He won't give me a straight answer. Which is what worries me.'

In La Victorine, Jean-Luc and I went on having our coffee breaks and lunches together. We didn't talk about what had happened at Vence. The closest we came to it was at the end of one lunch hour when he said out of the blue: 'You are a sneaky bastard.'

'What?' I didn't have to pretend to look surprised.

'You know what.'

He gave a short laugh, stubbed out his cigarette, stood up, and walked away. I took it to mean he had worked out what had happened, that I had hit my real target, and that I had used him and his comrades. But there was no sign that he had shared that information with anyone else. Nor, for that matter, that he held it against me. I thought I detected a touch of admiration rather than hostility or anger in his tone, but I might have imagined that.

After ten days I felt safe enough to retrieve the revolver, find Aviv in his guesthouse, and give it to him.

'More?' he asked hopefully.

I shook my head and advised him, pointlessly, to be careful.

The next morning, I strolled around the bench on the Promenade near the Hotel Suisse and saw a horizontal chalk mark summoning me to a meeting with Charles. I diverted to the

Monaco bus, got off at the Le Petit Afrique stop, and waited across the road. Charles pulled up at the appointed time and we dispensed with our previous identification routine.

'A message for you from Max,' he said as we drove back towards Nice. He paused for effect. 'Your woman friend has been released.'

'Really? That's great. How did he manage it?'

'Swapped her for a young Vichy diplomat who was also doing things he shouldn't have been doing in Washington.'

He overtook a couple of cyclists and eyed me on a short stretch of straight road. 'We look after our own,' he said.

'Glad to hear that.' I gave the expected response. And, indeed, I was more than glad to hear the news of Gertie's release. 'Where is she now?'

'Lisbon or Geneva, I imagine. But I don't know.' He changed the subject. 'What do you have for me?'

I told him about the end of the shoot at La Victorine and some of what had been appearing in the newspapers without mentioning Benetti. He picked up on my omission immediately. 'What about the shooting in Vence? Were you there? At the party?'

'No,' I said truthfully. 'They didn't bus us up.'

'What do those who were there think?'

'I don't know.'

'Nobody's talking about it at the studio?' He gave me a sceptical glance.

'Not much,' I said. 'They think it was a plot to kill the German.'

'They don't believe the newspapers?'

'Nobody believes the newspapers anymore.'

He took his eyes off the road to give me a sharper look. 'You were looking for guns,' he pointed out.

'Still am.' I met his look. 'Have you got some for me?'

'You planning something?'

'No. Just for protection.'

He dismissed that idea with a laugh. 'It's too soon. Like I told you last time, be patient. That day will come.'

We drove the rest of the way to Nice in silence. He stopped at Place Massena, reached into his inside pocket and handed me an envelope.

I got out of the car and sat on a bench facing the casino and looked at the letter. The envelope was blank. I tore it open and took out the single sheet of paper. The message was handwritten in an elegant Gaelic script but the Irish was like my own, a beginner's level with more than a hint of the classroom about it. 'I am going home,' it said. 'Thousand thanks.' It was signed with a single G in Roman script.

I refolded it and put it back in its envelope, wondering what she meant by home. Was she going back to Ireland, to Vienna, or even to America? It would be madness for her to go back to Vienna but I couldn't image her going home to any safe haven either. I'd be surprised if she could keep out of this war.

And what about myself? Where was home? And was I a participant in the war too?

The answers were all obvious. Home was in Nice, not least because there was no prospect of going anywhere else at present. And it was noticeable that my nightmare had not reoccurred since I had decided to take action against Benetti. Some part of my subconscious appeared to be satisfied that I had finally decided to stop running away, to come out of hiding from myself. I could no longer remain aloof from all that was going on around me. Or try to smother the guilt that followed that day in New York with detachment. There was no going back on what had happened then and there never would be. It would always be with me.

The noontime boom of the cannon on Castle Hill signalling lunchtime interrupted my thoughts. A small burst of white smoke appeared against the blue sky above the hill and expanded until it dissipated in the clear air. The sun was hot, warming the ochre colours of the square and the flurry of early lunch-goers emerging from shops and offices. Among them refugees in their cold climate clothes headed for the seafront. Across the road, the casino's doormen stood at ease in bright and braided uniforms, ready to greet those willing to take their chances on the roll of dice and the spinning ball of the roulette wheel.

I stood up, put Gertie's letter in my pocket, and headed to work.

Read Joe Joyce's ***Echoland*** spy trilogy set in neutral Ireland during the Second World War.

Paul Duggan, a young intelligence officer in the Irish Defence Forces, is finding his way in a new job and hunting for German spies as the country tries to maintain its precarious position between the Allies and the Axis.

Available as ebooks and paperbacks on Amazon and free to read with Kindle Unlimited.

More info and signed copies also available from www.joejoyce.ie

Printed in Great Britain
by Amazon